Georgie Crawley lives in Hertfordshire with her husband and their six dogs. She spends as much time as possible walking in the English countryside, and reading about her pet passion: the royal family.

Henry the Queen's Corgi

GEORGIE CRAWLEY

avon.

Published by AVON
A Division of HarperCollins*Publishers* Ltd
1 London Bridge Street
London SE1 9GF

www.harpercollins.co.uk

First published in Great Britain by HarperCollins*Publishers* 2017

A catalogue copy of this book is available from the British Library.

ISBN-13: 978-0-00-826313-3

This novel is entirely a work of fiction. The names, characters and incidents
portrayed in it are the work of the author's imagination. Any resemblance to
actual persons, living or dead, events or localities is entirely coincidental.

Typeset in Bembo 11.25/15 pt by
Palimpsest Book Production Limited, Falkirk, Stirlingshire

Printed and bound in the United States of America by LSC Communications

17 18 19 20 LSC/C 10 9 8 7 6 5 4 3 2 1

For every family, and their pets, this Christmas

Day 1

Saturday 14th December

HENRY

The thing about humans is, they take an awful lot of looking after. Oh, I'm not saying that they're not worth it. Just that, really, without us dogs, I don't know what would happen to them.

Take my family, for example. The Walkers.

Ever since I arrived here as a puppy, it had always been the five of us. (Okay, six, if you include The Cat. I don't, generally.) Jim, Amy, Jack, Claire and Me: Henry. (Fine, and Sookie. If you must.)

That is, until Bonfire Night, five weeks ago. (I remembered the date clearly, because it all happened in amongst the bangs and the flashes.) I was hiding under the chair in Jim and Amy's bedroom (like any sane creature would be on Bonfire Night) so I saw Jim shoving clothes and things into his bag. And I heard Amy sobbing, asking Jim why.

Sometimes, I think maybe she didn't understand what was going on any better than I did.

All I knew for sure was that Jim left that night, and he hasn't really been back much since. This wasn't like when he went out to work and I missed him, or even when they all went on holiday and left me at the kennels.

This was different. And I didn't like it one bit.

After Jim had left, I'd curled up beside Amy as she cried herself to sleep on the bed. It was only after her sobs had subsided and I was sure that she was asleep that I risked jumping down to check on the others. Jack and Claire were both still outside, watching the fireworks from the nearby school field. I braved the noise and the lights to check that they were okay, then headed back in to my basket to have a think about what was happening – and how I could fix it.

It was then that Sookie had slinked out from behind the sofa and looked at me with that awful, superior gaze that all cats seem to have.

'Well, that's you done for,' she'd said. I hadn't understood, and she wasn't willing to explain. But ever since, I'd been looking for clues, something to explain what was going on – and ideas on how to make things better.

The next morning, Amy had sat Jack and Claire down and explained things to them. I'd listened in, of course, but all I'd managed to understand was that Jim had gone away, and we all needed to help out and do our bit to keep things together.

Well. That was easy! I would be the most helpful dog they could ever wish for.

I started by checking in on Jack and Claire at bedtime. Sometimes, Claire would be crying when I stopped by her room, so I'd jump up on her bed and snuggle for a while, until she felt better, or fell asleep. (I wasn't really supposed to go on the beds, but I figured these were special circum-stances. Besides, Claire's bed is *really* comfy.)

Next, I made a point of helping keep the place clean and

tidy by eating up any scraps of food that found their way onto the floor. But then I decided that wasn't helpful *enough*, so I started jumping up onto the kitchen chairs to clean off the plates that got left there after meals, sometimes. They were always very clean by the time I'd finished licking them.

Amy didn't seem to appreciate this as much as I thought she would, and after a while, Jack started putting all the plates in the dishwasher as soon as they'd finished eating. So I started looking for other ways to help, instead.

One big worry I had was that there were a lot fewer walks for me. Jack would take me out to explore the park sometimes, but he usually met up with his mates and made me sit around on my lead while I waited for him to finish chatting. Claire was only allowed to take me as far as the local shop and back on her own, and I already knew all the scents along that route, so it was a bit boring. Also, sometimes Sookie followed us too – I always suspected that she was Claire's favourite.

Amy didn't seem to have time for walks at all, any more. But I knew that she always felt better after we'd been out for one, so I started grabbing my lead from the hook in the hallway, then dashing out the front door whenever it was opened, so she'd have to follow and chase me. By the time she caught me and clipped on my lead, and we'd walked home again, we'd both got some exercise and fresh air. Amy never seemed very grateful for it, but I knew it was helping, really.

Still, overall, the atmosphere in the Walker household was not as bright and cheerful as I was used to – and Jim hadn't been back once. Despite my best efforts, my family were suffering.

But then this morning, everything changed.

Amy sprang down the stairs with a sense of purpose, shoving things into her bag and making sandwiches by the loaf. Something was happening – and I really wanted to know what.

'Jack! Where's your blue rucksack?' Amy yelled up the stairs. I pressed closer to the table by the front door as I watched.

'Can I take my tablet?' Claire asked, holding up her electronic device.

'Definitely not,' Amy replied. 'Why don't you take that new book Gran bought you?'

'What blue rucksack?' Jack appeared at the top of the stairs, still wearing his pyjamas.

'Jack! You're not dressed!' Amy's face was turning a little red.

'Because I don't want to go,' Jack said. 'I told you that.'

'Well . . . tough. We're all going. It's going to be an adventure.' Adventure. I liked the sound of that word! 'Now, find that rucksack.'

'What rucksack?' Jack asked again. 'And why do I have to go? Take Claire.'

'I'm taking both of you,' Amy said. 'So go and find the rucksack I bought you for your Duke of Edinburgh trip and *get dressed.*'

Jack stared down at his mother for a long moment. I knew that look. He was deciding if he could push her any further.

Apparently he decided he couldn't.

'That rucksack is red,' he said, grumbling, but he headed back to his room to get ready, all the same.

Which just left me wondering – getting ready for what? Amy hadn't said. She'd said they were all going on an adventure – but did that include me? I hoped so. And if not . . . well, maybe I'd just grab my lead and follow after them! I wasn't going to miss out on what could be the most fun any of us had had in weeks!

'Well. This looks interesting.' Sookie brushed up beside me as she sat herself in her usual spot, next to the radiator. 'What do you think is going on?'

'We're getting ready to go somewhere,' I said, watching Amy as she bustled about between the kitchen and the hall, gathering things together.

'Obviously.' Sookie swept her fluffy tail from side to side on the wooden floor. 'But where?'

'An adventure.' I couldn't keep the excitement out of my voice.

Sookie rolled her eyes, and headed off towards the kitchen. 'Bo-ring.' Cats. They have no sense of adventure at all.

Amy reappeared in the hallway again, Claire trailing along behind her.

'If I had my own phone, I could play on that on the train,' Claire said. 'I mean, I *am* twelve now. All my friends have them, you know.'

'We said we'd talk about a phone when you're thirteen.' Amy didn't even turn to look at her as she replied. Given how many times they'd had this argument, I wasn't very surprised.

'I'm just saying, I'm *almost* thirteen.'

'You turned twelve in October. Two months ago.'

'And a phone would make a *brilliant* Christmas present,' Claire went on, oblivious to her mother's attempt to use logic against her.

Sighing, Amy turned back to look at her daughter. 'Claire,

we've talked about this. You know Christmas is going to be a little . . . different this year. And big presents like that, they're just not on the cards right now, I'm afraid.'

Claire's expression turned stormy. She often got that look just before she clipped on my lead and dragged me down to the shops full pelt. I like a walk as much as the next dog, but when Claire is on a full speed sulk there's no time to enjoy it.

'Fine,' she said, folding her arms over her chest. 'I'll just ask Dad, then.'

Amy looked away, a sudden sadness in her eyes. It made me want to go snuggle up against her, for comfort. 'You do that.'

The tension continued as Amy finished packing her bag – and Jack's red rucksack, after he tossed it down the stairs. Claire sat at the kitchen table, just within eyesight of the hallway, still glaring. Sookie wandered past to weave between Claire's legs as they dangled down from the chair, but Claire didn't even reach down to pet her.

I went to sit by my lead. We really needed this adventure. All of us.

'Right,' Amy said, sounding decisive again. 'Coats on, everyone. It's time to go!'

Jack thumped down the stairs and yanked his coat from the rack. Claire shrugged her puffy red jacket on, too, and Amy buttoned up her old duffle coat. The she picked up her rucksack, handed Jack his to carry and . . .

Yes! She lifted my lead off its hook and clipped it onto my collar!

A warm, peaceful feeling settled over me. Wherever my people were going, they wanted me with them. That was all that mattered.

'Guess you'd better just hope they bring you back with them, too,' Sookie murmured, as she brushed past us to run up the stairs.

I didn't pay her any mind. *Of course* they'd bring me home again.

I was an integral part of the family. Let's face it: they'd all be lost without me.

AMY

This was a good idea, Amy decided, finally, as she spotted the sign she was looking for in the distance.

Even as the train had pulled into Victoria station, she still hadn't been sure. Jack had been silent for most of the train journey – actually, he'd been silent for most of the last six weeks, ever since Jim left. But the silence seemed to be getting more pointed as the days went on without their father returning. At least she still got a few words out of him, sometimes. Jack wouldn't even talk to Jim when he called – he hung up every time he answered the phone to him.

And Claire – her sunny-natured, happy girl – was different these days. She argued every point, complained about any slight change to the usual routine . . . and there were plenty of changes. Even Henry's behaviour had been erratic since Jim left. The poor corgi seemed determined to remind everyone that he was still there, mostly by causing trouble. Before Jim had left, Henry had been a perfectly behaved dog. These days, Amy seemed to spend half her time shooing him off the beds, or chasing him down the road when he escaped, again. She'd even had to assign Jack to dishwasher duties, to stop Henry eating the leftovers right off the plate.

Still, she couldn't blame the little dog for being unsettled, maybe even a little scared. They all were. Things were very different now.

Jim had taken his salary with him when he left. He still paid his half of the mortgage, and had offered more for the kids, but Amy wouldn't accept it. Why should she? It would only make him feel better, like he was doing enough for his family.

He wasn't, not by a long shot.

His family needed *him* there. Not his money.

And if they didn't have him – well, then she would do it herself. All of it.

She'd prove to Jim that they were better off without him, anyway. That would feel better than slapping his stupid face. Apparently.

Her friends had had plenty to say about Jim's departure, of course – mostly scathing comments about him living the cliché, or not knowing a good thing when he had one. They all meant well, Amy knew, and it even helped a little, knowing she had all those people on her side. But the most useful advice she'd been given had actually come from a very surprising source – the new doctor at the surgery where she worked as a nurse. Dr Fitzgerald was new to the area and, according to the grapevine, recently divorced himself. Amy had seen him in the park by the surgery a few times, walking his pet Dalmatian, but they'd rarely spoken until last month. The week after Jim had left, he'd stuck his head into the room she was working out of, and asked if she was okay.

Amy had pasted on a smile and tried to put up a show of coping, but he'd seen through it immediately.

'Everyone is going to have a lot of advice for you,' he'd said, with a gentle smile. 'And some of it will probably be good, and some of it will almost certainly be terrible. The only thing I can tell you is: you're the only one who will have to keep living in your life once this is all over and everyone else has moved on. Once it all calms down, he'll still be your kids' father, whatever he's done. And you'll still be you, even if it doesn't feel like it right now. So grieve and rage for what you've lost, sure, but in the end, you have to focus on the long term.'

The long term. It seemed so far away still, but Amy was trying. Trying to imagine a future where things weren't so hard, where she was happy again – and so was her family.

That's what today was about. Starting the long term, right here. Creating the happy family future she wanted.

And where better to do that than at a Winter Wonderland?

'What do you think?' she asked, as they walked up from the station in the crisp December air, towards Hyde Park. At her feet, Henry trotted along beside her, content to stay close on the pavement and in the crowds, thankfully. She really didn't need him creating any of his mischief today!

Jack and Claire were slightly behind her, dragging their feet, so they didn't see the sign as quickly as Amy did. But when they spotted it . . .

'Mum! Are we going in? Are we really?' Amy smiled. For a moment, Claire sounded like her little girl again. God, she'd missed that sound.

Up ahead, the crowds were amassing, all streaming towards the enormous, brightly coloured gates. Even in the daylight, the place was lit up, and Christmas music filled the air. Beyond them, the giant wheel loomed over the whole park. Amy felt a rush of exhilaration at the very sight of it, and even Henry barked his excitement.

Yes, this *was* a good idea.

'Winter Wonderland?' Jack tried to sound cool and unaffected, but Amy knew him too well. She could hear that spark of excitement, hidden deep under his words. 'That's what we're here for?'

'Yep!' She grinned at the kids, her heart warming as they smiled back. She handed them the map she'd printed off ready for the day ahead. 'What do you want to do first?'

Jack and Claire held the map between them, talking over each other as they pointed out their favourite attractions. They'd wanted to come last year, and the year before, but Jim had always said it was too busy, too commercialised. He'd wanted to take them all skiing instead, but they'd never been able to afford it for the four of them – plus kennels for Henry and Sookie.

Winter Wonderland, thankfully, had free entry. Of course, there were plenty of things you *could* pay for inside, but that was why Amy had planned the whole trip so carefully. She'd budgeted and booked ahead for two of the bigger items – the Giant Wheel and ice skating by the bandstand. And by bringing Henry along, she'd ensured that she'd have to stay on the side with him, so they only needed two tickets. She'd kept enough money aside for the kids to choose one activity each on top of that, and brought their Christmas money from their Granny – donated early for the cause – if they wanted to spend any more.

They'd had an early picnic lunch on the train in, so they didn't need to buy food at one of the overpriced food stalls, and Amy had planned a dinner at an inexpensive Italian she remembered from when she and Jim were dating, after they'd walked through Oxford Street to see the lights. Add in a side trip to look at Buckingham Palace and they'd have had a full, memorable day – and Amy would still have money left to buy the food for Christmas dinner.

Not bad going, if she did say so herself.

The kids didn't seem to have noticed that everything they did was being done on the cheap, thankfully. Claire was mesmerised by the lights and sights of the Christmas market, and even Jack seemed engaged by the music and excited to see the views from the Giant Wheel. Henry stayed close by her feet – almost tripping her up a couple of times – but generally wasn't causing any trouble, which was a plus.

For a moment, it was almost like the last few months hadn't happened at all.

Except that Jim wasn't there.

Amy watched the huge wheel turning against the darkening London sky, and let herself imagine, just for a moment, how different things might have been if Jim had never hired Bonnie as his new secretary. Never fallen in love with her. Never decided to give up on almost twenty years of marriage in a heartbeat.

Then she shook her head. There was no point dwelling

on the past. She had to focus on the future – and making it perfect for her kids, without Jim at her side.

She didn't want Jack and Claire to hate their dad – adding more bitterness to the situation wouldn't help anyone. And Dr Fitzgerald was right – he'd still be their dad, once the divorce was all over and settled. But in her efforts to keep things civil and polite, Amy couldn't help but think she'd got the rough end of the deal. The fact that Jim had an affair and, when forced to choose, picked Bonnie for his future, meant that Jack wasn't speaking to his father. As for Claire . . . Amy wasn't even sure how much she knew about what had happened. After all, Jim hadn't introduced the kids to his new girlfriend yet.

But that couldn't last forever. Soon they'd have a new person in their lives, a new permanent situation to deal with. Someone to share holidays and special occasions with. Next year, they'd be scheduling out who got the kids when, who enjoyed Christmas Day with them and who got stuck with Boxing Day, and who was responsible for the stockings on Christmas Eve . . .

This year, though, they were still all hers. And she intended to make the most of that. Jack was nearly eighteen, after all – this could be his last family Christmas, if it came down to it. So Amy was determined to make this Christmas magical for them both. Give them one last year of being proper kids at Christmas.

Even if she had to do it alone.

Henry brushed up against her legs, and she reached down to pat him as the Giant Wheel came to a halt.

'We can do it, can't we, boy?' she murmured, as she watched for Jack and Claire disembarking.

Henry just rested his head on his paws, over her feet. At least she could be sure Henry wasn't going anywhere.

It was kind of nice to have at least *one* guy she could rely on.

Even if he was a corgi.

HENRY

I had to admit, there were a lot more interesting smells at the 'Winter Wonderland' place than at home in Redhill. There, it was mostly other dogs, children, cars, bins and the occasional squirrel in the local park. Here, there was chestnuts roasting (at least, according to the man who bellowed at us as we went past, that's what they were) and all sorts of sweet things, along with the biting scent of the ice and the cold air. Plus the smell of excitement, that ran through the whole place – I could even smell it on Jack, Claire and Amy, which was a lovely change.

Claire groaned when it was time for us to go, but she didn't make the kind of fuss we were all used to lately. Amy wrapped an arm around her slim shoulders and promised her there was plenty more fun ahead, and Claire cheered up again after that.

'So, what's next, Mum?' Jack asked, hardly a hint of his usual surly tones in his voice. I sat at his feet, my stumpy tail wagging in approval. I liked my Walkers happy, and this was the first time I'd seen it in months.

Maybe things were on the up again, for everyone.

'I thought we'd walk down past Buckingham Palace.' Amy

folded the map of the Winter Wonderland carefully, and placed it back in her bag. 'And maybe through St James's Park to see the pelicans. Then later, once it's dark, we can catch the tube back up to Oxford Street to look at the lights, before dinner. What do you think?'

Claire rested her head against her mum's arm. 'Sounds brilliant.'

'Great!' Amy beamed.

I trotted along contentedly at Amy's side as we wound our way past log cabin market stalls and ice skating children, the sounds of laughter and joy filling the air. Today was a very good day indeed – and I definitely liked the sound of St James's Park!

Parks, in my experience, were places for running and chasing, for seeking out new scents and hunting down squirrels. Amy was always relaxed in the local park – she knew that I knew my way around, so she didn't need to watch me too closely. Plus we always met interesting people there: the neighbour with the Yorkshire terrier, the new doctor who'd moved to town last month and had a really fun Dalmatian puppy. Even Claire's friends from school, or Jack's mates, were often to be found in the park. We always stopped to talk and, over the last month or two, having those people to talk to seemed to help my family's mood.

After all, while I was an *excellent* listener and comforter (unlike Sookie who disappears at the first sniffle), sometimes my humans needed other humans to talk to, too.

I was right – St James's Park was brilliant. Amy let me off my lead and I was free to romp around to my heart's content. Even the cold, frozen earth was gentler on my paws than the hard concrete of the pavements we'd walked to get there, so I enjoyed the freedom to just run and run.

'No chasing the pelicans now!' Amy called after me, as she and the kids followed. I barked a quick reply over my shoulder. What *were* pelicans, anyway? I couldn't commit to not chasing them until I'd found out. What if they were like squirrels? Squirrels were my favourite things to chase. With pigeons a close second. But I was willing to rejig the top two if pelicans were even better . . .

The humans stuck to the harder paths, while I zigzagged across the park, mostly on the grass, always keeping them within sight. Jack tossed sticks for me to hunt down, which was great fun. When we reached the lake, Claire pointed out to an island in the middle, just as I was contemplating if it was really too cold for even a little paddle.

'Look! Mum! There are the pelicans!'

I jerked my head up, ears pricked, scanning the horizon. The park was green, even in the depths of winter, and the lake hadn't frozen, so there was still plenty of wildlife around. I stared at where Claire was pointing, taking in the immense, ridiculous birds that apparently lived here in the park.

They were huge and a sort of dirty white colour, with giant, pointy beaks with a flappy pouch for the lower half.

Most pertinently, they were bigger than me.

I took a step or two back from the edge of the lake. Those things definitely looked like they could swallow a pigeon or a squirrel whole. I didn't want them trying their beak at a corgi.

'Who do they belong to?' Claire asked, still staring at the enormous birds. I felt a pang of longing for the sparrows and thrushes of our back garden, at home in Redhill. Those were proper birds. Birds that knew their place in the animal order.

'Well, St James's Park is one of the Royal Parks,' Amy said, slowly. 'So I guess they belong to the Queen.'

The Queen had very peculiar taste in pets, I couldn't help but think.

'The first pelicans here were presented to King Charles II in 1664 by the Russian Ambassador.' We all looked at Jack in surprise, and he held up his phone. 'The power of the internet. Now, come on, it's freezing! What's next?'

'We've seen the pelicans – let's go see if we can catch a glimpse of their owner,' Amy suggested. 'I read in the paper this morning that she was heading out from the Palace later today. You never know – we might get lucky.'

I wasn't sure how lucky it would really be to meet the owner of those terror-birds, but Claire hopped up and down on the spot, clapping her hands, so maybe I was missing something.

We trotted along the length of the lake, towards the edge of the park. Amy didn't put me back on my lead, which I appreciated. I stayed close anyway – at least, until I was sure we were out of sight of the pelicans.

This was one park I decided I could live without visiting again. I much preferred our own, local park, with all the people and dogs we knew, and some nice, plump squirrels for chasing.

At the far end of the park, we saw a mass of people, gathered around a set of railings. There was lots of chatter, filling the frozen air, and Amy hurried us all across a wide road. I tried to look around, to get my bearings, but all I could really see was legs – thin legs, thick legs, legs in heavy dark trousers and boots, or in jeans or tights. Legs everywhere, blocking my view.

'The gate's opening!' Claire cried, and suddenly the three of them rushed to get closer to the railings up ahead. I stuck with them, weaving through legs to make sure I didn't lose them.

'Come on, Henry,' Jack said, glancing down at me.

I still wasn't on my lead, I realised, but the Walkers were far too busy peering out through the crowd to think about that now.

Suddenly, the noise levels rose again. Through the legs, I could see a motorcycle leaving the gates, its lights flashing. Behind it, a long black car, also with lights, followed – and as it came past, cheers and shouts rang in my ears as the crowd went wild – it was worse than on Bonfire Night. I shrunk back, but there were more legs behind me, and the noise was everywhere, so loud I couldn't escape it.

But I had to. I wanted to dive under my cushion into my basket at home. I wanted to snuggle up with my mouse toy. I wanted Jack to pet my head and tell me that everything would be quiet soon.

I knew it wouldn't though. London had been loud all day – from the train to the crowds at the Winter Wonderland, to the squawks of the pelicans as they were fed their fish. But this crowd was the worst, and I needed to get away from it.

Whining, just a little, I backed away, fighting my way past the legs and the noise to reach the back of the crowd. I could wait for the Walkers there – they'd find me in no time once this was over.

Behind all the people the racket was a little less, but I still wanted to put my paws over my ears and hide from it all. I ran a little further, just to be safe, until I reached a patch of greenery I could hide in. As I pressed back into it, a large, fat pigeon hopped past. I studied it carefully, distracting myself from the noise by imagining how I'd catch it. The sounds of the crowd faded as I focused on my prey.

The bird, unaware it was being hunted, hopped closer. And closer again. Until I could almost . . .

At exactly the right moment, I lunged forward – and the pigeon flapped up into the sky in a panic. I watched, as it flew over the bush I was hiding in, landing on the other side.

Too easy.

The bush was even denser than the forest of legs, but so much quieter, and less inclined to stand on my paws. I pushed through the branches, pausing only for a second when I came up against two tall metal bars in the middle of the greenery, which wouldn't give way to my shoving.

Instead, I angled my head between them, wiggling my shoulders to fit through, followed by my back, my rear and my hind legs.

I shot out the other side with a pop, brushing through the last of the branches in time to see the pigeon hopping off towards a patch of grass on the other side.

The chase was on.

Pigeons are truly stupid birds. It never seems to occur to them that if they just flew high enough, or far enough away, I wouldn't be able to catch them at all. Instead, they get all flappy for a few moments, hovering in mid-air, then land again a short run away.

Like I said: stupid. But it does make the game more fun.

I dashed after the bird, barking happily. The loud cheering and shouting was almost inaudible from in here – where was I, anyway? It looked like another park, like the one with the pelicans, with lots of trees and greenery. That was okay, then. Parks were always a good place for dogs, and the Walkers would be sure to find me here once they'd finished doing whatever it was they were doing by the gates. After all, it wasn't like I'd gone very far.

Eventually, the pigeon had enough sense to fly up into a tree, and stay there, but I didn't mind. It just meant I could spend some time exploring this new park – while keeping an eye out for pelicans, of course.

I had a marvellous time investigating the pathways and the flowerbeds, the trees and the bushes. But after a while, even I had to admit my paws were tired. And, even worse, it was starting to grow dark. Hadn't Amy said something about dinner? Yes, that when it got dark we'd all go to look at some lights, somewhere called Oxford Street, and have a nice dinner.

I didn't want to miss that.

Yawning, I trotted back the way I'd come, heading back through the falling gloom, towards the big building the Walkers had been standing outside – what was it Amy had called it? The Palace. Buckingham Palace. Although, I had to admit, it looked a little different from this angle. No big gate and railings, for a start. But still, it was the same place, so the Walkers had to be around here somewhere, right?

Except there were no crowds on this side of the Palace. No guards with those funny hats. No people at all, actually.

I stopped, closer to the Palace than I'd remembered us getting from the other side. I just needed to find a way around, that was all. Back to the Walkers. I'd squeezed through a bush, hadn't I? So I just needed to do that again.

If only I could remember *which* bush.

'What are you doing out here?' A grumpy voice behind me made me hop with surprise. I spun around so fast I almost caught my stumpy tail, and saw a man in a dark suit and a white shirt glowering at me. 'You must be the new one, I suppose. I thought Her Majesty was taking you with her, but apparently not. No, you'll just get to run around here, getting under everyone's feet and having little "accidents" and we'll all have to pretend we love you. Just like the other three. Honestly. I thought there weren't going to be any new Palace pets, any more. But no, couldn't resist a corgi in need, could she?' He sighed, and opened a door to the Palace. 'I suppose it's not your fault. Come on. Let's get you back where you belong.'

My ears perked up at the last part. The bit about Her Majesty and accidents made no sense at all, but getting back where I belonged – with the Walkers, that was *exactly* what I wanted to happen. So I trotted dutifully through the door, prepared to follow the grumpy man in the suit to wherever I was sure the Walkers would be waiting for me.

My eyes widened the moment I stepped inside, though. I hadn't really understood what 'Palace' meant – except that it was clearly a very big house. But the room we entered wasn't anything like our hallway at home. For a start, there was no

24

straight staircase heading up, with items belonging to the family strewn on every step, waiting to be returned to their bedrooms. There was no telephone table, with the address book that was good for chewing. No coat rack, with baskets of mismatched shoes underneath.

No hook for a lead, either.

Instead, a huge room spread out from the doorway, with a dark red carpet, lots of dark red chairs and sofas (that I suspected I probably wasn't allowed on) and huge, tall columns made out of white-ish stone. On the walls were giant pictures of people wearing funny clothes. And in the centre of the room was an enormous Christmas tree, decorated with plush red decorations in the shape of crowns.

It was so imposing, I almost wanted to hide behind the heavy, red and gold curtains. Except then I'd never get back to my family.

'Well, come on, then,' the grumpy man said, ushering me forward. 'If you don't hurry up you'll miss your dinner, and then there'll be hell to pay.'

The man had a point. Amy would *not* be happy if I made them all so late they missed dinner. And I wouldn't be very pleased about missing a meal, either. (It wasn't like I'd actually got to *eat* the pigeon. And I had been doing an awful lot of running around. It was enough to leave a corgi famished.)

The only problem was, I had no idea where I was supposed to go.

The man sighed again, heavily. 'Right. You're the new one. Suppose you haven't figured out where everything is yet. Come on, then. I'll take you.'

I'd expected him to lead me straight to another door, and back outside, but instead we walked through ever more impressive rooms to a wide staircase, lined with golden banisters and even more gold on the walls. At the bottom of the stairs was a white statue, next to a huge ornate clock. Long, green garlands decked with shiny baubles trailed up along the banister.

This definitely wasn't like the Walkers' house.

'Right, upstairs, you.' The grumpy man waved a hand towards the stairs. I stayed sat at the bottom, looking from him to the steps. The Walkers couldn't be up there, could they? 'Go on. Up!'

All those puppy training lessons Jim had taken me to kicked in and, at the sound of the order in the grumpy man's voice, I hopped straight up and onto the first steps.

The man followed behind me as we climbed. I wondered what I was going to find at the top.

Hopefully, my family.

The upstairs corridors were just as ornate, and all decorated for the season. It made me realise that Amy hadn't even put up the Christmas tree yet this year. Probably because that was something that Jim always used to do.

I was glad to have the grumpy man to follow; without him, I'd have been lost in a heartbeat.

'Here we go.' He reached for the handle of the heavy, red door we'd stopped in front of. On it was a sign.

My reading isn't great. I'd learned a few words: Henry, dog, food and corgi.

The sign definitely said Corgi something.

The door opened, and three other dogs stared at me.

I stared back.

I was guessing the other word on that sign was 'room'.

It was a room full of corgis.

What on earth had I got myself into now?

AMY

'We saw the Queen!' Okay, so it had only been the briefest glimpse of a hat, and maybe a corgi's ear, as the big, black car had pulled away from the Palace, but Claire was still jumping up and down like they'd had a personal audience.

'And I got the whole thing,' Jack added, as he stopped filming on his phone. 'Granny will love this.'

'She will,' Amy agreed. Her mother, Granny Freida, was a huge fan of all things Royal. Jack had basically just secured the best Christmas presents for life in return for a viewing of that ninety second film and its half a second shot of Her Majesty.

Really, she couldn't have *planned* this day better. The kids were happy and excited, she felt relaxed for the first time in months, and now they'd go and look at the lights and get some dinner, and it would all be lovely and perfect and the magical Christmas she'd been hoping for.

Dr Fitzgerald had been right. Focusing on the future was the way to go.

'Where's Henry?' Jack asked, frowning, and Amy felt all that calm relaxation evaporate in an instant, as she was dragged back to the suddenly frightening present.

'What do you mean? He was right here . . .' Amy glanced

down to where Henry had sat at her feet, calm and content, all day. Even in the cold, her palms were sweaty as she checked the lead in her hand. It was a retractable one and it was, of course, fully retracted. No dog attached. Because she'd taken Henry off his lead so he could have a race around St James's Park, and then—

'I forgot to put his lead back on.' Amy's heart thumped so hard in her chest she thought it might break free. 'But . . . but he must be around here somewhere. He wouldn't just wander off.'

Would he? Henry had been to all the standard puppy training classes, and was usually sensible enough to stay close when things were busy – mostly to make sure he didn't miss out on any food. But an event like today, with all the noise and the pushing, and in such a strange place . . . Not to mention his recent habit of escaping out the front door whenever it was open. What if he'd run again?

And where could he have run to?

'He could be *anywhere*,' Jack said, sounding agonised.

She should have been more vigilant. More careful. More attentive. How could she have forgotten his lead? How could she have forgotten *Henry*, even if just long enough to watch the Queen drive away?

She'd failed him. Failed her family. She'd been an idiot to think she could do all this alone.

Despair gripped her as she looked desperately around her, hoping for the sight of a fluffy, stumpy tail, or a doggy grin.

Nothing.

No. Amy shook her head. She didn't have time for despair. She had to be a parent again. To take charge.

After all, she was the only one left to do that, now.

'We need to look for him. Call him,' she said, thinking her way through a plan. 'He always comes when he hears his name. Let's split up. Jack, you take that side of the railings, Claire and I will take this side.'

The crowd was clearing now, as much as it ever did outside Buckingham Palace, and they could at least see the pavement between people. Keeping Claire close – the last thing she needed was to lose a child as well as a dog – Amy made her way along the railings, calling for Henry.

'He couldn't have run out into the road, or we'd have seen him,' Claire said, following her. 'So he has to be around here somewhere. Doesn't he?'

'Absolutely,' Amy said, with much more confidence than she actually felt. 'And even when he runs away to the park, he always stops to look back and check I'm following. He won't have gone far. I'm sure we'll find him in no time.'

Three hours later, as the train raced them home along the tracks, Amy wrapped an arm around Claire's shoulders, her heart breaking at her daughter's tears. Across from them, Jack sat sullenly, staring out of the window. He hadn't looked her in the eye since the moment they realised Henry was missing.

The policeman they'd spoken to had been helpful, but not hopeful. London was just such a big city. Henry could be anywhere.

'He's microchipped,' Amy had told them, desperately.

'Well, if he turns up, at least they'll know who he belongs to,' the policeman had said, obviously trying not to emphasise the 'if'.

'He could have been stolen,' Jack said, suddenly, setting Claire off with fresh waves of sobs. 'Corgis are a popular breed. Someone could have dognapped him while we weren't looking.'

'Which means we'll never see him again!' Claire shot an accusing glare at her mother.

Amy didn't blame her. It was all her fault. She'd been so busy congratulating herself on organising the perfect, magical day for her kids, without Jim, that she'd lost sight of what really mattered – them all spending the day together.

Including Henry.

He must be so scared, alone in the city, or with total strangers. He wouldn't understand what was happening, or where they'd gone. He'd only know he wasn't with them. That they'd left him behind.

Never mind the kids forgiving her – she'd never forgive herself for that.

Jack had gone back to staring out of the window, into the bitter, winter night. He might not have said much, but Amy knew he had to be just as upset as Claire was. Henry was *his* dog really, his and Jim's. Jim had brought him home for Jack when Henry was just a puppy, and Jack only just turned ten. Ever since, training Henry, walking him, looking after him, had been something father and son had done together. But now, Jim had gone, leaving Henry behind to muddle through with the rest of them.

Jack had seemed to take his father's leaving well, to start with, but as the weeks had gone on he'd withdrawn more and more into himself. He'd always talked about becoming a vet, and researched exactly which courses he'd need to take, what work experience would stand him in good stead for getting a place on his preferred course. He'd worked so hard, for the last two years, determined to get his dream job. But in the last few weeks, he seemed to have forgotten that it was ever even important to him.

But Henry . . . Henry had always mattered, to all of them. As much as he might frustrate her sometimes, Amy knew that Henry loved them all with that unfailing devotion that dogs had. She might not like him climbing on the beds, but she knew Claire slept better with Henry beside her. Not just Claire – Amy had woken a few times over the last six weeks to find Henry curled beside her, keeping her warm in Jim's absence.

And Jack . . . Jack might not talk to her about how he was feeling, but she knew he talked to Henry, sometimes, when he thought no one could hear him. Who would he talk to now?

Amy watched Jack now, resting his head against the glass, his dark hair flopping over his forehead, and felt her heart ache for him. Her boy, almost all grown up – but not so grown up he didn't still need his parents.

Didn't need his father. And his dog.

Amy let her eyes close for a second, and tipped her head back to rest against the back of the seat. Just a moment to grieve and feel like all was lost.

Then she opened her eyes, straightened her spine, and got back to it.

Okay, so she'd reported Henry as missing, and made sure they knew he was microchipped. She'd searched the area, called his name, and tried to tempt him out with doggy treats.

She'd spoken to every tourist in the vicinity of Buckingham Palace who could understand her and asked if they'd seen Henry.

She'd done everything she could, on the scene.

So the next question was, what could she do from home to bring Henry back to them?

The Walker family had already lost enough this year. She wasn't about to give up another member of the family without a fight.

'Okay, kids,' she said, waiting until she had their full attention before continuing. 'What we need next is a plan.'

Day 2

Sunday 15th December

HENRY

For a moment, when I woke, I wasn't sure where I was. The basket I'd fallen asleep in felt too soft, too comfortable, to be my own, battered one. And the room was too quiet – no radio blaring out from the kitchen, or Jack thumping down the stairs.

It didn't feel like home at all.

Then I opened my eyes, and everything that had happened the previous day came back to me.

After the grumpy man had deposited me at the Corgi Room, it hadn't taken me long to realise the mistake he'd made. He thought I belonged here, at the Palace, so he'd brought me to where all the other dogs lived – instead of taking me back to the Walkers like I'd hoped.

Where were they now, my family? Had they left without me? Or were they still waiting, searching for me?

What if they thought I'd *meant* to run off and leave them, like Jim had? I hoped they all knew I loved them far too much to ever do that.

Spending a night in a Palace might be a very big adventure for a rather small dog, but it did make me miss my real life, and my family, just a bit. Who knew what sort of trouble they'd all get into without me there to look after them?

Who would make sure Amy took her daily walks? Or curl up with her to watch romantic movies on Friday nights? Who would eat Claire's leftovers at dinner, when she smuggled them under the table when Amy wasn't looking? Who would keep Claire company at night, when she was sad and needed a snuggly, furry body beside her for comfort? She might be too old for teddy bears (most of the time) but she certainly wasn't too old for me. And most important of all, who would listen to Jack talking about how he missed his dad? I knew he didn't want anyone else to know that he felt that way. But he needed someone to talk to. He needed *me*.

They all did.

But it looked like the Walkers would have to learn to manage without me, at least for a little while. Just until I could straighten out this mistake and find my way home.

And in the meantime, since I *was* in the Palace . . . I might as well make the most of it. It couldn't be long now before someone realised what had happened and Amy arrived to take me home again. Yes, there was nothing to worry about.

Not yet, anyway.

Stretching out in my super-soft basket, I took in the rest of the room around me.

Given how grand the Palace was, maybe I shouldn't have been so surprised that the Corgi Room was every bit as luxurious – but I was. Each of the dogs had its own wicker basket, raised a little above the ground for some reason. It made me wonder whose basket I'd borrowed – and when they'd be back to claim it.

Of course! The moment that happened, that was when the humans at the Palace would realise they'd made a mistake, and then I'd be taken home to the Walkers. It was only a matter of time, really.

Except, of course, that while the humans might not have realised they had the wrong dog yet, the other dogs were a lot smarter. It wouldn't take them nearly as long, I was sure.

There were, as far as I could tell from my observations the evening before, three other dogs in the Palace – one corgi like me, and two others who looked a little like corgis, but not quite. They had longer faces, and bodies, and sat even lower to the ground than I did. I'd intended to ask their breed, but given the suspicious looks they'd given me at dinner the night before, I'd decided to hold off until they got to know me better.

But apparently the Palace dogs didn't like to wait.

Sitting bolt upright in my basket, I realised the other three dogs were staring at me, no friendliness at all in their gazes.

'So. You're the new dog, then,' the corgi said, spitting out the word 'new' like it was a mouldy dog biscuit.

'Um, sort of?' I needed to find out what the situation here was before I let slip the truth about my unorthodox arrival.

'Thought you were supposed to be going with Her on the trip,' one of the other dogs said. 'Special treatment and all that.'

Hadn't the grumpy man yesterday said something about thinking I'd gone with Her Majesty? 'There was a change of plan,' I said, thinking how very true that was.

'Not so special after all, then,' the third dog said. 'Well, suppose we'd better get used to you being around. I'm Candy.

That's Vulcan, and this' – she nodded towards the corgi in the middle – 'this is Willow.'

Candy seemed friendly, so I decided to try to get some more information out of her. 'Great names,' I said. 'And it's always lovely to meet another corgi. What's your breed, Candy?'

'Vulcan and I are Dorgis,' she explained. 'Half dachshund, half corgi.'

Well, that explained the low to the ground thing.

'It is customary, when someone gives you their name, to return the pleasantry,' Willow said, in a very high and mighty voice. She almost sounded like *Sookie*.

'The what now?' I asked, having not quite followed the question.

Vulcan rolled his eyes. 'Your name. It would be polite for you to tell us your name, now you know ours.'

'Oh, sorry. Henry,' I said, automatically. 'Pleased to meet you.'

Willow's head shot up at that, and she stepped forward to study me more carefully. 'Henry, is it? We were told the new dog was called Monty.'

Ah. Now I was for it.

I gave a wide, doggy smile, and prepared to charm my way out of it – the way I did with Amy when the odd songbird ended up dead in the back garden. 'It's sort of a funny story, actually.'

I related the events of the day before in as entertaining manner as I could. Willow, Candy and Vulcan didn't find it very funny, unfortunately.

'So you're an imposter,' Vulcan said, staring down his long nose at me.

'An intruder, even,' Candy added. She'd seemed like the friendliest of them all to start with, but now she looked anything but. Her eyes had turned cold, and there was no hint of a wag in her stumpy tail.

'I like to think of myself more as an . . . unexpected guest,' I said, trying to make it sound like a joke.

'We don't let just anyone into Buckingham Palace, you know,' Vulcan said. He seemed by far the grumpiest of the dogs, and with the shortest legs. Maybe he had short dog syndrome, I mused. A need to feel more important than he was.

Mind you, he was a Royal Pet. That had to count for something.

Candy and Vulcan turned to Willow, presumably for guidance on what to do next. The only other corgi in the room was clearly the leader of the pack – understandably. Corgis are always the dogs you want to turn to for leadership and good sense.

I just hoped that Willow would come down on my side. She didn't seem any happier about my presence in the Palace than Vulcan was.

'Well, I suppose this will all get cleared up when She returns, and tosses you back out onto the streets where you belong.' Willow sniffed. 'Until then . . . it does indeed appear that we have an *unwelcome* guest.'

Candy and Vulcan echoed the sniff, and turned their backs on me, all three of them padding off towards their own baskets. Willow had made her opinion clear – and the others would follow it.

So much for my making new friends while I was at the

Palace. The dogs all hated me and She, whoever she was, would be throwing me out again in no time.

It seemed I was unwanted, unwelcome, and worst of all – unable to get home to my family.

Well. They might have ideas about the sort of dog I *wasn't*, but clearly they had no idea what sort of a corgi I *was*.

Because I wasn't the sort of corgi who gave up that easily. And they'd all learn that soon enough.

'I bet you lovely creatures are ready for breakfast, right?'

I raised my head from my paws and saw a blonde human with a bag of dog food standing in the doorway to the Corgi Room.

My saviour!

Who needed the pampered Palace pets, anyway? All I needed was a human that could see sense. I bounded over towards her, hoping I could make her understand, somehow, that I wasn't meant to be there. That I needed to go home.

She smiled, and bent down to pat my fur. 'You must be our new boy! I heard you'd decided to stay with us at the Palace after all. Good choice. What was your name again?' Lifting the tag from my collar, she read it out. 'Henry. Very royal. Very appropriate. Well, I'm Sarah. Sarah Morgan. Pleased to meet you, Henry.'

She held out a hand and I raised a paw to meet it, glad that shaking hands was the one trick Jack had insisted I learn. It meant I didn't feel totally out of my depth here, even if everything about Buckingham Palace was new and strange – and Willow had ideas about how a corgi was supposed to behave that I apparently could never match up to.

Pulling four silver-coloured bowls from the shelf on the wall, Sarah laid them on the floor in front of us.

'Now, I believe there's a very strict order for this,' she said, smiling. 'But I'm afraid I'm new here too, so you'll have to forgive me if I get it wrong.'

She shook the dry, meaty food into the first bowl. It didn't look like the food we'd had at dinner the night before, but to be honest I'd been too scared and lost to even notice what I was eating then. In fact, I'd left most of it – meaning I was starving now.

I would have jumped forward at once to start eating, but the other three dogs held back, so I waited too. Obviously this was another Palace rule I didn't understand. I mean, really – who waited for food?

Once the bowls were filled, Sarah stepped back and looked at us. 'Do I need to say something? Um . . . eat?'

I jerked forward, but Vulcan and Candy both barked at me. 'Not you,' Candy said, sharply.

I backed off, and Willow stepped delicately forward, dipping her muzzle into the bowl before her and eating.

Looking more closely at the bowls, I realised they all had a name inscribed on the front of them – all except mine. Maybe they hadn't got around to engraving the missing Monty's bowl yet – or maybe they'd taken it with them and this was a spare. I didn't know.

I did know it was still empty. And I was beginning to think it might be a while before it was my turn.

I was right. Next up was Vulcan, and then Candy. Both

took their time eating their breakfast – probably just to annoy me. Then, finally, Sarah filled my bowl and the other dogs moved aside to let me tuck in.

Sarah laughed as I demolished the food. 'You were hungry, huh, boy?'

I would have barked a yes, but I was too busy eating. The food was fantastic – even for dry food. Meaty and moist and filling and tasty. *Just* what a hungry and lost corgi needed.

Eventually, the bowl was empty. I looked up pleadingly at Sarah. It was my best look, the one that made Amy crumble every time, but Sarah was already putting the food bag away.

'Sorry, Henry,' she said. 'I might be new, but even I know that rule. Only one bowl of food, and that's it until dinner.' She placed the bag back on the shelf and collected up the bowls. 'See you guys later, if I'm lucky. I'm hoping that, with Her Majesty away, I might be allowed to feed you your dinner, too. I heard the chef is making you rabbit, tonight.'

She turned and left, my stomach rumbling at the very *idea* of rabbit. In fact, I was so distracted by the idea of dinner, it took me a moment to realise that she'd left the door open, and the other three were trotting towards it confidently.

Was this a mistake? Maybe Sarah didn't know that the door was meant to be closed. Or, were we really allowed to go out and explore the Palace? It seemed unlikely – the whole place was too ornate, too special, for four dogs to just go wandering around. Wasn't it?

Willow, Candy and Vulcan obviously didn't share my concerns. They were already through the open door and out into the corridor. I paused for just a moment before following them.

Unsure of where to go, I padded along behind the other three until we reached the stairs I'd climbed up the day before.

Vulcan looked back over his flanks. 'Where do you think you're going?'

'Um, downstairs?' I hazarded a guess.

'Okay then,' Candy said and, before I could figure out what was happening, all three of them had turned tail and were heading along the corridor in the opposite direction to the Corgi Room. As I watched, a man in the same sort of suit Grumpy Man had worn the day before held a door open for the procession of one corgi and two Dorgis. They trotted through, imperiously, as if they were the Queen themselves, rather than just the Queen's dogs.

The man looked at me curiously, obviously waiting to see if I'd follow. But I couldn't. I wasn't going to go anywhere I wasn't wanted.

Which meant I just needed to find somewhere that I *was* wanted.

Turning away from the door, I padded down the stairs, front paws then back to manage the wide steps. Maybe downstairs would be more fun.

I took a few wrong turns before I found my way to the red room I'd entered through the day before, and then I found the door I'd come in through was closed. I looked around for a helpful man to open it, but I couldn't see any.

Pressing my nose up against the glass of the door, I stared out at the gardens longingly. They'd been so tempting yesterday, I couldn't help but follow that pigeon into them. Even now, I knew, if someone opened this door for me I'd race out and run around for all I was worth. I'm an outdoor dog, you see. As luxurious as this Palace was, the gardens were still my favourite bit so far.

Even if they had taken me away from my family.

Were they looking for me? I hadn't really gone so far from where they were. I'd have thought they'd have just knocked on the door and asked if anyone had seen me. Then the grumpy man might have realised his mistake and given me back.

Sookie would be glad I was gone, anyway.

The thought of Sookie made me smile for a second, unexpectedly. Sookie, moggy that she was, would have loved the Palace. She'd have thought it was exactly where she belonged. She could do imperious even better than the Royal Dogs.

Sookie would fit right in at Buckingham Palace; I didn't think I ever would.

No, I couldn't think like that. If I'd found a way into the Palace, I could find a way out, too. A way home.

I knew that Buckingham Palace was a lot larger than my home, but I had no idea how much bigger until I started exploring. I stayed on the ground floor to start with, padding through luxurious room after luxurious room, all of them far bigger than any room at the Walkers' house.

Everywhere I looked something sparkled gold or silver, or shone with lights. Under my paws, the carpets were deep and soft, and mostly a dark, rich red.

Every person I saw moved out of my way to let me trot past, like I really was one of the royal pets. And as much as I wanted someone to realise that I didn't belong there, the fact that they didn't gave me the confidence to continue my expedition.

Somewhere, there had to be a door that was open. One that I could escape through and find my family again. I just had to find it.

On my travels, I came across a room with a large, dark wood table in the centre, piled high with shiny silver objects. As I approached, I saw a woman wearing the same uniform that Sarah had on that morning, bustling the other way, muttering something about polish. Intrigued, I headed in.

The stack of silver on the table looked like pirate treasure from one of the movies that Jack loved to watch when he was younger, all gleaming in the sunlight from the windows. At the top of one pile, I spotted a silver bowl that looked a bit like the ones Sarah had fed us our breakfast in. Tilting my head to the side, I considered it.

It was unlikely that it still had food in it, all the way up there, right? But it would be silly not to check. Just in case. After all, once I found my escape route, I'd need all my energy to get home. A little extra food wouldn't go amiss, in that case.

Hopping up onto a nearby chair, I pressed my front paws up against the table and peered up at the pile of silver. Still too far away to tell if there was any food waiting at the top of that pile of treasure.

In Jack's movies, the treasure was always worth the risk it took to get it. I figured the same probably applied here.

With a quick glance around to make sure that no one was watching, I hopped up onto the table itself, and tentatively began to climb the pile of silver, trying to reach that bowl at the top. I balanced myself carefully between the items, making sure to keep my weight even as I climbed. The only thing I hadn't counted on was that silver is slippy. And loud.

Just as I came within a whisker of that elusive bowl, my back paw slipped on a plate below, and suddenly everything was moving. I grappled with my claws against the dishes and plates, but it was no good – with an enormous crash, the pile of silver I was scaling smashed to the floor – sending me tumbling after it.

The bowl I'd been aiming for landed smack bang on my head.

It was empty.

'What on earth!' Another two members of the Palace staff came racing in to see what the commotion was, and so I decided that it was probably time to scarper. Racing between their legs, I headed back the way I'd come.

Maybe one of the other dogs would know of a way out of the Palace. They seemed as eager for me to leave as I was.

Of course, I had no idea where they were, so I had little choice but to head back to the Corgi Room and wait for them.

My paws felt heavy as I climbed the stairs back to the Corgi Room. I'd barely explored a fraction of the Palace, but already I knew there was far more to this building than I could hope to see in one day.

The door to the Corgi Room was open, at least, so I slunk in and found myself alone. Settling down into my basket, I curled up and waited for one of the others to come back and help me find a way out.

But as I lay there, another, terrible thought occurred to me.

Willow had said that when She returned – whoever She was, but I was guessing probably the Queen – I'd be thrown out into the streets the minute they realised I wasn't the real Monty. Which was fine by me, as I'd get to go home.

Except . . . I didn't know my way around London, and I certainly didn't know how to get back to the Walkers' without help. I knew we'd come in on a train, but how would I tell which one? And even if I could, I was fairly sure they wouldn't let me on without a human.

My grand plan of escaping was a bust – even if I could find an open door.

No, I had to try and make the best of things here at the Palace until Amy could find me – if she was even looking. And if she wasn't . . . well, I was a charming dog. Maybe if I made enough friends here, they'd let me stay.

Which meant winning over Willow and the Dorgis.

Not likely.

Before I could follow this line of thought any further, a shadow appeared in the doorway. Willow.

'Where are your henchmen?' I asked, getting to my paws.

Willow shook her head. 'They're not henchmen. They're family.'

'And I'm not. I get it.'

'You're . . . not like us,' Willow said, with more diplomacy than I'd heard from her so far. 'But apparently it seems you're going to be staying a while.'

'You just figured that out?' I said, channelling my inner Sookie to get the sarcastic tone just right.

'I heard one of the footmen talking,' Willow explained. 'The one that held the door for us by the stairs. He said that the new dog didn't seem to be fitting in very well, and perhaps She should have taken you with her after all.'

'So?'

'So, I'd assumed that the humans, like us, would have been able to see through your lack of breeding and realised you weren't Monty. Apparently I was giving them too much credit.'

'Sarah didn't notice,' I pointed out. 'Why would you think a footman would?' Presumably, the grumpy man from yesterday was a footman, then. There seemed to be a few of them running around the Palace. I wondered what their jobs were.

'Well, she's like you, isn't she?' Willow said.

'You mean new?'

'I mean . . . an outsider. She wasn't born to this. She doesn't know how it all works, yet.' Willow hopped up into her own basket, turning around a few times before settling down. 'She'll learn, or she'll leave.'

Also like me, I realised. If I wanted to stay here long enough for the Walkers to find me, I needed to fit in, so they didn't realise I wasn't Monty. Which meant learning more about the place.

And I knew just the person to teach me.

'So, tell me about Monty,' I said, jumping down to pad over towards Willow's basket. I settled myself on the carpet below where her wicker basket rested just a little above the ground. 'And this place. How come you all get your own room? And what's with the baskets not being on the floor?'

All valid questions, I thought – and I had plenty more. But Willow gave me a look like I was the stupidest dog in the world. Which she probably thought I was.

'Monty is the latest addition to our pack,' Willow said. 'We haven't actually met him properly yet, but given his pedigree, and his previous owners, I'm sure he'll fit in fine. He'll understand the hierarchy, for a start.'

'The hierarchy?' Maybe I really was as clueless as Willow thought. I had no idea what that word even *meant*.

'Of course. The dog who has been here the longest – me, in this case – is the leader. The queen, as it were. The others follow in the order in which they arrived.'

'So Vulcan, Candy then me,' I guessed. 'That explains the order for breakfast and such. I didn't even notice last night.'

'Well, you were late,' Willow pointed out. 'Another mark against you. Punctuality is a virtue – especially where dinner is concerned.'

That, we could both agree on. 'So, Monty would be at the bottom of the pack too, then?' I supposed that made sense. Sookie had been with the Walkers for a year longer than I had, and she always made it clear that she thought she was the leader, too. Of course, Sookie would probably have done that even if I'd been there years before her. That was just Sookie.

Was it weird that I was actually starting to miss that mean old cat?

'Of course. Besides, Monty isn't really a *Royal* Pet, you know.' Willow leant out of her basket slightly, talking down to me as if exchanging top-secret information (like where the treats were kept). 'She decided a few years ago that She wouldn't get any more pets – I mean, obviously we were companionship enough for Her, so why would She need them?'

'But She got Monty.'

'Yes.' Willow pulled a face. 'But only because She's so kind-hearted. His previous owner was a friend of Hers – an earl, of course – and when he died She offered to take him in. She explained it all to us first, of course.'

'She sounds kind,' I said. I'd never really thought all that much about the Queen before, but given the luxurious surroundings She gave her dogs, I supposed She must be.

'She is the kindest human, or owner, any dog could hope to have,' Willow said, firmly, as if daring me to doubt it.

I didn't.

'It was Her mother, you know, who set out our routine.'

'Her mother?'

'The Queen Mother,' Willow clarified, although it still meant nothing to me. 'She recognised our superior qualities, as a breed, I suppose, and made sure that the Royal Dogs would live a life suited to their status.'

'Such as baskets raised off the floor?'

'To avoid draughts.'

'And I suppose you get all sorts of treat foods and things, right?' I said hopefully. Maybe something good could come of this adventure, after all. 'Scraps from the Queen's table, doggy chocolate drops, that sort of thing?'

Willow looked scandalised. 'Not at all! We have a very strict diet, developed specially for us and our well-being. She would never dream of doing anything less.'

I sank down onto my haunches. 'Strict diet' didn't sound like a lot of fun, if I was honest.

'It's not what *you're* used to, of course,' Willow said. 'I suppose you must – what? Hunt for your own food? Raid the bins, or what have you?'

Now it was my turn to look horrified. 'Of course not!' Although, actually . . . 'Well, not if I don't want to.'

'So you *have* an owner, then.'

'Yes, of course I do. I told you this morning – the Walkers.'

Willow looked at me blankly.

'My family. Jim and Amy and Jack and Claire.'

Willow gave a small shrug. 'I thought they were just like our walkers. People who walk us, when She is busy.'

'They're much, much more than that,' I said. 'They're like She is to you.'

'I wouldn't go that far,' Willow said.

'I would.'

'Hmm.' She eyed me carefully for a few moments. 'I suppose you want to get back to them, then.'

'Very much.' I'd spent a restless night imagining how they'd all be coping without me. And whether Sookie had stolen my favourite squeaky toy yet. 'The last place I saw them was just outside the Palace, before we got . . . separated. I've spent today searching for an open door out of here . . . except I realised, I don't know where I'd go if I found one. So instead I'm hoping that Amy will keep looking for me, and realise I must be here in the end, and come calling to pick me up.'

'Which means you have to stay here long enough for that to happen,' Willow surmised.

'Exactly.'

She gave a doggy sigh. 'Well, in that case, I suppose I'd better fill you in on how we do things around here. See if we can stop you standing out *quite* so much.'

'Is it really so obvious that I don't belong here?' I asked. Surely, when you got down to it, a dog was as good as any other dog, after all.

But Willow laughed. 'Of course! Only truly *special* dogs get to live the life of a Royal Pet, you know.'

And, I realised, in Willow's eyes, I was nothing special at all.

Showed what little she knew, right?

Later, when dinner time came around, I was prepared. And also starving.

Willow had patiently (and patronisingly) talked me through a day at the Palace, giving me a little history along the way. Tomorrow, she promised, she'd take me with her so she could 'train me up properly' – a phrase I disliked immediately. After all, the Walkers had already trained me. I didn't need some posh corgi telling me how to do things.

But then Willow had added, 'If you're going to be a Royal Pet, you're going to have to learn a whole new lifestyle, you realise.' She surveyed me, and sighed. 'I've never had to work with such raw material before, but I suppose I'll see what I can do. A good teacher should be able to instruct even the roughest of dogs, and you are, at least, a corgi.'

The one thing we had in common. Our breed. But even that didn't seem to be enough to satisfy Willow. Willow, I'd realised quickly, was a snob. And her snobbishness had rubbed off on the other two dogs, too.

'So gracious of you,' I'd muttered. Oh well. At least following the other dogs around might be more entertaining than being shunned and ignored by them. 'Now, why don't you start by telling me about dinner?'

I already knew about the order for eating, but now I understood a little more about why.

'Normally, we'd eat dinner in Her sitting room, and She'd feed us Herself,' Willow had explained. 'But She's away at the moment, which is why we have the rather unsatisfactory Sarah feeding us instead.'

'Does She go away often?' I'd asked.

'Yes,' Willow had replied. 'But normally She takes us with Her.'

I could tell that this was something of a sore point for the other dogs. They weren't used to being left behind, and the idea that the New Dog, Monty, had got to travel with their beloved Queen when they hadn't was obviously ruffling their fur.

That could be my way in, I decided. A way to make friends with these dogs. They'd been left behind, too – although not in quite such a spectacular manner as I had. But still, it was the one thing we had in common.

I just hoped it would be enough.

At dinner time, Sarah arrived, smiling again – although her eyes were a little bit red.

'How are you settling in, Henry?' she asked, leaning down to pat my head. I nuzzled into her hand, happy for the contact. None of the other dogs had let me close enough to touch them, and none of the footmen or other humans I'd encountered on my jaunt around the Palace had wanted to get near me at all. It was as if they thought I might bite them or something!

But Sarah had no such concerns. She took time to give my ears a good scratching, and when I rolled over onto my back she even rubbed my tummy.

It was the happiest I'd been since I arrived at the Palace.

Even if the others were looking on disapprovingly, I didn't care if I'd broken *another* rule.

Soon, there was a knock on the door and Sarah said, 'Time to go!'

We were led along the corridor a little way to outside a door that – according to Willow's information – must lead to the Queen's sitting room. Sarah and a man in uniform laid a plastic sheet over the carpet, then set out the four silver bowls – three with names, one without.

'Is that straight, John?' Sarah asked. 'Sorry, it is John, right?'

'It is.' The man straightened the plastic until it lay perfectly against the carpet, lined up with the wall on both sides. He didn't ask her name, I realised. Candy and Vulcan probably wouldn't approve of that.

But I wasn't bothered about protocol, right then. Already, I could smell something wonderful. Rabbit, Sarah had said. But this smelled richer, meatier, than any dog food I'd ever sniffed at before.

The man – John – filled the bowls with the juiciest looking food I'd ever seen. My mouth watered just at the sight of it. But I knew from earlier that I couldn't just dive in and eat – as much as I wanted to.

But what if the others ate my food too? Or dragged out their own meals so long that there wasn't time for me to eat? I wouldn't put it past them. It was the sort of thing that Sookie would try – and these dogs reminded me an awful lot of Amy's cat. (And no, that wasn't a compliment.)

These thoughts tugged at my brain and, as much as I tried to resist, I couldn't help lunging forward, desperate to taste the delicious food in front of me.

'Ah-ah!' John said, sternly. 'In order, please.'

Chastised, I slunk back, saliva practically dripping from my jaws. I could hear the other dogs muttering uncomplimentary things about me behind my back.

'It seems so mean, making them wait,' Sarah said, as Willow stepped daintily forward to begin her feast. 'They look so hungry.'

John gave her a scornful look. 'These dogs are the most spoilt and pampered pooches in the land. Look at them, they eat better than I do!'

'Don't you eat here at the Palace too?' Sarah asked, innocently. 'I think the food here is just marvellous.'

'That's not the point. The point is . . . they're dogs, not princes and princesses. They get their special raised baskets, their specially designed menu, all cooked from scratch by the chef with the finest ingredients. They get to go wherever they like in the Palace, with no one to stop them, even when they have their little accidents on the carpets and *somebody* has to clean up after them. And they get brushed by the Queen herself! Trust me. There's no need to pity these dogs.'

'I suppose not,' Sarah said, but she didn't sound completely convinced.

Her bowl licked clean, Willow stepped back, and the man called Vulcan forward for his turn. I shifted from paw to paw impatiently.

'You'll get used to it,' John said to Sarah, suddenly. 'Life here, I mean.'

'Or I'll leave,' she said. 'I've heard it already.'

The man shrugged. 'It's not like any other job, working in the Palace. Some people are born to it. Others . . . aren't.'

He gave her a sideways look. 'Of course, you had the family connections, didn't you?'

'You mean my godfather,' Sarah said, and sighed.

'Butler at Windsor Castle, I heard.' John raised an eyebrow. 'Must make it easier, when you've got an in like that.'

'I applied for the position the same as everyone else.' Sarah sounded offended. 'And I worked hard to get it, thank you very much.'

John threw up his hands in mock surrender. 'Okay, okay. Sorry, then.'

Sarah sighed again. 'No, I'm sorry. It's just . . . some of the other girls, they've been saying the same thing. Like I can't ever be one of them, because of who my godfather is.'

'I wouldn't worry about them,' John said, dismissively. 'They'll get over it.'

'Maybe,' Sarah said, but she didn't sound very certain.

Finally, after Vulcan and Candy, it was my turn to eat. I waited, panting, for John to give me the signal, then dove onto my bowl. I didn't care about dinner manners, or protocol. I was starving!

The food was worth waiting for, though. Succulent, tasty – and all coated in a gravy that was like nothing I'd ever tasted before. As I savoured my last mouthful, I remembered that Willow had said that the Queen held the secret recipe for it herself.

No wonder everyone was so in awe of Her. It all made sense now.

I stepped back from my empty bowl, already knowing there wouldn't be any more. John might think we were spoilt, but I'd give a lot for a doggy chocolate drop right then.

As John and Sarah packed up the plastic sheet, and took the bowls to be washed, the other dogs headed back to our room to sleep off the meal. I trotted along behind, uncertain of what else to do.

'See you all tomorrow,' Sarah called to us. I looked back to see John rolling his eyes at her, but Sarah didn't seem to notice.

That night, as I curled up in my comfortable, draught-free basket, listening to the other dogs snoring and snuffling, I had a thought.

Willow might have spent some time explaining to me how things at the Palace worked, but I was under no illusion that she actually wanted me there. And Candy and Vulcan were even worse. But they weren't my only options.

If the Palace dogs didn't want to be my friends just yet, I'd just have to make friends with the humans, instead. Starting with Sarah.

Maybe she could help me get home to my family.

AMY

'No, I understand. Thank you for your time.' Amy rubbed her forehead as she hung up the phone, sure that the officer on the other end must think she was a complete idiot. *Of course* she understood that London was a big city, and that finding one small dog in it was an almost impossible task. It was just that the facts didn't stop her hoping.

What she couldn't explain to the officer – who probably wouldn't care even if she could find the words – was that Henry wasn't just one more dog in a city that was full of them. He was special. Important.

How could she make the authorities understand how empty the house felt without Henry there? How Claire had cried herself to sleep again last night, but without a furry friend to comfort her. How Jack had gone completely silent – and stopped filling the dishwasher now Henry wasn't there to tackle the plates. How cold and lonely Amy's bed had been that morning, when there wasn't a wet little nose pressing against her neck, hoping for some breakfast.

Amy glanced up at the hook where Henry's lead hung, unused and unnecessary.

How had she never realised how much of a hole Henry

would leave behind in their lives? Until now, when it was too late.

The phone in her hand beeped again, and she sank down to sit on the stairs to listen to the voicemail, left when she was on the phone to any one of a number of authorities in Greater London she'd been checking in with throughout the day.

Maybe, just maybe, one of them would be calling back to tell her they'd found Henry, at last.

She scowled automatically as Jim's voice came on the line. One of the hardest parts about focusing on the future was the way the past kept interrupting her efforts.

'Hey, Amy. Um, look, about this Christmas. I know we talked about me having the kids on Boxing Day, but a friend of Bonnie's has this great cabin in the Alps, and they've invited us to go spend Christmas out there, skiing. I figured you wouldn't mind – I know how you love having Christmas at home with the kids, so really, this all works out, right? Anyway, I thought I'd come see the kids Tuesday evening. Drop off presents and all that. Yeah? Okay, see you then.'

And just like that, all her plans were pushed aside, ignored, and Jim had assumed her agreement with all of them. Really, it was just like they were still married.

Oh. The thought washed over her as Amy realised something – she was *glad* they weren't married any more. When Jim had first gone, she'd been distraught, wondering how she'd cope without the man she'd thought would be her partner for life.

Somehow, over the past six weeks, she'd come to see that being alone was far better than being with someone who didn't want to be there.

Her life was wide open now – her future still to be written.

Except for the part where her ex would be stopping by on Tuesday.

Jabbing at the phone screen, Amy deleted the message, and sighed. Future later. First, she had to prepare her kids for not seeing their father at all over Christmas. And for seeing him on Tuesday.

She wasn't entirely sure which one would go down worse.

Sighing, she checked her watch. Still too early for wine.

'Kids?' she called up the stairs, waiting for a thundering of footsteps or a yell to tell her they'd heard her. 'Can you both come down here a moment.'

Might as well get it over with. Like pulling off a sticking plaster. Or a really painful bikini wax.

'Have they found Henry?' Claire asked, as she bounced down the stairs. 'Is he coming home?'

Amy winced. 'No, sweetie, I'm sorry. I just checked in with the authorities again, and there's still no sign.'

Claire's face fell, her blue eyes wide and sad. Amy reached out and wrapped an arm around her shoulders, pulling her close against her. With Claire on the second step, and Amy on the floor, Claire was almost as tall as her.

It won't be long before she's grown up and leaving, too, Amy realised. Jack would be off to university in September – at least, he would if he knuckled down and got back to work. Since Jim had left, his homework had been erratic, to say the least.

Something else to worry about.

Jack appeared at the top of the stairs, his usual scowl firmly in place. 'What's the problem?'

'No problem,' Amy said, as cheerfully as she could manage. 'Just . . . could you come down here a moment?'

Jack rolled his eyes, but complied. Amy led them through to the kitchen, her arm still around Claire's shoulders.

Didn't she have some mince pies somewhere? Talks always went better with something sweet to eat.

As she rooted around in the cupboard, Jack and Claire settled themselves at the kitchen table. Amy glanced over at them and smiled. It was almost like when they were little, again. Jack doing his homework at the table, while Claire sat close by with her colouring or stickers, asking how long it would be until *she* could do homework.

Of course, the novelty of that had soon worn off.

But those days, the three of them in the kitchen, the kids busy while she cooked, waiting for Jim to make it home from work, Henry barking for treats at her heels . . .

Amy grabbed the box of mince pies and slammed the cupboard door.

Times had changed. She had to remember that. Even if she still had hope that Henry would be home, begging for snacks again, soon.

'So, your dad called,' Amy said, nonchalantly. She placed mince pies on two plates, added some squirty cream from the can in the fridge, and handed them over to Jack and Claire.

Jack didn't meet her gaze as he took the plate. 'So?' he asked, halfway through his first mouthful, spraying crumbs everywhere.

'So . . . there's a few changes to the plans for Christmas.'

Claire looked up, alarmed. 'Like what? No presents?'

Of course that was her first concern. Amy sighed. 'I'm sure

there will be presents. In fact, you might even get the ones from your dad early. He's coming by on Tuesday.'

'Great!' Whether Claire was more pleased about seeing Jim or the prospect of presents, Amy wasn't sure.

Jack clearly wasn't happy about either of them. 'I don't want to see him. We have to go there on Boxing Day. Isn't that bad enough?'

Well, at least there was one part of the plan he'd be pleased with. 'Actually, there's been a bit of a change there, too. Your dad's actually going away skiing for Christmas now, so we'll have a bit longer together before you go to spend time with him.' And Bonnie, she assumed. Not that they'd talked about it.

They should, Amy knew. And soon.

'Brilliant. Then I'll be out on Tuesday and I won't have to see him at all. Perfect.' Jack shoved the last half of his mince pie into his mouth.

'Jack . . .' Amy started, but Claire spoke over her.

'So, we're not seeing him at all at Christmas?'

'You're seeing him on Tuesday,' Amy said, brightly. 'In fact, we could get his presents wrapped tonight, ready to give to him. We'll put a Christmas film on, really get in the festive mood . . .'

'Have you told him about Henry yet?' Jack asked.

Amy winced. 'I haven't actually spoken to him. He left a message on my phone.'

'Meaning that you didn't want to speak to him either,' Jack said, astutely. 'So how can you nag me about having to see him when you won't?'

She didn't have a good argument for that, not really. Only

a thousand emotions that battered her heart, none of which she could put into words.

So instead, she said another true thing.

'I'm still hoping Henry will have come home by the time we see Dad.'

'Me too,' said Claire, her voice very small.

Jack looked away, and Amy saw his Adam's apple bob, hard, as he swallowed. 'Yeah. Me three.'

Oh Henry, Amy thought. *Where are you tonight?*

Day 3

Monday 16th December

HENRY

I woke the next morning from a deep sleep, after doggy dreams about chasing rabbits through puddles of gravy.

The other dogs were already awake, so I hopped down to stand beside Willow.

'So?' I asked, nudging her side to get her attention. Because even though they weren't the friendliest I wasn't ready to give up on finding some allies in the palace who at least understood me. 'What's the plan? You said you were going to let me join in with your Palace Dogs routine today, right?'

Sighing, Willow turned slowly towards me. 'Fine. But really, without Her here, it's a pale imitation of the real thing.'

'Well, I've never spent a day with Her Majesty, so I doubt I'll really notice the difference.' I was just excited to be included. I'd spent a lot of the previous day trying to imagine what the other dogs might be doing – what adventures they were having. Did they spend time chasing rabbits in the gardens? Or taste-testing the gravy? Were there Royal Pet duties I knew nothing about, like greeting important guests? Or special meals I'd missed out on somehow, like the afternoon tea Amy took Claire to with Father Christmas when she was smaller?

I wanted to know it all.

'First, we have breakfast,' Willow said, turning away again. 'I trust you can remember how that goes?'

I did, and this morning, when a new housemaid came to feed us, I waited patiently for my turn before eating. I didn't want to give Willow any excuses to shut me out again.

'Now what?' I asked, the moment the housemaid had gone.

Willow, Candy and Vulcan all exchanged annoyed looks.

'Are you going to be like this all day?' Vulcan asked.

'Like what?'

'Vulgarly excited,' Willow answered. 'And yes, I rather suspect he is.'

Candy rolled her eyes. 'It doesn't do, you see, to get too excited about things here in the Palace. Apart from anything else, you're supposed to be used to this sort of life, remember?'

'Oh. I see.' I supposed Candy had a point – I wanted to fit in here well enough for no human to notice that I didn't belong, at least until Amy could find me. 'So, what? I just sort of wander around looking superior?'

Vulcan laughed at that. Rather unnecessarily, I thought.

Willow, however, decided to continue with my instruction. 'Soon it'll be time for our morning walk,' she said. 'If we wait here, someone will come and fetch us, soon enough.'

Waiting. One of my least favourite things to do.

But a walk sounded fun, at least, so I hunkered down until a footman appeared with four leads – and some sort of jacket things.

'Cold outside today,' he said, as he manoeuvred Willow,

then Vulcan into their padded jackets. They looked like something Claire would make Sookie or me wear to take videos of us and post them online.

I did not approve.

'Do we have to wear those ridiculous things?' I whispered to Candy.

She shrugged. 'They keep us warm, outside in winter.'

'I prefer to keep warm by running around,' I said.

But apparently my fate was sealed. Soon enough I found myself outside in the Palace gardens again, this time wearing a stupid coat.

'Come on, let's make this quick,' the footman said, shivering, as he led us around the garden on the path.

I'd hoped for a chance to explore the gardens again – to run wild and stick my nose in every interesting scent I could find. Instead, the other dogs sedately stuck to the path, only departing onto the grass to take care of business. We were back at the doors to the Palace again in no time.

'Is that it?' I asked.

Willow looked at me like I was crazy. 'It's cold. Of course we don't want to stay out there too long.'

I looked longingly back out of the window at the gardens. All those pigeons left unchased. All those fascinating smells unsmelt. It seemed such a waste.

Still, maybe the next part of the corgis' agenda would be more interesting.

'So, what's next?' I hopped up the stairs beside Candy. She seemed like the more relaxed of the three dogs, so far. Willow just wanted to make sure I did everything the way *she* thought it should be done, and Vulcan just wanted rid of me as soon as possible. But Candy, although she followed the others' leads, seemed just a little more friendly.

And friendly was what I needed right now.

'Next?' Candy looked surprised. 'Well, I suppose we usually stay with Her as she goes about her business – keeping Her company in Her study, or following Her to meetings and the like. Then in the afternoon, we take tea with Her – sometimes we even get some scones. Then She might brush us, or walk us again before dinner. That sort of thing.'

Candy seemed to be missing one very important point. 'But She isn't here.'

'No,' Candy agreed, sounding forlorn. 'She isn't.'

I thought about Amy, Jack and Claire – I understood how Candy felt, but I didn't want her to feel sad so I gave her a nudge. 'So what do you do when She isn't here?'

Willow, passing us on the stairs, replied, 'We behave in the manner She would expect us to.'

'But by doing what?' I asked, chasing her towards the Corgi Room.

The answer, it seemed, was Not Much.

Without the Queen at the Palace, the other dogs were at a total loss for what to do.

'You could give me a proper tour of the Palace,' I suggested.

Willow shook her head. 'It all looks much the same after a while.'

'Well, we could find the kitchens. See if we can figure out the recipe for that brilliant gravy they serve at dinner.' That would definitely be a memento worth taking home from the Palace.

'Why would we do that?' Vulcan looked down his long

nose at me. 'They already make and bring the food for us. Why on earth would we need to know what's in it?'

'Fine.' Sighing, I sank down to my paws, and watched as the others curled up in their baskets, apparently ready for a nap.

I'd really thought today was going to be more fun than this.

Well, if I wanted fun, I'd just have to find it myself.

'Where are you going?' Willow asked, sleepily, as I passed her basket.

'That footman last night said we're allowed to go wherever we like in the Palace, right?'

Willow nodded. 'That's right.'

'Well then,' I said, lifting my nose to take in the air outside the room, 'I'm going everywhere. I'm going to explore every inch of this Palace, find all its secrets and seek out adventure!'

Vulcan snorted inelegantly at that. I ignored him.

'Who's with me?' I asked, directing my words at Candy in particular. If any of them were likely to come on an adventure with me, it was Candy the Dorgi.

But Candy looked between Vulcan and Willow, both of whom were rolling their eyes, then back at me. She gave a small, apologetic shrug, and settled down into her basket.

'Fine.' I could adventure on my own. 'Don't wait up for me.'

And with that, I strode off into the Palace corridors, an intrepid explorer. I wouldn't come back until I'd seen every last room in the Palace. (Or until it was time for another meal. Whichever happened first.)

Of course, when I made my plan, I hadn't realised quite how much of the Palace there really was to see. The parts I'd seen so far were, apparently, just the start – the top of the

rabbit hole, so to speak. (Rabbit holes always looked interesting until you realised they went much deeper than you
thought, and the rabbits were always out of reach. Of course,
by that time your muzzle was well and truly stuck, and Sookie
was sitting on the grass beside you howling with laughter.)

I padded through corridor after corridor, and room after
enormous room, all of them lavishly decorated with huge
paintings on the walls, surrounded by golden frames. And
everywhere, there were Christmas decorations, sparkling in
the winter light like snowflakes.

I saw a few people – mostly men wearing the same uniform
as John had the night before, and the grumpy man the day
before that. I snuck up on a few of them, hoping to make
friends, but mostly they just jumped back and swore when
I got close. I learned a few new words, anyway. (I could guess
their meaning easily enough!)

The funny thing was, every time, after I'd been sworn at,
the men would look around, like they were checking no one
had seen them.

In one long, long room, lined with huge paintings hanging
on a rail at the top of the red flocked walls, I came across some
other people – a small boy with blonde hair, riding a wooden
trike over the creamy patterned rugs, his little sister toddling
after him, trying to catch up. At the far end, their mother stood
laughing, her dark hair hanging around her pretty face.

They looked like a nice family. I wondered, if the Walkers
never came back for me, if those three needed a pet.

But then the boy on the trike came careening towards
me, and I hopped through a doorway into another room to
avoid being squished.

This room was even more magnificent than the ones I'd seen before. Decked out all in red and cream, everything about it was extravagant – oversized and made to impress. Huge crystal chandeliers, with white candles placed in them, hung from the ceiling along the length of the room on both sides – plus another giant one in the middle.

At the far end of the room there were three red carpeted steps up to a raised platform – with two ornate chairs with red cushions and backs, gold legs and gold embroidery on the backs. Behind the chairs hung a dark red velvet curtain.

I looked around. No one else seemed to be watching, and those chairs did look particularly comfy.

Willow *had* said we were allowed anywhere we liked. Surely that included the furniture?

I padded up the steps, my paws a little sore from all my exploring. I was sure no one would mind if I just had a little rest on one of the big chairs . . .

As I was drifting off, I heard an amused snort from the doorway. I opened one eye to see a red-headed man standing at the other end of the room. 'Granny really does let you dogs rule this place, doesn't she?'

I snuffled my agreement as I fell asleep.

When I awoke from my impromptu nap, my stomach was rumbling. Hopping down from my seat, I set out again – this time, following my nose, hopefully towards some food. The footman, John, had said that all the dog food was prepared in the kitchens – including that fabulous gravy. This Palace might have a lot of unfamiliar rooms – like the Big Chair Room or the Painting Room, never mind the Corgi Room – but even I knew what a kitchen looked like.

All I had to do now was find it.

Fortunately, corgis are in possession of an exceptionally fine sense of smell. Even in a Palace of this size, I could find a scent trail to follow. (The smell of the rabbit from last night was very memorable.)

My nose led me down a different staircase from the one I'd used before – one at least twice as big. It was as grand in its way as the Big Chair Room.

From the landing where I stood, awed, I could see that the stairs split into two, each set curving around to the ground on either side. The banister was twisty, patterned gold, and the carpets – of course – were red. And there were more huge paintings of people. I wondered if all the people on the walls were the people who lived here – and where they'd all gone. There were enough rooms in the Palace for all of them, for certain.

I pondered the question as I padded down the stairs, still chasing the delicious scent of food. Maybe they were all the people who'd lived here over the years. The family of the Queen, I supposed. Just like all the photos Amy kept on the wall by the stairs at home.

I was still thinking about Amy, and *my* family, as I trotted into another huge room, and stopped, staring.

There, placed at either side of another small set of stairs, and at the top of the stairs, were three enormous Christmas trees – at least fifteen dogs high – all decorated with bright lights and tiny red and gold crowns.

Stepping closer to the nearest tree, I tilted my head to look up at it.

Most years, Jim went out with Jack and Claire, a few weeks

before Christmas, while Amy made mince pies ready for when they came back. They would always return with a big, bushy green pine tree to put up in the lounge, and I'd dance around their feet as Jim unravelled strings of lights and Claire ate too many mince pies.

But even the biggest of those trees wasn't a patch on these three.

This year, Amy had brought back a not-real tree from the supermarket, along with a couple of boxes of mince pies. Jack had refused to help decorate it, and Claire had declared that she didn't like those mince pies, so the tree was still in its box when we left for London the other day.

I looked up a little further, and spotted something else – a big bunch of green leaves with white berries. Mistletoe. Amy always used to hang a bunch of it by the front door at Christmas, and Jim would always kiss her under it, every time he left the house, and when he came home again.

When had they stopped doing that? Was it last year? The year before? I couldn't remember.

I wondered again how they were all managing without me.

I hoped it was better than I was managing without them.

No. I wasn't going to mope. I was going to explore. Have adventures.

And besides, the smell of the pine was blocking out the scent of the kitchens, so I carried on my way to find the food.

No point pining on an empty stomach.

AMY

Monday morning, life went back to normal – or as normal as anything ever was, these days, without Jim or Henry there to share it. Amy started the day by waking up to the shrieking alarm, and fumbling for the light switch, only to remember that Henry wasn't there to take for his early morning walk.

She collapsed back onto the bed, and tried to feel grateful for the extra half hour's sleep. It wasn't the same as having a furry companion to brighten her morning, though.

It was the last week of the school term, which meant there were carol concerts to get through, assignments due in, friendly fallings-out over presents, and what seemed like endless requests for money or food or bottles from the school. Stumbling out of the bedroom twenty minutes later, Amy tripped over Sookie on her way to the bathroom, and bit her tongue to keep from swearing. Loudly.

At least someone seemed to be making the most of the dogless house. When Henry had been at home, Sookie had gone out of her way to avoid him. Now, the cat seemed to be underfoot all the time.

'I think she's missing Henry,' Claire said, bending down to

pet the cat — instead of getting her coat on ready to leave for school.

'I think she's gloating,' Jack answered. 'She's probably glad that she's the only pet.'

'I think it's cold outside and she likes to be inside by the radiators,' Amy said. 'And we need to get going, so will you two hurry up!'

Eventually, they were ready to go, and Amy got the joy of forcing her way through traffic to drop them off at two different schools — the local secondary for Claire, and the nearby sixth form college for Jack.

The kids safely at school and college — where she hoped Jack would be staying for all his classes, for once — Amy raced to the doctors' clinic where she worked and prepared to try and get through another day.

The only problem was, focusing on the patients she was trying to help was growing harder and harder as her first break approached.

She needed to call Jim. She knew that. She needed to tell him about Henry. And she absolutely had to do that before he arrived at the house the next evening and realised that Henry wasn't there.

Of course, she had quite a few other things she'd like to say to Jim too, but they might have to wait until after they'd dealt with the immediate crisis.

'Amy? Do you have a moment?' Dr Fitzgerald appeared in her doorway, in between patients. He always looked faintly rumpled, Amy thought, in a distracted, absent-minded professor sort of way. But she'd sat in with him on meetings with a few patients, and she knew he was sharp as anything when it came to medical issues. Even better, the patients liked and trusted him. That went a long way.

'Of course.' Amy pushed her chair away from her desk and turned towards him. 'What's up, Doctor?'

'Please, call me Luke.' He waved a sheet of paper vaguely at her. 'Somehow, I've got stuck with booking the table for the surgery Christmas dinner.'

Amy grinned. 'Newbie privilege.'

'And I'm sure I feel very honoured,' Luke said, drily. 'You're coming though, aren't you?'

Amy pulled a face. 'I'm not sure . . .'

'Oh, come on. Please? For me? If this dinner is a failure I'll probably have to leave and find a new surgery, just to get over the shame. And I like it here. My flat is a five-minute walk from work and, apart from anything else, Daisy loves exploring the park across the road.'

'Daisy's your Dalmatian?' Amy asked. 'I've seen you walking her a few times, when I've taken Henry out in my lunch break. She's gorgeous.'

'Thank you. And Henry . . . he's a corgi, right?'

'Right.' Amy's smile dimmed. 'Actually . . . he's missing at the moment. We took him to London on Saturday and he ran away.'

Luke's expression was stricken. 'Oh, Amy! I'm so sorry. Is there anything I can do to help? Put up posters, make calls, anything.'

'You're very kind.' Amy felt tears pricking behind her eyes. It seemed like a long time since anyone had been that kind to her.

'I just know how much it hurts to lose a pet you care

about,' he said. 'When I got divorced . . . my wife kept our dog. That's when I got Daisy. But much as I love her, it doesn't make up for the dog I lost. So seriously, anything I can do, just ask.'

'Thank you.'

'And I'll put you down for the Christmas dinner,' Luke said, backing out of the room to let a mother with a small baby in. 'You need something fun to look forward to!'

How could she argue with that?

Ten minutes later, Amy waved goodbye to a red-eyed baby who'd just suffered through his injections (and his teary-eyed mother who'd watched and held him). Once they were gone, Amy checked in with the reception desk to make sure she had time to take her break – and phone Jim. She tried to pretend that she wasn't hoping for some sort of emergency or walk-in patient that meant that she didn't have to make the call. But there was none.

With a sigh, she headed back to her desk and stared at her mobile phone.

She had to tell him. And really, what right did he have to be mad? She might have lost their dog, but he'd walked out on them all first.

In fact, she'd never have taken them all to London if Jim hadn't left to run off with Bonnie.

Which meant that, really, this was entirely Jim's fault. Just like everything else that seemed to be going wrong in their lives at the moment.

That thought made it a lot easier to press the right buttons to place the call.

'Amy?' Jim sounded just as he always had when she'd called

him at work – impatient, and slightly annoyed. 'Is this important? Only—'

'Yes,' she said, quickly. If they didn't have this conversation now, it would only be worse later. 'It's important.'

Jim gave a heavy sigh. 'Is it money? Or the kids? Is it—'

'It's Henry. He's missing.' Her heart clenched again as she said it out loud.

'Amy, can't you deal with this? I really don't have time—'

'And I do? I'm already looking after everything else you left behind here, remember.'

Jim was silent for a moment. Then he said, 'Have you tried looking in next door's garden? You know he loves hunting the squirrels there.'

'We lost him in London. On Saturday.'

'In London? What the hell did you take him to London for?'

Because I was trying to make Christmas special again. Because I'm doing it all on my own here, and that's your fault. Because Henry deserved a day trip too – because he's more a part of this family than you are, these days.

Amy took a deep breath, and held all those thoughts inside. 'Does it really matter now? What matters is getting him back.'

'Right. Right, sure. Okay.' Jim exhaled slowly. 'So, what have you done so far?'

Glad to be back on firmer, factual conversational ground, Amy explained all the steps she'd taken to try and find Henry – and how none of them had worked.

'Okay, so you've done all the obvious stuff,' Jim admitted. 'That means we need to come up with something new. Something innovative.'

'Great,' she said evenly, trying to hold her tongue at his implication that she'd only done the basics. 'Any ideas?'

'Not yet.' Jim sighed down the line. 'How are the kids taking it?'

'Not great,' Amy admitted. 'You know how much they love that dog.'

'Yeah.'

The door to the office Amy was using opened, and Shireen from the front desk stuck her head in. 'Sorry,' she whispered, pulling an apologetic face as she motioned towards the phone. 'But Lacey's just called in sick – stomach flu, so she'll be off a couple of days. Do you think you could stay and cover the after hours slots tomorrow night?'

Three months ago, Amy would have said, let me call my husband, I'm sure it'll be fine. Now, working late had become a logistical nightmare – and Shireen knew it, which was probably why she was looking so guilty about having to ask. Amy sighed. She knew her friend wouldn't have asked if she wasn't desperate. They seemed permanently short-staffed at the surgery at the moment, and Shireen was the one who had to try and make the whole thing work.

Pretty much like Amy was stuck doing at home.

'Tell you what,' Jim said, unaware of Amy's new dilemma. 'I'm on some course that finishes early tomorrow. I'll come round earlier than planned, get there for when Claire comes home from school, so I'm there when Jack arrives too. Maybe they'll have some ideas, and we can work on them together.'

'Are you sure?' Amy asked. 'Only, they need me to work late tomorrow night. So if you could stay with Claire until Jack gets home, at least . . .'

'No problem,' Jim said, firmly. Then, more quietly, 'It would be really nice to spend a bit longer with Jack and Claire, actually.'

Amy smiled, a little sadly, and nodded at Shireen, who gave her a grateful thumbs up.

'That's great,' Amy said. 'So, I'll see you tomorrow then, I guess.'

'Yep. See you then.'

'Bye.' It wasn't until she'd hung up that Amy realised she'd forgotten to warn him that his son might not be entirely happy to see him.

Oh well. He'd figure that one out for himself, soon enough.

HENRY

It turned out that, although the Palace chef daily made the most delicious meals known to dog for the Palace pets, he wasn't actually a fan of corgis. Or at least, not of me.

All I did was stick my nose around the door and sniff, taking in all those delectable smells. And, okay, I might have snuffled around the floor a bit looking for scraps. And maybe I tried a little too hard to climb up near one of the surfaces to get a taste of whatever it was that smelled *so* good in the pan. And perhaps – just perhaps – my little legs weren't quite up to the task, and I might have knocked a few utensils to the ground as I tried to pull myself up.

Still, there was no need for the sort of language the Palace chef used, in my opinion. And I am sure he wouldn't use it if *She* was around.

As I was chased out of the kitchens, the sound of frying pans clattering to the floor still ringing in my ears, I realised that Chef was clearly *not* the person to go to for unauthorised snacks and treats.

I raced through the corridors and adjoining rooms as fast as my stumpy legs could carry me – so fast, that I stopped paying any attention to where I was going. Which meant, in no time at all, I was well and truly lost.

Certain that I was far away enough from the kitchens that any pans that Chef tried to throw at me wouldn't reach me, I slowed to a walk, panting heavily as I took in my surroundings. I was back upstairs, I knew that much – I remembered scampering up some wide steps, but the staircase itself had been unfamiliar to me. Which meant I was probably in a part of the Palace I'd never visited before.

I wandered through another huge door, and found myself in yet another long, high ceiling room with paintings on the walls. In fact, it was so familiar that it took me a moment to realise what was different about this room: unlike the human portraits I'd seen everywhere else, here all the paintings were of dogs!

I paused in front of the nearest one, staring up at a very regal looking King Charles spaniel – his nose in the air, his coat glossy and healthy, and those distinctive ears hanging either side of his head. Next along was a painting of a pack of hunting dogs, chasing down a rabbit. After that, a picture of a well-groomed corgi, not unlike myself. I cocked my head to one side. It wasn't Willow, I was sure of that much, but there was a definite resemblance. Maybe one of her ancestors?

It seemed the Royal Family had a long association with dogs. It definitely made me like them more. (Okay, maybe it was the food that did that first.)

Suddenly, I heard laughter from the other end of the room. 'Admiring your forebears?' someone said.

I spun around, briefly worried that the Chef had sent

someone to follow me with a frying pan, but when I looked, there stood Sarah Morgan, her hands on her hips, smiling at me.

Smiling. At me. Like she was pleased to see me. Happy that I was at the Palace, even.

I barked with happiness as I realised I'd already found the friend I needed at the Palace! Sarah had been kind to me, right from the start. And she was new here too, so she understood how it felt. And, most importantly, she was in charge of the food, sometimes.

She was perfect.

Now I just needed to persuade her to help me.

I trotted over to her side, and she reached down to pet me, but only briefly.

'Sorry, no time to play at the moment,' she said, waving a duster at me. 'Too much to do. It wouldn't do for any of these lovely paintings to get dusty now, would it?'

She moved towards the first painting and began dusting the frame. I followed.

'Maybe once I'm done here, I can take you on your afternoon walk,' Sarah suggested, reaching up to clean a groove in the patterned frame. 'I'll need some fresh air after all this dust!'

As she moved on to the next painting, I followed again, sitting at her feet while she worked. Looking down at me, she laughed again.

'Well, I suppose there's no harm in you keeping me company while I work, is there? As I understand it, you dogs have the run of this place, anyway. I should be asking *your* permission to go places!'

Sarah, it seemed, was the chatty type. I liked it – it reminded me of Amy. She always chatted to me, when we were alone in the house, as she was going about her jobs. Sarah carried on a one-sided conversation with me as she worked, too.

Sometimes, I wished that I could speak to humans, so I could respond properly. But, on the other hand, they probably said more to me because I couldn't. And it wasn't like I couldn't make myself understood when it mattered. Like at mealtimes.

'So, how are you finding the Palace?' Sarah asked, as if I could really answer her. 'I hope the other dogs are being nicer to you than the staff are to me.'

I frowned. That didn't sound good. Why on earth wouldn't people be nice to Sarah? She was lovely.

'Oh, I shouldn't say that.' Sarah waved her duster around vaguely, as if to brush away her comments. 'It's not that they're *mean*, exactly. Well, not most of them, anyway. And I'm so lucky to be here! It's the job I've always dreamt of but never believed I could have. And I worked *so* hard to get here. I really should just be grateful that I made it and stop whining.'

She sounded like she was trying to convince herself, more than me. Like Amy had, that night Jim had packed his case and gone, as she sat on her bed and said, 'Of course he'll come back. This is only temporary.'

It hadn't worked then, and I was pretty sure it wouldn't work now. So I waited at Sarah's feet to see what came next.

With a huge sigh, she deflated, her fake smile fading as she sank down to sit on one of the many upholstered chairs that lined the edges of the room.

'The thing is, Henry, that it isn't really what I was expecting.

Oh, not the work – I knew exactly what that would be, and what would be required of me. I don't have a problem with working hard, or starting at the bottom and working up. It's not that at all.'

I nudged up against her legs, and she put her duster down to pat my head.

'The thing is . . . I grew up listening to my godfather telling me stories about what it was like to work at the Palace. He's a butler at Windsor Castle, now, but he used to work here. And he always made it sound so magical – not just the surroundings, but the . . . the Palace family, I suppose. Not the Royals, exactly. But the household. The way you all belong here, together, and it's more than just being colleagues. It's deeper. More special.' She sighed again. 'That's what I wanted when I moved here. That's why I worked so hard for it.'

I looked up at her, making my eyes big with sympathy. I might have even whimpered a little. She just looked so sad! Her blue eyes were wide and a little watery, and there was no sign of that lovely smile that had first let me know we were destined to be friends.

Sarah, I realised, was a human in need of some cheering up. Luckily for her, I had a lot of experience in that, lately.

'I think my parents thought I was just running away,' Sarah went on. 'And maybe they're right. But is that so bad? At least I was running *towards* something. And I figured that anywhere had to be better than where I was.' Something in her expression tightened, her jaw suddenly set hard. 'And I was right. It might be difficult here, and maybe the other girls *do* make fun of my accent when they think I can't hear them, and talk about how I only got the job because of who my godfather is. But it's still a million times better than staying with David, right, Henry?'

I had no idea who David was, but Sarah sounded so determined all of a sudden that I found myself barking my agreement anyway.

'Exactly.'

Jumping to her feet, Sarah began dusting again with new vigour. I followed her as she worked her way around the room.

'I deserve better than a cheating, manipulative, cruel, verbally abusive . . . *idiot* like him.' As she spoke, she punctuated each word with a wipe of her duster, until the painting she was cleaning swayed on its chains. 'Whoops,' Sarah said, with a small giggle, when she noticed.

She stepped back from the painting, and smiled down at me. 'You're a good listener, Henry. And you're right – or I am, I suppose. I'm much better off here. I mean, I even get to help look after you beautiful creatures, don't I?' She bent over to scratch my ears. 'Now, come on. The sooner I get this room dusted, the sooner we can head out to find the others on their afternoon walk, right?'

It didn't take Sarah long to finish her work, now she had cheered up. I padded along beside her as she cleaned, wondering if the afternoon walk might also involve some sort of snack. Either way, it would be good to get outside and explore again – especially if Sarah was there with me.

Suddenly, I had a thought. If I could lead Sarah to the bush where I'd entered the Palace gardens, maybe she could help me find a way back out – or at least realise the truth about what had happened. Eventually someone was going to notice that the dog who was supposed to be here – Monty – wasn't, or that I had the wrong name on my collar tag. Although no one other than Sarah seemed to be too keen to get close enough to check my collar.

I'd rather it be Sarah who sussed it out anyway, I decided. Already, I trusted her to help me find my way back to my family – rather than just tossing me out on the street. She knew how it felt not to belong somewhere, and I was certain she'd want to help me.

I just had to make her understand what the problem was.

Sarah led me out into the gardens on a lead, just like the footman had that morning.

'Sorry, Henry,' she said, as she clipped it on. 'I'm sure I could trust you not to run off. But it's just that, with you being new, I can't risk it. Not that you'll find it easy to escape from these gardens! They go on forever, it seems like, to me. Maybe once you're used to them I'll let you run free a bit more.'

Free sounded good. And, of course, I already knew just how extensive the gardens were – it was exploring them that kept me busy so long that I forgot to go back to the Walkers.

Still, I didn't mind staying with Sarah. She chatted to me as we walked, and it was comforting just to hear her voice – to know that someone, at least, was glad that I was there.

We were halfway around the gardens before we bumped into another human. Literally, in Sarah's case. We turned a corner, around one of those large, evergreen bushes (that *wasn't* the one I'd squeezed through – I checked) and suddenly – crash!

'Oh gosh, I'm so sorry!' she said, looking flustered.

The man she'd slammed into gripped her elbow to steady her, and smiled. 'No harm done.'

'Are you sure?' Sarah asked. 'I didn't hurt you? Oh! And Henry!' She crouched down quickly to check me over. 'Are you okay, Henry? You didn't get hurt did you? I'd never forgive myself . . .'

The man chuckled. 'You're in the right place, if you like dogs,' he said. 'You can't get away from them in Buckingham Palace.'

'But why would you want to?' Sarah, reassured that I was just fine, stood up again. 'They're such lovely creatures. Back home on the farm, my parents have springer spaniels, so corgis are new to me – but Henry is *such* a friendly dog.'

'I'm glad one of them is.' The man bent down to rub between my ears. 'The other footmen are always complaining about how yappy they are. And snappy, for that matter.'

'Not Henry,' Sarah said, loyally. 'He's a darling.' I barked my agreement. Amy was always saying that about me.

'Henry, huh? You must be our new guy. Funny, I thought his name was something else.' He frowned for a moment, like he was trying to remember, then shook his head. Poor old Monty. He hadn't even made it to the Palace properly yet and everyone had forgotten his name already. 'Anyway, pleased to meet you, Henry. I'm Oliver Kinchen-Williams, Senior Footman here at the Palace.'

'Oh!' Sarah said, suddenly. '*You're* Oliver. I didn't realise . . . my godfather, he told me to introduce myself to you when I started here. But with one thing and another . . . I hadn't. Yet. I'm Sarah Morgan.'

Something in her tone didn't quite ring true to me – I have a good ear for lies and half-truths. I didn't think Sarah was really deceiving Oliver, or anything, but I wondered what her reasons *really* were for not introducing herself sooner. I suspected it had something to do with the less than friendly attitude of the other staff she'd met so far.

If the other staff were treating Sarah the same way Willow and the Dorgis were acting with me, then Sarah would definitely need my cheering up efforts. I could help her make friends around the Palace, I was sure – not everyone could be mean and horrible, could they? And Amy always said what a friendly dog I was. It would be easy!

'I am pleased to finally make your acquaintance, Sarah,' Oliver said, with a confused smile. 'Now, who on earth might your godfather be that he knows me? I'm not exactly a big name around this place.'

'To him you are,' Sarah said. 'He calls you his protégé.'

Understanding flooded Oliver's face. 'There's only one person that could be! How is old Tom? Still ruling the roost at Windsor – at least, when the Royals aren't in residence?'

'He is,' Sarah replied, grinning. 'I don't think he could bear to be anywhere else, really.'

'It's an odd life, in royal service,' Oliver admitted. 'Either you're made for it, or you're not. But if you are . . .'

'Why would you be anywhere else?' Sarah finished for him. 'I've heard Tom say that a lot!'

'He does have his sayings, doesn't he?'

'And he says them often,' Sarah agreed.

I was glad that Sarah had found someone to talk to, someone who shared her interests, and knew her godfather.

That was a really good start for my Cheer Up Sarah campaign.

But unfortunately, the conversation itself wasn't quite as interesting to me as the pigeon that had just hopped across the path.

I gave a tug on my lead, without even meaning to, and Sarah looked down at me. 'Sorry, I promised Henry a proper walk, and we're still only halfway round.'

'And I need to get back to work, anyway,' Oliver said. 'But it was very nice to meet you, Sarah.' I gave a sharp bark, trying to tell him not to go – to stay and talk to Sarah some more. But it only made them both laugh.

'And you, too, Henry,' Oliver added. 'I hope I'll see you both around the Palace again, soon.'

'I'm sure you will.' Sarah gave a sunny smile, and suddenly the day didn't seem quite so cold.

Oliver headed back towards the garden doors, and Sarah and I stood and watched him for a moment.

Then she gave a little sigh. 'He seemed nice, didn't he? I knew there *had* to be some nice people here at the Palace somewhere.'

I barked, and pulled on my lead again. If Oliver was gone, why were we still standing here?

Sarah laughed. 'Come on, then, you. Let's see if we can catch up with *your* friends, too.'

Day 4

Tuesday 17th December

AMY

The cold, sharp air felt fresh against Amy's face as she crossed the road from the surgery to the park on her lunch break. She'd got so used to spending her lunchtimes out in the fresh air, walking Henry, that she'd felt cooped in and stuffy-headed staying in the office when she could be outside.

Besides, outside she didn't get any pitying looks from the other staff – not just for the loss of her husband, but now the loss of her dog, too.

Amy wasn't entirely sure how to tell them she couldn't decide which one she missed more.

Sinking down to sit on a bench under a bare-branched tree, she sighed. That wasn't true, anyway.

She definitely missed Henry the most.

As she sat and watched the park – the people walking, with and without dogs, the squirrels scampering with the last of the nuts, the birds searching for sandwich scraps – it was almost as if Henry was there with her. Any moment now, he'd bound forward after a pigeon, or start snuffling around the base of that tree to figure out what smelled so interesting.

Except, of course, he couldn't. Because he was lost.

'Still no sign of Henry, then?' Luke settled onto the bench beside her, Daisy sitting patiently at his feet in a way that Henry never would have managed.

'Not a whisker,' Amy said, sadly. 'I've been calling everywhere I can think of, asking them to check the microchips of any corgis that have been found in the Greater London area . . . but nothing.'

'I'm sorry,' Luke said. 'But have faith. He'll come home eventually.'

'How can you possibly know that?' Amy asked. Luke's optimism was kind, but she couldn't help but worry that it was misplaced.

But Luke gave her a sunny smile. 'With family like you, how could he possibly stay away?'

Amy smiled back, her day suddenly a little warmer.

'So, you and Daisy are enjoying Redhill, then?' Amy asked. It seemed that she'd been telling Luke a great deal about her life recently, and not learnt very much about his in return. Perhaps it was time to redress that balance.

'Very much,' Luke said. As if to agree with her owner, Daisy gave a small bark, and trotted a little way apart from them in the direction of a bustling squirrel. 'Everyone at the surgery has been very welcoming.'

'We're just grateful to have a full complement of doctors again!' Amy laughed. 'The last few months since Doctor Shah retired have been *very* busy.'

'I'm glad to have been able to help.'

'Oh! Not that that's the only reason we're glad to have you, of course,' Amy said, quickly. 'The patients all seem to love you, and, well, you're a nice guy.'

'Compliment of the century, right there,' Luke said, with a grin. 'But I'll take nice guy. Better than the alternative.'

'Most definitely,' Amy agreed. In fact, Luke seemed like *such* a nice guy, it was hard to imagine why his wife would have divorced him.

Unless he had a hidden dark side, of course . . .

'What just happened then?' Luke looked at her curiously. 'Your face just went from "nice guy" to "serial killer" in ten seconds flat.'

Amy shook her head, and laughed. 'Just trying to figure out what your dark side is.'

'Not serial killer, I promise,' Luke replied. 'I mean, I'm not the world's tidiest person, and you already know that my handwriting is atrocious. But I'm kind to children and animals, and I cook a mean curry.'

'The good does seem to outweigh the bad, then,' Amy admitted. There must be some way to ask 'how did your marriage end' without it sounding like an accusation, right? She just couldn't think of it.

'If what you're really asking is "why did my wife leave me", that's easy,' Luke said, putting her out of her misery. 'We got married very young, before we were done growing up really, and we never talked about the future in the way we should have.' He shrugged, although Amy could still see the pain in his eyes as he talked about it. 'Turned out, we grew into very different people – and we didn't like the other person so much any more. Not to mention, we both wanted very different lives. So really, divorce was sort of inevitable. When she left me, I was hardly even surprised. Which doesn't mean it didn't hurt like hell at the time, of course.'

'I'm sorry.' Amy placed a hand briefly on his, and he smiled up at her.

'It's fine. Well, it's sad, of course – I thought I had life sussed out, and now I'm back at the start again,' he said. 'But actually, there's something quite liberating about that. I get to design my future myself, as the person I am now – not the boy I was at nineteen. That's exciting.'

'It sounds it.' Maybe she should be thinking of her life that way, too. Jack would be off at university next year, and Claire would follow a few years later. Amy had her whole future ahead of her. How did she want to spend it? Who did she want to be, without Jim there to help shape her decisions?

'What about you?' Luke said. 'If you don't mind me asking.'

Amy gave him a small, half smile. 'Oh, that's even easier. My husband fell in love with someone else.'

It felt good to say it – to admit that truth. Not 'he left me', or 'he cheated on me', or even 'he abandoned me'. Yes, he'd done all of those things, and the pain he'd caused wasn't going to fade away completely for a very long time.

But in the end, Amy realised, it hadn't been about her.

She hadn't done anything wrong, she hadn't been the wrong wife for him, she hadn't driven him away.

Jim had fallen in love with someone else. It was sad, and it hurt – but it wasn't her fault.

'He's an idiot, then,' Luke said.

'Oh, absolutely,' Amy agreed. 'But honestly? I think it's all going to work out just fine. In the end.'

After all, hadn't it been Luke who'd told her to focus on the future?

And suddenly, that future was looking a lot more exciting.

'Good,' Luke said.

Together, they sat and watched Daisy chase around the park for the rest of their lunch break.

HENRY

My days at the Palace were already starting to settle into a sort of routine. Willow and the others assured me that once She came home, things would be even better – except, of course, we all knew I probably wouldn't be around to experience that.

As it was, I was content enough adventuring around the Palace alone – or with Sarah. I'd decided that it was definitely worth staying with the other dogs until after the morning meal – just to make sure I didn't miss out on those meaty dog biscuits. Then, I'd go exploring – roaming the halls and the rooms of the Palace and getting to know them all. I was building a scent map of the place, slowly but surely, until I could find my way around with my eyes shut. (Not that I'd want to, of course, but it was a useful way of making sure I didn't get any more lost than I already was.) I tried to get Candy to come adventuring with me, and I thought she might be starting to waver, but every time Vulcan or Willow gave her one of those superior Looks, she'd change her mind and slink back to her basket.

Never mind. I'd win her over eventually. I was a charming dog, remember.

Anyway, after I'd explored a new area of the Palace, and around the time I started getting bored of more paintings and more golden-legged furniture, I went in search of Sarah.

Sarah seemed to have lots of different duties around the Palace, mostly to do with cleaning, and she always seemed happy enough to be doing them. As I pottered along beside her, she'd talk to me, and so I learned all about her life before she came to the Palace, and what she'd left behind.

It didn't take long for me to come to the conclusion that she was right – she was far better off here with me, than back at home with her ex, David.

'It's not that I don't miss it there,' Sarah said, that morning, as she dusted another vase. 'Home is . . . well, it's home, isn't it? I think you always miss it, just a bit. But I'd outgrown it, maybe. It was time to move on, anyway. After everything happened with David . . . I decided it was time to find the real me again. The happy, enthusiastic me. So that's why I came here!'

It seemed to me that the change of location had worked for Sarah. Most of the time she *did* seem happy and enthusiastic. Except when one of the other staff said something mean – like copying her accent, or making a comment about her godfather.

The only other times she seemed sad was when she talked about David – or when she was thinking about him. I could always tell when that happened, because she'd start cleaning slower, and her eyes lost all their sparkle.

'I don't know why I still get sad about it. It's not that I miss him, exactly,' she said, slumping down to sit on one of the red upholstered benches in the room she was cleaning.

'It's more that I miss the life I thought we were going to have together. Which is silly, because I know now that the life *I* dreamt of never even existed.'

That was my cue to get to work on cheering her up, I decided.

The best way to do that, in my experience with Amy and Claire, was to get Sarah outside. So, the moment she'd finished her jobs, I persuaded Sarah to take me out to find the other dogs on their midday walk, before she had to go back in to eat her lunch.

So far, I hadn't had any luck in leading Sarah to the bush I'd entered the gardens through. Not least because I couldn't remember where it was. And, to be honest, all big, green shrubs look sort of the same from corgi level.

Still, maybe today would be the day!

'You're ready for your walk then, I assume,' Sarah said, laughing when I appeared with my lead in my mouth. I'd found a whole stash of them hung by one of the garden doors the day before, so now I knew just where to go when I needed a walk.

'Come on then,' Sarah said, clipping the lead to my collar. 'I suppose this room is as clean as it's going to get, anyway.'

Outside, Sarah's mood brightened almost immediately – especially when I did some of my best funny tricks for her. It's hard not to be happy when there's a corgi gallivanting around for your pleasure, chasing squirrels halfway up trees before slipping back down again, or hopping over stepping stones and skipping into bushes to look for fun treats to bring back for you.

By the time we met up with the other dogs, and Sarah

handed me over to the footman walking them so she could go and eat her lunch, she was beaming away again. Good.

After the midday walk, and all my exertions entertaining Sarah, I took advantage of the Corgi Room for a small snooze before dinner. I wanted to be well rested to really appreciate all the effort that Chef had gone to (while still staying well out of the reach of his frying pan).

My plans for the rest of the afternoon were light. A bit more socialising with the other dogs – I was still trying to win Candy over at least, and I could definitely feel her softening. Perhaps I'd get my coat brushed by Sarah or one of the other staff (during which Willow and the others would inevitably moan, because they were used to having it done by the Queen herself), and before long it was time for bed.

All in all, it wasn't a bad life – for however long I got to live it.

But that night, I awoke suddenly to the sound of crying. Not human crying, but dog crying. The sort of whimpering and whining that let me know whoever was doing it was in real distress.

In the darkness, I hopped down from my bed, and twitched my ears to get a firm lead on the direction of the sound. Then I followed it, all the way to Candy's basket.

'Candy? Candy?' I tried not to make too much noise, for fear of waking the others, but I soon realised that Candy was still asleep.

She was dreaming. But whatever she was dreaming about, it sounded utterly terrifying.

I've had some scary night terrors over the years, often to do with there being no more food, ever again. Or being chased by a ten foot tall version of Sookie. Or . . . well, anyway. I'd never had any dream as scary as Candy's sounded.

Tentatively, I jumped up, leaning my front paws against her basket, and said her name again, close to her ear. Still nothing, except more whimpers. I was starting to think I was actually making things worse.

I reached out and pressed my nose to her side, nuzzling her gently until she started to stir. Her eyes fluttered open.

'What on earth are you *doing*?' she asked, obviously outraged.

'You were having a bad dream.' I pulled back to look her in the face. 'You were whimpering. Crying. I thought I'd better wake you up.'

'I do not *whimper*.'

'Fine, if you say so.' I dropped back down to all four paws. 'But that was what it sounded like.'

I turned to head back to my own bed, but Candy's voice stopped me. 'Wait . . .'

Pausing, I twisted my head to look back over my flanks at her. 'Yes?'

She looked nervous, all of a sudden. Scared, even. 'Could you just . . . stay? Just for a little while?'

Whatever that dream had been, it must have really freaked her out if she was accepting my company over being alone. Or maybe she was softening to me more than I'd thought.

'Of course.' I put my paws up on the edge of her basket again and, this time, she shifted over to make room for me to get in there too. So, after a moment's pause, I did.

Candy nuzzled into my side as I settled down. One thing I'd noticed since I arrived, the Dorgis were definitely smaller, with shorter legs than me and Willow. And Candy was even smaller than Vulcan, so there was plenty of room for us both in the spacious basket provided by the Palace.

I wanted to comfort her. To cuddle up to her and tell her everything would be okay. Why was it that I could cheer up humans easily, even though they couldn't understand me, but I couldn't seem to get close to these other dogs, who understood every word I said?

Still, Candy had let me in. She was scared and alone, and she'd welcomed me into her basket – which meant it was my job to make her feel better.

If only I knew how.

'Could you do something for me?' she asked, already sounding sleepy again.

'Anything,' I said. 'What do you need?'

'Tell me a story?' she said.

'A story?' I knew lots of stories, but they were mostly human ones. Books that Jack and Claire had brought home from school and been made to read out loud, when they were younger. Or TV shows and films that I'd watched with the family on movie nights.

I knew all about happy endings, and how to get two people who were perfect for each other to fall in love. I even knew exactly what Christmas should look like, and how human best friends cheered each other up when they were sad.

But I didn't know many stories about dogs, that weren't really about their human owners. And I didn't know what story to tell Candy to chase her nightmares away.

'What sort of a story?' I asked.

Candy yawned. 'Tell me all about your life before you

came to the Palace. About the world out there. And your family – what were they called?'

'The Walkers.' I had a lump in my throat just saying their name. I'd been having so much fun exploring the Palace, and making friends with Sarah, I'd almost forgotten about them, just for a day, but now I thought about them the emptiness opened up inside me again.

'Yes, the Walkers. Tell me all about them,' Candy ordered.

I knew why she was asking. She didn't really care about me, or my life before the Palace. She just wanted distracting from whatever her bad dream had been.

But I wasn't one to leave another dog scared and alone. Jack wouldn't do that, and neither would I.

'Jim and Amy brought me home with them when I was just eight weeks old,' I started. 'I was a present for Jack's tenth birthday, and from the moment we met, we were best friends.'

I told her all about the Walkers, and Redhill, and the parks and the people and the squirrels. I talked and talked, until I realised Candy had fallen asleep.

By then, I was far too tired to make it back to my own basket. Especially when Candy's was so comfortable, with her in it to make it extra cosy.

So I fell asleep there, too, my nose pressed against her side hoping that I might just wake up next to Amy in the morning, my time at the Palace only a dream.

AMY

Why was it that late shifts always ended up running even later than they were supposed to? First it had been a number of complicated appointments running over all through the afternoon, then a problem with the computer system, and finally the burglar alarm had been playing up. All in all, Amy rather thought the day was out to get her.

She'd phoned home during the afternoon, to check that the kids had got back from school okay, and that Jim had been there to meet them. She'd spoken to Jack, who had seemed in a worse mood than ever.

'Why didn't you tell me *he'd* be here early?' Jack had whined, the minute he realised who was calling.

Because you'd have gone out of your way not to be there, Amy had thought, but didn't say.

'*He* is your father, Jack,' she'd said instead, sighing. 'Whatever has happened, whatever happens next, he's still your dad. And Claire's too. And this is the only chance the two of you have to spend time with him before Christmas. So make the most of it? Please?'

She wasn't sure if her pleading had done any good, but at

least she knew she'd done her part. Jim couldn't blame her if Jack didn't want to be around him.

Finally, the surgery was all locked up, and Amy could head home. To her dogless house, her grumpy children, and her cheating almost ex-husband. She was just living the Christmas dream. Really.

She made herself remember Luke Fitzgerald's smile, and his total confidence that everything would work out. It didn't make her feel as good as it had in person, but it was a start.

As she pulled into her street, she realised how dark her house looked compared to the others. In other years, Jim would have put up lights on the roof, or at least around the ground floor windows. Somewhere at the back of the garage was a wicker reindeer that Claire had always loved, with tiny fairy lights strung around its antlers. She should find the reindeer. Make an effort. Focus on their future – her Christmas with the kids.

Maybe tomorrow.

At the very least she should finally put up the fake tree she'd picked up at the supermarket. It was so small it wouldn't take too many decorations to cover it. Which was just as well; most of the ones in the attic had too many memories attached to them for her to want to put them on the tree this year. Like the glass hearts she and Jim had bought in Venice on their honeymoon, or the angel decorations Jim had bought her over the years – one every December, to add to her collection.

Until this year.

Maybe she should just buy all new decorations. Have a festive fresh start, so to speak.

Exhausted, Amy rooted around in her pockets for her keys, only to have the front door yanked open before she could insert them into the lock.

'Where have you been?' Jim asked, sounding annoyed. 'I called your mobile half a dozen times.'

'I was working,' Amy pointed out. 'And I called home earlier – I spoke to Jack.'

'And told him it was okay to go out, even though this was my only night with the kids before Christmas? What happened to not bringing the kids into this? If you're mad at me—'

'Okay, stop right there,' Amy snapped. Surely the best thing about not being married to Jim any more was that she didn't have to answer to him. Or anyone else, for that matter. She was her own person, she got to make her own decisions, her own future – and she definitely didn't have to put up with being spoken to like that. 'First of all: *if* I'm mad with you? Jim, you walked out on nearly twenty years of marriage so you could be the ultimate cliché and run off with your secretary. Trust me, I'm not going to stop being mad with you for a hell of a long time yet.' She kept her voice down, aware that Claire was somewhere in the house. But that wasn't going to stop her telling the truth.

Amy took a breath, pleased to see that Jim had stepped back, and looked suitably guilty as she brushed past him into the house.

'Secondly, it was your decision to spend Christmas skiing with said secretary.' Amy slipped her coat off her shoulders and slung it over the end of the bannister, instead of hanging it up on the coat rack. That had always driven Jim crazy. 'I told you that if you wanted to spend Christmas with your kids, that we'd make it work here. *You* chose to go away.'

'Bonnie said—'

'Bonnie isn't part of this family.' Not yet, anyway. She suspected eventually she'd be Jack and Claire's stepmother, and Amy would have to learn to get along with her. But for now, she wasn't part of this argument. This was still about *their* family, for the time being 'And I'm not done talking.'

'Right. Sorry,' he said looking shamefaced.

'Thirdly, I'm not bringing the kids into anything. I told Jack to be here tonight – and I certainly didn't tell him that he could go out.'

Not that she was hugely surprised that he'd wanted to. Jack had been very clear about his feelings for his father, over the last couple of months.

'You didn't?'

'No, I didn't.'

They stared at each other for a long moment, weighing up the meaning of that. Amy couldn't help but take in the changes in Jim since he'd left. She'd known something was different for months before it happened. It wasn't just the secretive phone calls, or the extra work trips away. It had been the changes in *him* – the way he dressed, the care he took over shaving or styling his hair. A sudden interest in country music that had never existed before.

She'd known, Amy admitted to herself at last. She'd known he was having an affair, and she hadn't confronted him about it, not because she was scared to lose him, but because it was easier for their family if she just turned a blind eye and kept things together.

But sometimes easier wasn't better, she realised. Sometimes, you needed the big changes to move forward. To find a better future.

She just wondered what other changes she'd be called on to make.

'So, Jack played us,' Jim said, eventually.

'He played *you*,' Amy corrected him. 'If you'd called me to check—'

'I did call!'

'Before or after Jack walked out the door?' Amy placed her hands on her hips and waited for the answer she already knew.

'After.' Jim scowled. 'He didn't really wait for me to give permission.'

Amy sighed. 'He's seventeen, Jim. He's almost an adult. Another nine months and he'll be off to university, and soon enough it'll be up to him if he even wants to see us at all. If you want to keep him in your life, you have to give him a reason.'

'I'm his father!' Jim protested. 'Isn't that reason enough?'

Not when you don't act like it. Not when you abandoned him. Not when you tore our family apart . . .

Amy shook her head. She couldn't think like that.

She knew, deep down, that Jack and Claire would both be better off with Jim in their lives. He was, it turned out, a rubbish husband – but he'd always been a good dad.

Until now.

'You really have to go skiing?' she asked. 'I think it would mean a lot to them to have you here, this first Christmas.'

'It's all booked,' Jim said, weakly. 'And Bonnie's so excited about it.'

'It's your choice,' Amy repeated. At the very least, she could make him take responsibility for his actions. 'Where's Claire?'

'She ran off upstairs when Jack and I were arguing.'

'So, what, about an hour ago?' Amy guessed.

'Yeah, I suppose so.'

'Did you at least feed them dinner?'

Jim looked affronted. 'Of course I did! I haven't totally forgotten how to be a parent in the last six weeks, you know.'

Amy didn't grace that with a reply.

Trudging up the stairs, she called out for her daughter, but got no answer. As she reached her bedroom door, she found it ajar, and nudged it open enough to peer through the gap.

'Claire?'

'What?' The response came from under a pile of blankets on the bed. Amy could just make out the torchlight through the sheets, and Sookie, curled up on the pillow.

Amy perched on the edge of the bed, and peeled back the covers enough to find Claire's face. Sookie, obviously sensing she was no longer needed, hopped down and headed for the door.

'What are you reading?' Amy asked, nodding at the book in Claire's hand.

She held it up so her mum could see the cover. *The Lost Puppy*.

'Been a long time since we read that one together.' It had been Claire's favourite book in the world when she was six. They'd read it over and over again for months. Now, at twice that age, she was obviously finding comfort in it again.

And thinking about Henry, Amy was willing to bet.

'Do you think Henry will ever find his way home? Like

Rusty does in the book?' Claire's voice was small, lost. It made her sound about six again. Amy missed those days, when both her kids were small enough for her to hold them in her arms and imagine she'd never have to let them go.

'I don't know, sweetheart.' Leaning over, Amy kissed the top of her daughter's head and plucked the book from her hands. Comfort reading or not, she had a feeling it wasn't helping tonight. 'But I hope so. And we'll keep doing everything we can to get him home.'

'But nothing we try seems to be *working*,' Claire whined.

She was right. Having faith that Henry would find his way home was all well and good. But that didn't mean they couldn't help things along . . .

'Come on,' Amy said. 'Let's go downstairs and talk with your dad. Maybe he can think of some new things for us to try to help find Henry.'

If nothing else, at least he could start earning his keep as a father again, while she got out that Christmas tree. And maybe by the time they were done, Jack would be home – and they could start mending that bridge, too.

'We need a new plan,' Amy announced, as she and Claire walked into the kitchen. 'A plan to find Henry.'

'What sort of thing were you thinking of?' Jim asked, looking uncertain.

Amy shrugged, trying to resist the urge to roll her eyes at her ex-husband. 'That's what I was hoping you'd be able to help with. I told you, we've notified the authorities, we're checking in regularly, we've made sure everyone who is anyone knows that he's microchipped and missing . . . I don't know what else we can do.'

'But there has to be something,' Claire said, looking much more like her almost teenager self again, rather than the scared little girl she'd been ten minutes before. 'Because what we've done so far isn't working. We need something that does work.'

'Well . . . if he was lost around here, I guess we'd put up missing posters and such, right?' Jim said.

'Are you suggesting we go pin a poster to the gates of Buckingham Palace?' Amy asked, eyebrows raised. 'Because I believe that sort of thing is discouraged by the guards . . .'

'No, no, of course not,' Jim said. 'But there has to be something similar we can do. Like, online.'

'A Facebook hunt?' Claire suggested. 'Like a picture of him, saying when and where we lost him, and asking anyone who was there that day to think if they might have seen him?'

'A Hunt for Henry.' Jim clicked his fingers. 'Exactly!'

'But you'll have to set it up,' Claire said. 'I'm not old enough for Facebook. Apparently.' She rolled her eyes in Amy's direction as she said it.

'And I don't have an account any more.' Amy didn't look at Jim. She didn't want him to know that he was the reason she'd deleted it. She couldn't bear seeing everyone else's perfect Christmases – perfect lives – while hers was falling apart around her. And she really didn't want to see scenes from Jim's new life, every time he hung out with one of their mutual friends. That sort of thing was better off unknown.

'Fine. Bring me your laptop?' Jim asked Claire, who dashed off to fetch it from her room.

'Do you think it will help?' Amy asked, moving across the

kitchen to flip on the kettle. This sounded like the kind of endeavour that would be made easier with tea. And maybe another of those mince pies, if Jack had left any. 'The Facebook thing, I mean.'

Jim shrugged. 'Gotta be worth a shot, right? And besides . . .' He glanced out into the hallway, obviously making sure that Claire wasn't hanging around to listen. 'It'll make her feel better, just knowing we're doing *something*.'

'You're right,' Amy said, surprised. 'The most frustrating thing is how little we can do except wait.'

'Well, you always were a very patient person.' Jim gave her a small half-smile, and Amy realised that might have been the nicest thing either of them had said to the other in months.

'I just hope he comes home. I miss him.' It felt weird to admit that. When they'd been together, Henry had always been Jim's dog, not hers. Something that he and Jack shared. She and Claire had had Sookie instead.

But it seemed that Henry had wormed his way into all their hearts. And without him . . . the house felt even less like home than it had since Jim left.

'I hope so too,' Jim said, seeming a bit upset for the first time about Henry being missing.

Claire came racing back through the door with her laptop, and Amy turned her attention back to the kettle and mince pies, while they got it set up. Placing cups of tea and sweet treats on the kitchen table, she left them to it while she went and dug the fake tree out of the garage and dragged it through to the lounge.

It didn't take too long to set up, thankfully. In the bag she'd stashed with it, Amy found a selection of discount baubles she'd picked up at the same time, and a small string of fairy lights. They weren't much, but once they were all on the tree at least the lounge started to look a little bit festive.

By the time she made it back through to the kitchen, the tea and the mince pies were long gone – and there was a Hunt for Henry Facebook page up and running. Amy grabbed the packet of mince pies and replenished the plate.

'It looks great,' she said, leaning over Claire's shoulder to take a look at the webpage. Claire had included a lovely photo of Henry from last Christmas, wearing a paper crown and the fancy red collar she'd picked out for his present in the pet supplies shop. Just looking at it made Amy miss his furry little face all over again.

'Claire did all the hard work,' Jim said. 'I just provided the log in.'

'So, what do we do now?' Amy asked.

'Wait, mostly.' Jim gave a small shrug. 'These things can take a while to pick up. We'll just need to keep an eye on it over the next few days. See if we get any responses – sightings, messages and so on.'

'I'm going to keep watching it now,' Claire said. 'I need to know how many hits we get.' She reached for a second mince pie. 'How many likes, how many shares. The more people who see this post, the better. I mean, people visit Buckingham Palace from all over the world, right? So we need this post to get shared far and wide. Someone must have seen *something*.'

Amy and Jim exchanged a look. They might have focused Claire's attention on taking action, but Amy sincerely hoped that they hadn't raised her hopes for nothing.

At that moment, the front door slammed open, crashing against the telephone table in the way Jack knew she hated. Still, she bit her tongue. They were going for family unity tonight – and she knew her son. The harder she nagged, the further he'd pull away. In the grand scheme of things, one slammed door wasn't important.

His relationship with his father was.

'Jack, you're home,' she said, as he appeared in the kitchen door, hovering half in, half out of the room, the way he always did when he knew he was in trouble. 'I didn't know you'd be going out tonight.'

She saw Jack glance over at his father, saw their gazes meet.

Please, Jim. Just this once, play along. Of course, if she'd ever had any telepathic powers with her husband, they might not be in this mess in the first place.

Or maybe they'd have just been in it a lot sooner.

To her relief, Jim held his tongue. Later, she and Jack would be having a talk – a talk about respect, about playing parents off against each other, and about making time for family.

For now, she just wanted him to *actually* make time for family.

'Uh, Toby called and asked me over to help him with something,' Jack said. Then he caught sight of the laptop screen Claire was still staring at. 'Hey, what's that?'

'It's a "Hunt for Henry" page,' Claire said, her eyes never leaving the screen. 'Dad helped me set it up. It's to try and find someone who might have seen what happened to Henry at the Palace last weekend.'

'That's . . . a good idea,' Jack said, looking at Jim in surprise. 'Any luck yet?'

Claire shook her head. 'But we've got ten shares already, and over fifty hits. Plus a few comments from Dad's friends who work in London saying they'll ask around locally if anyone has seen him.'

'It's a start,' Jack said, reaching for a mince pie off the plate. 'Hang on, let me share it in a few groups I know. See if that gets any traction. In fact, let's add me as an administrator to the page – that way I can do more with it.'

Soon they were working on it together: Jack on his phone, Claire still on the laptop. Jim caught her eye and smiled, and Amy couldn't help but smile back.

Maybe, just maybe, they'd all get through this.

And maybe Henry would come home to share it with them.

Day 5

Wednesday 18th December

HENRY

I woke the next morning warm and cosy in a way I hadn't been since I left the Walkers' house. It took me a moment to figure out why, and by that time Candy was awake and yelping for me to get away from her.

I rolled my eyes and hopped down, stretching out my back as I landed. Apparently I was fine company in the night, when she was scared and needed a friend, but not in the daylight hours when the other dogs might see.

Well. She'd learn I am *excellent* company all the time, soon enough, I was sure.

Another day in the Palace, and already I thought I knew what to expect. This was a place that ran on tradition, order and routine. Even for us dogs, the days proceeded in an order set down years ago, with very little variation.

Which is why I was so disturbed when I couldn't find Sarah after breakfast.

I checked all the usual places, all the rooms she normally took care of, racing through the halls and the galleries hunting her down. I couldn't even catch a whiff of her scent.

I did come across some other new people, though, in one of the larger rooms, shifting furniture around and laying out new tables and chairs that hadn't been there before. Obviously something was going on. Was Sarah caught up in it?

Eventually, I tracked my friend down by pure chance – I met her coming the other way down a corridor I'd never explored before.

'Henry!' Sarah sounded delighted to see me, which is always gratifying. 'I wondered if you'd find me this morning. It's my day off.'

A day off. When Amy had one of those, or Jim, they tended to be spent out of the house. But when the house in question was as big as Buckingham Palace, maybe Sarah didn't feel the need to leave.

'I thought I'd spend it catching up on a few things – like Christmas cards,' she said, as I turned around to trot alongside her as she walked. 'I've been writing them all morning. It's funny, when you realise how many people you normally wish a Merry Christmas in person, and then try to write to them all. I ended up doing just one card for the village church, and another for the pub – otherwise I'd have been there all morning!'

From the stack of envelopes in her hand, I could see she clearly hadn't thinned out the list that much. It reminded me of when Claire was smaller, and Amy used to have to bribe her with chocolate to write cards to all the other children in her class at school. It always seemed a little ridiculous to me – all these pieces of card sent out into the world, and just as many coming back in. Amy would attach them to ribbons and hang them from the stairs – and I got into all sorts of trouble when I tried to play with them. Then in the New Year they'd all go out in the green bin anyway. What a waste.

This year, most of the cards we'd received were still sitting in a pile on the kitchen counter – or at least, they had been when I left. And I hadn't seen Amy writing any at all.

'So now I'm off to the Post Office to post them,' Sarah said, cheerfully, breaking through my memories. 'Are you coming with me?'

I stumbled to a stop.

I wanted to, of course. Sarah was fast becoming my best friend – maybe only friend, if you discounted Candy last night – in Buckingham Palace. But Post Offices, I knew from queuing with Amy in previous years, were in shopping centres, or on the high street in the town. And while I might be allowed to roam anywhere I liked in the Palace, I'd seen no indication that I was allowed to go outside the grounds – in fact, Willow had made that quite clear. I didn't want Sarah to get into trouble for taking me outside.

Sarah looked down at me and laughed. Then, as if she could read my mind, she said, 'Don't worry, silly. You don't have to leave the Palace. There's a Post Office right here in the building, you know!'

That, I didn't know. Clearly Willow hadn't thought it was important information to share.

Cheered, I hopped forward again, eager to see the Palace Post Office.

'Apparently there's a swimming pool and a cinema too,' Sarah said, as we carried on walking. 'I thought I might go for a dip later, if the pool is free. And I want to see about joining the Palace Film Club, too. I mean, if I want to make friends, I've got to get involved, right?'

I hoped she was right about that. I hated seeing Sarah sad

because she hadn't made any friends amongst the other housemaids or footmen. She was such a lovely person, but I knew the others made fun of her, for her accent more than anything. Personally, I liked the way Sarah spoke. It was warm and welcoming – and a lot more friendly than any of the other voices I'd heard around the Palace.

There had to be some other staff at Buckingham Palace who would appreciate all the *good* things about Sarah, instead of picking at the parts they thought were bad. Didn't there? They couldn't all be mean and nasty. Chances were, it was just like when Claire joined her new school last year and three of the girls there were horrible to her. Claire had assumed that *all* her classmates were awful, but actually, after a few weeks, she'd made fast friends with some of the nicer ones.

It was just a matter of finding them. And if Sarah couldn't do that here, maybe I'd have to give her a helping hand.

I followed Sarah all the way to the Palace Post Office, where there was a queue for the counter. Apparently it wasn't all that much different from the normal Post Offices I was used to, after all.

As we entered the Post Office, I eyed up the other staff members hanging around the counters. After a moment, I spotted a woman about Sarah's age, with dark hair and even darker eyes, who was sticking stamps on a stack of envelopes. Hmm, how about her? She looked friendly.

Pushing past a few pairs of legs, I headed towards the woman, knowing that Sarah would follow me. Then I brushed up against the woman's legs until she looked down.

'Oh!' she said, surprised. 'Hello, you.'

'Henry . . .' Sarah made it through the crush of people to join us. 'Sorry, he's oddly excited about being at the Post Office, it seems!'

'That's okay.' The woman smiled at us both. 'You're Sarah Morgan, right? The new housemaid?'

'That's right.' I could feel Sarah bracing herself – probably for another joke about how she spoke, or a jibe about her family. I sat on her feet and tried to reassure her. She just had to trust me.

'It's lovely to meet you. I'm Harriet.' The woman stuck out a hand for Sarah. Sarah, a surprised smile on her face, shook it. 'I hope you're settling in here okay – I can see you've already made friends with the most important residents!'

Sarah laughed. 'I rather think that Henry has adopted me, actually!'

Harriet stuck the last stamp on her cards, then waved goodbye as she moved to post them in the tall red box in the corner.

'Maybe there are some nice people here, after all,' Sarah murmured, and I barked my agreement. 'Come on, Henry. Let's join the queue.'

I followed her to the line of people, snaking around the room. As we settled into the queue, the man in front turned around to face us, and I saw Sarah's face break into a huge smile.

'Oliver!' she said.

Of course. Oliver Kinchen-Williams. *He'd* been nice to her, hadn't he? And Sarah's godfather had even told her to seek him out and introduce herself. That *had* to count as a personal recommendation.

Oh, I was good. This was *two* new friends for Sarah in one morning!

'Hello, you two,' he said, bending down to pat my head. 'He really has taken a shine to you this one, hasn't he?'

Sarah blushed prettily. 'He seems to have. But then, I'm pretty taken with him too.'

'Lucky boy. So, posting Christmas cards?' Oliver asked, nodding to the stack of envelopes Sarah was clutching.

Sarah nodded. 'It's the first Christmas I've ever spent away from home,' she admitted. 'When I took the job . . . well, it doesn't matter.'

'Of course it does,' Oliver said, his tone kind.

'It's just . . . I was so excited about being here for Christmas, when I first got the job. All the decorations, the celebrations . . . everything. But the nearer we get to the big day, the more homesick I seem to feel.'

'It's a strange thing, being far from home at Christmas. Trust me – I know.'

'Are you from far away?' Sarah asked, curiously. 'You sound like you were born and bred in the Palace – not like me!'

Oliver laughed. 'I like your accent. Devon?'

'Close,' Sarah admitted. 'My parents own a farm in Somerset.'

'How brilliant!' Oliver said. 'My parents actually emigrated to New Zealand a few years ago, to run a sheep farm in their retirement. So, while I grew up not very far from here, I still feel a long way from home, sometimes.'

'That's because home is more about the people than the place, I suppose,' Sarah said. I knew what she meant. Buckingham Palace would be the most fantastic home anyone could hope for. But without my family there . . . I just couldn't feel like I belonged.

'So, which people are you missing this Christmas?' Oliver asked. 'Because that's an awful lot of cards.'

'It was almost a lot more! I figured that people would get a real kick out of seeing a card with the Palace postmark on it, so I sort of wanted to send one to everyone.' Sarah fanned the cards out so she could read off the names. 'There's one for my parents, and my grandparents, of course. My best friend Rachel, and a few other old school friends who've moved away now. Everyone at the local church and the local pub – but only one card each for them! Some aunts and uncles, cousins, my godfather Tom, of course, and . . .' she trailed off, looking at the last card in her hand.

'Who's Debbie?' Oliver asked, reading the name upside down from the envelope.

'My ex-boyfriend, David's, Mum,' Sarah said, quietly.

'Ah.'

'Yeah. I wasn't sure whether to send it . . . we broke up a few months ago and, well, it wasn't very pleasant.' Sarah shook her head, as if shaking away the bad memories. From all the things Sarah had said about him, I had a very bad feeling about this David bloke. 'But the thing is, I actually knew Debbie before I met David. She runs the local farm shop, you see, so we worked with her a lot, my parents and I. We were friends. Then David came home from university after he graduated, and we got to know each other and, well, the rest is ancient history. But I did feel bad about losing Debbie as a friend, when things ended between David and me.'

'Then it's kind of you to send a card,' Oliver said. 'Christmas is the time for mending bridges, after all.'

'Yes,' Sarah said slowly, looking up at Oliver with dawning realisation on her face. 'Yes, it is. And maybe . . . maybe building new ones, too.'

'Definitely,' Oliver agreed.

After the Post Office, I followed Sarah around the Palace for a while as she discovered the whereabouts of the swimming pool and the cinema, carefully noting down the times for the next showing.

'Ooh! *Miracle on 34th Street*! That's my favourite,' she exclaimed, when she saw the poster for a special Christmas cinema night the next day. 'I wonder if they let dogs in there,' she added, smiling at me.

I decided they probably would. After all, I was allowed everywhere else. And I'd always enjoyed film night with the Walkers. It was the one time that everyone sat down together, without anyone having to rush off to work or school or friends' houses or to do homework. I could curl up on the sofa between them and be sure of a good hour or two of petting and fussing. Absolute bliss. Plus there were always really good snacks, and Jack and Claire were good at sharing them with me.

I felt a little homesick again just thinking about it. It was good that I had found Sarah – at least we could be homesick together. And maybe she'd meet some more friends at the cinema night – people who liked the same sort of things she did.

Films – at least the ones I'd watched – always seemed to

be about bringing people together, especially if they were set at Christmas. Even the ones Jack liked, where the world was about to be blown up by aliens or whatever, usually featured a group of people who became friends through working together.

That was what Sarah needed – a friend in the Palace who wasn't canine. As much as I liked being her best friend, I knew it wasn't the same as having someone who could actually talk back to her. Besides, hopefully I'd be going home soon, and I didn't like the idea of leaving Sarah all alone at Buckingham Palace when I left.

No, I needed to find Sarah a proper human friend. Maybe Harriet from this morning, or one of the other housemaids, or someone from the kitchen staff. Someone she could go swimming with, or take to the cinema to see her favourite film.

'I wonder if Oliver likes films,' Sarah said, her voice soft and her cheeks pink.

It was then that I realised. This wasn't one of Jack's disaster movies. It was one of the films that Amy and Claire tended to choose for film night – one where a man and a woman kissed under the mistletoe on Christmas Eve, or he chased her through the rain to tell her he loved her. One where everyone lived happily ever after, because they'd found that one person who could make them happier than anyone else in the world.

Sarah deserved more than just some people at the Palace who didn't make fun of her. She deserved love. Romance. Someone to make her see how special and lovable she was.

And Oliver might just be the perfect person to do that, I thought. I had a nose for these things.

Now I just had to figure out how to make him see that.

I shook my ears out. How hard could *that* be? Humans in movies managed it all the time – and I was much cleverer than them.

All I needed was a plan . . .

AMY

'How's it looking?' Amy called from the kitchen counter, where she was hastily assembling packed lunches for the three of them. It was cheaper than buying school lunches, of course, but the effort of making them – not to mention finding enough variety to keep Claire happy – was wearing her down all the same. Would it really kill her to just eat cheese and cucumber sandwiches every day, like she had for four years of primary school? Now it had to be pasta salad or chicken wraps or whatever.

Amy had made herself a cheese and cucumber sandwich instead, mostly out of nostalgia.

'One thousand shares overnight!' Claire squealed. 'We're definitely getting the word out.'

'That's brilliant, sweetheart.'

As she hunted for the least dried out clementine to put in Claire's lunchbox, Sookie twining around her legs and almost tripping her over, Amy's mobile beeped. She sighed without even checking it. It would be work – again. Flu season had well and truly hit, which meant they had the double whammy of people desperate to get the flu jab they should have got months ago, as well as sick people who wanted to see their doctor or nurse – even if all they would be told was to go back to bed and look after themselves at home. Add in a stomach bug that had knocked out a few of the staff, and work didn't look like it was going to get any less manic this side of Christmas.

'Let me see.' Jack swung into the kitchen, his school bag hanging off his arm as he grabbed the chair next to Claire.

'Jack, do you want to get your lunch together?' Amy asked, hoping that, while she was sure the answer was 'no', he might just do it anyway. Just to give her a hand.

'In a minute, Mum.'

Amy sighed. She knew what 'in a minute' meant. It meant 'I'm just going to leave it so long that you end up doing it anyway so we're not all late getting out the door.' She'd been here before.

'Jack, we don't have time for this. Claire's already dressed and ready to go, that's why she's on the computer. Have you even had breakfast?'

'Not yet. I'll grab something in a minute.'

Amy's phone beeped again, somehow sounding more insistent this time, so she grabbed it rather than responding to Jack again. Maybe if he went to school hungry, he'd listen next time. Except, probably not.

Flora's sick now, so I can't get in today, the text message from Shireen, the surgery receptionist read. Flora was her three-year-old daughter. Can you get in early to open up? I've got cover, but they won't be in until 9.

Amy's gaze flicked to her watch. Early? She was going to be lucky to get out of there on time, at this rate.

I'll do my best, she texted back, anyway. Wasn't that what she always did? Her best?

She just wished it felt like it was enough more often.

'Okay, guys, we really need to get a move on now. Jack, if you want a lift to school you need to be ready to go in fifteen minutes. Claire, same for you.'

Neither child responded. Of course.

Sighing loudly, Amy slammed the last of the packed lunches together and slung them onto the kitchen table along with various other 'must not forget' items.

Her phone beeped again, and Amy glared at it – until she opened the message.

Any news on Henry yet? Luke had written. Oh, and just got Shireen's message about Flora. I'm on my way in now, so will be there to open up – don't worry if you're running late.

Smiling, Amy typed a reply. Usual morning chaos here, and still no sign of Henry. Thanks for opening up. Don't know why you're so good to me!

Luke's reply was almost instant. Because you deserve it.

Amy read the message several times before shoving her phone in her pocket, and turning her attention back to her children.

'A thousand shares is a start,' Jack was saying, as he took over the laptop trackpad. 'But we need something more. Something to really catch the public imagination. I mean, London is huge, and Henry could be anywhere. We need to get people out hunting for him, somehow . . .'

'Or we could all get ready for school and work,' Amy suggested, and Jack and Claire both glared at her. 'Look, I'm as desperate to find Henry as you two are, but that doesn't mean that the rest of the world stops while he's missing. You still have to go to school. I have to go to work. Meals still need cooking, the house still needs cleaning . . . We're doing everything we can to find Henry, okay? But it doesn't mean we can give up on everything else.'

There was another beep, and Amy reached for her phone again – but this time, it was coming from the computer.

'Hang on . . .' Jack made a few clicks, his expression getting more excited with every one. 'Wait. Wait. This is it!'

'This is what?' Amy asked, as Claire tried to elbow her brother out of the way, saying, 'Let me see! Dad left *me* in charge of this page, remember? It's my name on it! You're just an admin.'

'What is it?' Amy asked again, impatiently.

'A message! From someone saying that they've seen Henry!' Claire was practically bouncing in her chair with excitement.

'They say they found him wandering around St James's Park . . . and they've got him safe!' The same excitement was clear in Jack's voice, too.

Amy hurried over to look at the screen. 'Did they send a photo? Or any other details?'

'No . . .' Jack scanned the rest of the message. 'He's asking if there's a reward for finding him. We can give a reward, right?'

Money. Of course. Didn't everything come down to money?

Amy shook her head. Something about this message just didn't feel right – and she didn't have the time right now to figure out what it was.

'I don't know. This person could be anybody,' she pointed out. She hated to burst their bubbles of hope so soon, but she didn't want them to get carried away, either. 'We need to talk to your father – he set up the page, he might be able to get some more information about who they are.' And if they wanted a reward, and they really had Henry, well they were definitely going to have to talk to Jim. She barely had enough money to make it through to the end of the month.

'But what if Henry runs away again?' Claire asked. 'We need to get him right now!'

'Right now, we all need to go to school and work,' Amy said, firmly. 'Jack, forward the message to my email address, and I'll try to speak to your dad today. Or you could,' she added, as the thought occurred to her. Jack was quite old enough to handle these things with his dad, but she wouldn't want him dealing with it alone. 'Then tonight we'll decide what to do about it. Together. Okay?'

'Fine,' Jack said, sulkily. 'I'll call Dad.'

'Great. But after school.' She grabbed her handbag and her lunch from the table. 'Come on, we're all going to be late!'

The kids glowered as they sullenly gathered their things. Amy sighed. She didn't want to be this person – the nagging mum who made her kids life miserable. But she didn't want them all to be late or show up to school with no lunch. There had to be a balance, somewhere . . .

Suddenly, Amy grinned, as a memory from Christmas pasts came to her.

'Tell you what, I'll put the Christmas CD on in the car.'

Jack groaned, but Claire perked up a bit.

'The one I made last year?' she asked.

'Yep,' Amy confirmed. 'And we can sing along as we drive.' A good sing-song *always* lifted the spirits, right?

'You're going to open the windows at traffic lights and traumatise the people in the next cars, aren't you?' Jack was rolling his eyes, but Amy knew that secretly he loved it as much as they did.

'Absolutely!' she said, and Claire squealed with delight.

Maybe the day wouldn't be a complete disaster, after all.

HENRY

I was still thinking about ways to get Oliver and Sarah together when I returned to the Corgi Room after dinner that night. I knew that it was the right thing to do, but how? It wasn't easy when I couldn't just talk to them and make them understand.

No, this was going to take some work. Some thinking, and some planning.

I wished I had Claire and Amy's DVD collection to help me, but as it was, I'd have to rely on my memory. I didn't think I'd even *seen* a TV in any of the rooms I'd explored in the Palace. They had to be there somewhere though, right?

In fact, I was so distracted by my thoughts, that I didn't notice that Vulcan and the others had stopped just inside the door. I stepped in and, in a flash, Vulcan was on me, snapping his jaws near my side – not close enough to hurt, but enough to give me a scare.

'Hey!' I jumped back. 'What's that for!'

Vulcan circled around me, teeth still bared. The Dorgi sat so close to the ground he was a good few inches shorter than me, and his stumpy legs made it hard for him to look threatening. But he was definitely trying.

'Okay. Why don't we calm down and talk about this,' I said, taking small steps to stay out of Vulcan's range. I was a lover, not a fighter. Well, I wasn't much of either, but I was pretty sure there was no way to look good after a fight with a stumpy Dorgi who'd hardly ever even left the Palace.

'Yes, let's,' Vulcan snarled. 'Let's talk about how you're bringing our reputation as Royal Pets into disrepute. About how you're an embarrassment to your breed.'

'An embarrassment? Me? How?' Now I was totally baffled. I'd been doing everything just the way Willow had told me – making sure I was there for meals on time, exploring the Palace like I had every right to be there, and taking walks in the grounds. What was I doing wrong?

'Fraternising with *servants*.' Vulcan spat the last word like it was one of those Amy never let Jim use when the children could hear. 'We saw you, walking in the garden with the housemaid. And talking with that senior footman. It has to stop.'

'This is about Sarah? And Oliver?' I shook my head, still confused. 'What on earth is wrong with spending time with the humans?' They'd been a lot nicer than the dogs had to me, for a start.

'They're not just any humans though, are they,' Willow put in. She was sitting off to one side, watching my encounter with Vulcan with obvious interest. And I was in no doubt as to whose side she was on.

I looked around for Candy. She sat huddled a little further back, near her basket, also watching. But her expression was far more conflicted than Willow's.

'Sarah's lovely,' I said, stubbornly. 'She's kind and friendly, she takes me out for walks, and she even feeds us most of the time! Why on earth wouldn't I want to be friends with her?'

'Because she's not one of *us*,' Willow said, calmly.

'What? A dog?' This was all very confusing.

'She's a *servant*,' Vulcan snarled. '*We* are Royal Pets. Part of the Royal Family. We rule this Palace.'

'Exactly,' Willow agreed. 'We are important. Everyone else – everyone outside the family – they're our inferiors. Here to serve us – not to be our friends.'

'I don't understand,' I admitted.

'Of course you don't.' Willow gave a small shrug. 'Because you don't belong here.'

So we were back to that. 'Maybe I don't. But at least I've got to know some of the people who keep this place running. At least I don't just expect them to open doors for me and feed me and walk me and clean up after me, without giving anything back at all.'

'But that's the point,' Candy said, her voice softer than the others. 'That's what they're here to do. They're not our owners – the Queen is. Nobody else matters to us, except Her.'

'Well, I've never even met the Queen. And the moment I do, she'll probably be kicking me out. So I think I'll make my friends wherever I can find them.' I turned my back on them, preparing to head back out. I'd had enough of this nonsense.

'Maybe we should try and get rid of you sooner then.' Vulcan lunged forward again, his jaws wide open and his teeth flashing as he launched himself at my side.

I hit out with my paw, trying to protect myself, but Vulcan was determined. Every time I managed to dodge his mouth, or his claws, he'd just regroup and attack again. I didn't want to hurt Vulcan – and even if I did, I knew that if I injured another dog that would probably be the end of my stay at Buckingham Palace.

On the other hand, I really didn't want to get mauled either.

'Wait!' I half expected that to be my voice, but it wasn't. It was Candy.

'Vulcan, don't.' She darted forward and put her trembling body between me and the other Dorgi. 'Don't hurt Henry. He didn't know he was doing anything wrong.'

'I still don't,' I grumbled, and Willow looked at me with amusement. Apparently this whole situation was very funny indeed to her.

Candy shot me a 'shut up!' glare, and I did as I was told. For once.

'Look, Henry won't be here long, right? And as soon as people realise the mistake, they'll know he wasn't one of us anyway. So what difference does it make who he's friends with?' Candy sounded persuasive, but Vulcan didn't look like he was buying it.

'It matters,' he said, stubbornly. 'What if the other humans get *ideas*? That senior footman of his *always* takes his morning break at that time. I always see him, coming back in just when *we're* going out to enjoy the gardens. Yesterday, he even said "hello" to us! What if he starts trying to stroke one of us? Or, worse of all, thinking of us as *his* pets?'

'You *are* pets!' I said, a little too loud.

'But not *their* pets,' Willow said, agreeing with Vulcan. Of course. 'They don't own us, you see. And they can't start getting ideas that they have any authority over us.'

This was an alien idea to me. As much as I was part of the Walker family, I knew that Jim and Amy were in charge of me – much the same way as they were in charge of Jack and Claire. The thought of the *dogs* having the power over the humans in the Palace – except for the Queen, of course – was just weird.

'I think the thing is,' Candy started, and everyone turned to look at her, 'Henry is just a friendly dog. He makes friends with everyone. He can't help it.'

'Why are you defending him?' Vulcan asked, suspiciously.

'Because . . .' Candy sighed. 'Because he was friendly to me, even though I'd given him no good reason to be.'

I looked down at the ground, a little embarrassed. 'You needed a friend. What else was I supposed to do?'

'Ignore me. Leave me alone. Pretend I hadn't woken you up with my bad dream.' Both Willow and Vulcan looked slightly guilty at Candy's words. I'd assumed they'd just slept through Candy's nightmare, but now I wasn't so sure.

'Yeah, I couldn't do that,' I admitted. 'It's just not in my nature.'

'And that's what I mean,' Candy said. 'See? He's just a friendly dog.'

Vulcan huffed disapprovingly. 'Fine. But as far as I'm concerned, the sooner She gets home and kicks you out onto the street, the better.'

'Understood,' I replied. At least I knew not all the Palace Dogs felt that way.

Willow didn't say anything, but she did look at me curiously. I wondered what she made of all this.

But most of all, I wondered what their owner, Her Majesty, would say when She found out everything that had been going on in Her absence.

Later that night, once we were all tucked up in our baskets, I heard Candy jump down and pad across the Corgi Room towards me.

'You can come up, if you like,' I murmured, when she paused beside my basket. 'Unless you're worried about what your *friends* will say.'

With a long sigh, Candy hopped up and joined me.

'They just don't know what to make of you,' she said, as she settled down, curling around my body as easily as if we did this every night.

'I'm a dog, the same as them,' I pointed out. 'There's really not all that much to be confused by.'

Candy gave a muffled laugh. 'Are you kidding? You're from a whole different world.'

Was I? I suppose I was. My life with the Walkers was nothing like their life in the Palace. Although, I had a feeling that if they ever met Amy and the others, they'd see that our relationships with our owners weren't as dissimilar as they thought.

'Has it always been just the three of you?' I asked. Maybe if I understood *them* better, I could help them understand *me*.

'No.' Candy's voice was small and sad. 'There used to be lots of us. When I was first born . . .'

'Wait, you were born here at the Palace?'

144

'Of course!' Candy looked surprised I'd even asked. 'Where else would I have been born?'

'I don't know. I just . . .' I couldn't remember the place I'd been born, where I'd lived before the Walkers brought me home. But it must have been *somewhere*. I knew, from hearing Amy and Jim talking, that I'd had a mother, and siblings.

I just couldn't remember them being family to me the way that the Walkers had, ever since.

'The Queen . . . she breeds us, you see. Or rather, she always used to. We come from a long line of Royal Dogs, you know. Can trace our ancestors back generations and generations.' Candy gave a small smile. 'Which is why we think they're so important, I suppose.'

'Family are important,' I agreed. 'I just don't think it really matters if that family is human, canine, or any other sort of family.' I thought about Sookie. How was she coping without me there? Even when we fought, or when she was cruel, she was still family. We were still the only two animals the Walkers had to look after them.

Could Sookie really do that, all on her own? Especially now, when things were so strange at home?

I hoped so.

Remembering something Willow had said on my first day at the Palace, I frowned. 'Willow said that the Queen wasn't getting any more pets. That Monty was an oddity.'

'Yes?'

'But there used to be more of you. If you were bred here, I mean, there must have been other dogs. Older dogs, or brothers and sisters?'

Candy's smile didn't reach her chocolate brown eyes. 'Time was, there used to be lots of us. Someone once described us as a moving carpet, there were so many dogs, running along in front of Her. But now it's just the three of us. The others all passed on, one by one.'

'I'm sorry.' Losing a friend – a family member – that must be incredibly hard. It wasn't just like Jim not coming home. This was never seeing someone you loved, ever again.

I could hardly imagine it. Or, I couldn't have, before I came to the Palace.

Even now, I knew that, if I never made it home, the Walkers would go on without me. And while that was true, there was always the hope that we'd meet again, somehow.

Candy didn't have that hope.

'Holly was the last,' Candy said, softly. 'She was a corgi, like Willow – and you. She and Vulcan, they were very close. I think he misses her most of all. I don't think he's been truly happy again, since she passed.'

I felt an unexpected surge of sympathy for Vulcan – something I didn't think I'd ever experience. No wonder he'd hated me so much on sight – another corgi coming in, taking the place of his best friend. He probably wouldn't like Monty all that much more, either.

It didn't change how Vulcan had treated me. But at least it helped me understand him a little better.

Candy yawned again, her jaw cracking with the effort.

'You should get some sleep,' I said.

Candy nodded. 'Night, Henry.'

I waited for her to jump down and go back to her own

basket, but instead she snuggled up beside me and closed her eyes.

After a moment, I did the same.

Looked like I'd made one doggy friend at the Palace, after all.

Day 6

Thursday 19th
December

HENRY

I woke the next morning with a plan to help get Sarah and Oliver together fully formed in my head.

In the end, it was something that Vulcan, of all dogs, had said that gave me the idea. He'd said that Oliver always took his morning break around the same time, so he was coming back into the Palace as the dogs were going out for their late morning walk. Sarah had been taking me for my walk a little later (apart from that first day when we met Oliver in the gardens) as that fitted with her work schedule better.

But this morning, we needed to go out earlier. That was the only way that she'd definitely get to see Oliver.

The first rule of romance in all of Amy's movies was that the man and woman had to be in the same place. (Well, apart from that one about Seattle.)

Once again, I lamented the fact that humans couldn't speak Dog. Life would be so much easier if I could just explain to her what I was doing.

As it was, I had to find other ways to make her understand.

The minute that breakfast was over, I rushed off to find Sarah, in the hope of chivvying her along to get her work finished earlier.

'Morning, Henry!' she said, cheerfully, as she passed me with her cleaning basket. 'Come on, we're dusting in the White Drawing Room to start with today.'

Which one was the White Drawing Room? There were so many rooms in this Palace, I couldn't keep them all straight, although listening to Sarah talk about them as she cleaned had helped. (For instance, I now knew that the Big Chair Room was actually called the Throne Room.)

I trotted along behind her, hoping that it was one of the smaller rooms – not like the giant Ballroom or the long Picture Gallery. That way she'd be done quicker, and I could encourage her to take a break. Outside. With me and Oliver.

'Here we go,' Sarah said, stepping inside and putting down her basket.

I followed, then stopped in the doorway.

No. Absolutely not. This was no good at all.

The White Drawing Room, it seemed, was more gold than white. There were gold sofas and chairs, gold raised patterns on the walls, gold on the ceiling and another huge crystal chandelier with white candles and gold trimmings. And, most importantly, it was filled with endless decoration and furniture – candlesticks and desks and cabinets and mirrors, to name but a few – all of which I was sure would need dusting by Sarah. This was going to take far too long.

'Isn't this room fantastic?' Sarah did a little twirl in the middle of the room. 'I've heard so much about it, you know. My godfather, Tom, used to tell me stories about the Palace when he worked here, and this was always his favourite room. In fact . . .' She rushed across to one of the tall, tall mirrors that stood either side of the ornate, white fireplace, above which hung another huge painting of a woman in a white dress.

Reaching under the top shelf of a cabinet below the mirror, Sarah felt around for something. Intrigued, I moved closer to see what she was looking for.

Then, all of a sudden, the wall moved.

I jumped back, out of the way, hiding behind Sarah. The last thing we needed was for us to break the Palace – that would definitely get both of us kicked out!

'Aha!' Sarah said, beaming happily. Then, suddenly cautious, she checked over her shoulder to make sure no one was looking. 'It's right where he said it would be!' she whispered.

Since Sarah wasn't alarmed, I decided I shouldn't be either. So instead, I stepped forward, nosing my way to where the wall had shifted.

In fact, I realised, it wasn't the whole wall. It was just the cabinet with the mirror above it. Because, I realised suddenly, it wasn't a wall at all. It was a door!

Beyond it, I could see another door, but that one was shut.

'That leads right to the Queen's private rooms,' Sarah said, softly. 'You could probably go in there, if it's unlocked, but I think I better not!'

As easily as it had swung open, Sarah shut the secret mirror door, then wiped off her fingerprints.

'My godfather told me that when they hold receptions in this room, the Royals will be through there in another, small drawing room called the Royal Closet, having their own pre-function drinks. Then, when they're ready to join the party – magic! A footman presses the button and they just appear! Can you imagine how exciting that would be?'

For the first time, I could see exactly why Sarah had wanted to work at Buckingham Palace. She was fascinated by the building, by the culture, and by the people who lived here.

I just wished she felt more at home, now that she was here.

'Anyway. I'd better get cleaning.' Sarah picked up her duster, and got to work. I watched for a moment or two – it didn't take any longer than that to come to an obvious conclusion: Sarah was never going to finish in here before Oliver came back from his break.

Which meant I needed to be more persuasive.

With that thought, I turned tail and raced back out of the White Drawing Room, and headed for the Corgi Room.

The next part of the plan required props.

'Oh, you're back, are you?' Sarah asked, when I returned a little while later. 'I thought you'd got bored of my Palace trivia and wandered off.'

She stepped down from the stool she was standing on to clean some of the higher up decorations and took a good look at me. Then she laughed.

'Is that a hint?' She pointed to the ball in my mouth. I barked my agreement, and the ball fell out, rolling across the floor of the White Drawing Room.

'You're going to have to wait until I've finished in here, Henry, if you want to play.'

That wasn't going to work for me. If we waited too much longer, Oliver would have finished his break, and she'd miss her chance to talk to him.

Okay. Step two.

Leaving the ball at Sarah's feet, I dashed back out again and down to the garden door. Carefully, I lifted a lead off the hook there, and raced back up the stairs to the White Drawing Room.

Sarah was *still* dusting. The ball had been picked up and put in her cleaning basket, I noticed.

Holding my lead between my teeth, I carried it across the room to her, and laid it at her feet.

'I won't be too long, Henry,' she said, reassuringly. But then she added the lead to the ball in her basket.

Okay, time to bring out the big guns.

I whined. Pathetically.

Well, you have to go with what works, right?

Sarah sighed. 'Do you really need to go outside that badly?'

I barked the affirmative.

'Well . . .' She looked around at the unfinished room. 'I suppose if you decided to go to the toilet here in the White Drawing Room that wouldn't be good for anybody. And I'd be the one who had to clean it up!'

She was wavering, I could tell. I gave one last whine for good measure.

Sarah rolled her eyes. 'Okay, then. Just let me stash my cleaning basket, and I'll take you out. But only quickly! And then I'll have to work through my break later to make it up, so I hope you know how good I'm being to you.'

I nuzzled her leg to tell her I appreciated it. Of course, she didn't know it yet, but she was going to appreciate it even more.

Sarah clipped on my lead as we reached the garden door, the ball safely in her other hand. I dragged her outside, heading towards where we'd bumped into Oliver the other day. Hopefully he would be easy to find; the gardens were huge, but I thought I could probably recognise his scent.

I was right. I picked it up just outside the doors, and followed it all the way along the path, dragging Sarah along behind me.

'Henry! I thought you wanted to play fetch?' She waved the ball at me.

I wavered. I really *did* want to play fetch.

But I wanted Sarah to be happy more.

I kept my nose to the ground and dashed after the scent trail, not wanting to lose Oliver. I was so busy following his scent, I barely even noticed when we came to a large tree in the middle of the path. I sidestepped at the last moment, pulling Sarah with me, only she tripped on a tree root and—

Crash.

'Oh my word, I'm so sorry!' Sarah, flustered, hurried to her feet – and off the man she'd crashed into. I danced alongside her, my lead getting tangled in her legs, as I tried to make sure she was okay.

'It's fine.' The man sat up and, at last, I got a look at his face. It was Oliver! 'Fancy seeing you two here,' he said, with a rather dazed smile.

'Oliver!' Sarah held out a hand to help him up. 'I really am *so* sorry. Henry was just racing along and I was following him and not looking where I was going, and then there was this tree . . .'

'It's fine. Really.' Oliver sounded surprised, but pleased to see us.

Actually, now I thought about it, this was perfect. Just like a scene from one of Amy's movies!

'For a Palace so huge, we do seem to be bumping into each other a lot, don't we?' Sarah said.

If only they knew how much work that had taken. But Sarah seemed far too happy with the outcome to be even faintly suspicious about my part in it.

'Quite literally, it seems!'

Sarah winced. 'Did I say sorry?'

'Many times. How about you make it up to me by letting me join you for your walk?' Oliver suggested. 'I often take my break around now, and I like to spend it in the gardens when I can.'

'Of course!' Sarah fell into step beside him as they walked along the path, me trotting along at their side congratulating myself on a job well done.

'I have to say, I was sort of surprised you were happy to talk with me,' Sarah admitted, glancing up at Oliver from under her lashes. 'You might have noticed, most of the other staff aren't so keen.'

'Then they're idiots,' Oliver said, with a shrug. 'Why on earth wouldn't I want to be friends with you?'

'Mostly it seems to be my accent putting them off. That, or the fact that they think my godfather got me the job.'

Oliver shook his head. 'It doesn't work like that any more, you know. It used to be that getting a job at the Palace was all about who you knew. These days, you have to prove you deserve it.'

'That's better, don't you think?' Sarah asked.

'Definitely,' Oliver agreed. 'Although if a letter from your godfather had been all that was required, I'm not sure I'd have complained!'

Sarah laughed. 'I suppose not. But . . . I like knowing I earned my place here, even if the others don't believe it. That I worked hard and got here on my own merit. It makes me feel . . . I don't know.'

'Proud,' Oliver supplied. 'And so you should. It's hard enough to get a job at the Palace, and harder still to do it well. You *should* be proud of yourself.'

'Are you?' Sarah asked. 'Proud of yourself, I mean?'

Oliver considered for a moment before answering. 'Yes,' he said, finally. 'I am. I didn't always want to be a footman, you know. I wanted to be a pilot. But my eyesight wasn't up to it, and so . . .' He shrugged.

'You had to find a Plan B,' Sarah guessed. 'I can understand that.'

'I was a little lost, for a while. Didn't know what to do with myself, really. But then I saw the advert looking for Palace staff, to train to be footmen and, well, I grabbed it. That was a few years ago now. I worked my way up to Senior Footman – with your godfather's help. And now I can't imagine doing anything else.'

'You've done brilliantly,' Sarah said, beaming up at him. She looked happier than I'd ever seen her.

I *knew* this was a fantastic plan!

'So, if Buckingham Palace was *your* Plan B too, what was Plan A?'

Sarah's smile faded at Oliver's question. 'Oh, you know. The usual.'

'Piloting for the Red Arrows? Or is that just me?'

'That's just you,' Sarah said, with a hint of a chuckle. 'No . . . I just wanted the boring things most people in my village wanted. A happy marriage, kids, to carry on helping at the family farm, and to win the quiz at the Fox and Duck on a Monday night. Like I said, the usual.'

'But something changed?'

'Would you believe me if I told you that I finally realised we were never going to beat the Quizzy Rascals?'

'No.'

Sarah's grip was tighter on my lead than normal, I realised. Like she didn't want me to run away without taking her with me.

Except I wasn't running anywhere. I wanted to hear her *real* answer as much as Oliver obviously did.

They walked in silence for a while, nearly finishing the lap of the park before she sighed. 'Let's just say that I realised there was more to life than I had going for me at home. A lot more.'

Oliver stayed silent, obviously waiting for her to say something more, but she didn't. 'Well, whatever brought you to Buckingham Palace, I for one am very glad that it did.'

'Me too,' said Sarah, with a grin.

It was perfect. Just like the movies.

Then Sarah glanced at her watch, and the moment was broken.

'Oh goodness! I need to get back,' she said, sounding flustered.

'Me too.' Oliver checked his watch too, and his eyes widened. 'I hadn't realised we'd been out here so long!'

'Neither had I.'

'I guess you're just really easy to talk to,' Oliver said, with a smile.

'Maybe we could . . . talk again, sometime?' Sarah's cheeks were pink as she asked.

'Definitely,' Oliver agreed. 'In fact, if you're free tonight, there's a special film club night in the cinema. They're showing—'

'*Miracle on 34th Street*!' Sarah finished for him. 'It's one of my favourites. I'd love to go.'

'With me?'

'With you,' Sarah confirmed, with a smile.

Well, wasn't that just ideal? If anything was going to help me bring these two together, a nice Christmas movie should do it perfectly!

I trotted back into the Palace feeling a little smug. I sensed that my work here was done.

Honestly. Where would humans be without us dogs to sort out their lives from time to time?

AMY

Amy stared around the bar, taking in the brightly coloured drinks, the sight of old Dr Evans wearing a Santa hat with mistletoe hanging from it, and her friends all having a brilliant, festive time.

Luke had done a great job of turning their normally dull Christmas dinner into something so much more by booking a great venue – a fun new bar that Amy hadn't even known had opened in town, that had a back room filled with large tables for groups to eat at, and a dance floor with Christmas karaoke running next to the main bar. Something for everyone – even Dr Evans, who was sweet-talking one of the barmaids into a kiss. He might look a hundred and seven, but apparently the guy had moves.

She hadn't been sure that coming was a good idea, despite Luke's insistence that she needed a night out. But it wasn't just him – *all* her friends and colleagues had teamed up to talk her into it. And they'd been so persuasive! Especially Shireen who, after dealing with Flora's stomach bug for the last couple of days, was desperate to hand her over to her husband and get out of the house for a few hours.

It's Christmas! We haven't been out together in months and months. What's the point of putting up with a seventeen-year-old if he can't babysit for one night a year? When was the last time you did anything just for you?

And, the most persuasive of all was Luke's gentle encouragement: *Just take a night off, Amy. Take a couple of hours away from the real world and relax.*

So here she was. Relaxing. At least, until the real world caught up with her again.

'Are you going to sing?' Luke slid into the chair beside her, and pushed a fresh glass of white wine her way. 'They're just getting the karaoke started. I brought the song list . . .' He waved the thick file with all the different songs available in front of her. 'There's a whole page of just Christmas songs. I think Shireen and Nathan are planning on duetting on "Baby, It's Cold Outside".'

'I can't remember the last time I sang karaoke.' Jim had always made fun of her love of singing along to music, but she enjoyed it. It made her feel happy. Especially when the music in question was Christmas songs. Belting out the classics in the car with Claire, while Jack rolled his eyes and pretended not to be humming along, was one of her best festive moments this year.

Maybe it was time to make another one.

Luke flicked open the song list, and ran his finger down the Christmas page. 'How about this one?' He pointed to a familiar song, and Amy smiled.

'I probably shouldn't,' she said, that last vestige of doubt still playing on her mind. What if Jim was right? What if she would just make a fool of herself.

'Oh, I think you definitely should,' Luke replied. 'In fact I'm going to go and put your name down, right now.'

'Okay, then,' Amy said, giving into the inevitable.

But no sooner as he had left, her phone buzzed on the table.

Jim.

Her ex-husband's name flashed up on the screen and for one brief and confusing moment she wondered if he was calling to complain about her singing in public.

Probably not.

Amy stepped away from the table where her friends were emptying a second bottle of wine, and held her phone tight to her ear as she tried to hear over the noise of the bar.

'Amy? Where are you?'

'Jim? What's the matter?' She had to shout to even hear herself, let alone hope Jim could hear her.

She needed to get out of here. Signalling to Luke as she passed the bar that she was stepping outside to take the call, she weaved her way through the crowds of people to the front door, and stepped out into the bitter winter night's air.

Why was he calling *her*, anyway? Whatever problems he had were no longer her concern.

'Do you know where our children are right now?' The anger in Jim's voice was suddenly stark and clear in the quiet of the outside, and Amy's heart jumped. Except for the kids. They were still their mutual problem.

'At home,' she said, hoping to God that was true. 'Jack agreed to babysit Claire for me so I could go on a Christmas night out with work friends.'

'Well, they're not there now,' Jim said.

Amy felt her heart sink down into her stomach, as she leant back against the wall of the bar for support.

'What do you mean?'

'I just checked the Facebook account for the Hunt for Henry. There was a message from some dodgy guy claiming he'd found him and asking about a reward.'

'Yeah, it came through yesterday morning,' Amy remembered. 'I didn't see it myself – I was trying to get everyone out the door to school.' And singing in the car.

'And you didn't think it was important enough to tell me about?'

'It's your account, Jim! I figured you'd see it, if you cared.' How was this her fault? Setting up the damn page had been his idea in the first place! 'Besides, I told Jack and Claire not to respond, or do anything at all, until they'd spoken to you about it. It didn't feel right.'

'Well, they didn't speak to me,' Jim said. 'Instead, Jack messaged him back earlier today and arranged to meet him.'

'When he knew I'd be out and wouldn't be there to stop him.' Amy turned and rested her forehead against the brick-work feeling panic burning in her stomach. 'Damn it. Do you know where they are?'

'Fortunately, yes. Shall I come and get you?'

'Yes please.'

Amy reeled off the address of the bar she was at, then hung up and went inside to tell her friends that her fun was over for another year.

Luke met her, just inside the door. 'What's the matter?'

'The kids. They've run off to chase some probably fake

lead on Henry.' She shuddered, imagining them alone out in the night. *Why* couldn't they have waited?

'Do you need me to take you to them?' Suddenly, the fun, relaxed Luke who wanted her to sing karaoke was gone, and in his place was the serious, capable doctor she knew from work.

'Thanks, but Jim's already on his way to get me.'

Luke nodded. 'Okay, good. I'll go fetch your stuff, you look out for his car.'

Amy nodded, and watched him go, imagining, just for a moment, a world in which this night might have had a very different ending.

Maybe even with mistletoe.

The drive was every bit as miserable as Amy had expected it to be. Tense, and silent, as she realised that – after twenty plus years together – they had absolutely nothing to say to each other. Nothing except 'this is your fault'. Which was both a lie, and unhelpful.

So Amy kept quiet, and stared out of the window, hoping for any sign that her children were okay.

Eventually, though, Jim slowed the car as the satnav told them they'd reached their destination.

'I guess this must be it.' Amy peered out of the windscreen at the dark, empty bus station. 'Why on earth would they agree to meet here?'

Or anywhere, for that matter. Nothing about this evening made sense. Her kids were sensible, even when they were being typical teens or pre-teens. What on earth could have possessed Jack to bring his little sister all the way out here, late at night, to meet a stranger?

Jim pulled the car into an empty space alongside the pavement, and they both got out, looking around cautiously for any signs of people. Or dogs.

'Hey!' At the shout, Amy and Jim exchanged a glance.

'That's Jack,' Amy said, as she started running.

Jim followed, catching her up in a few strides, then keeping pace as they headed to where the shout had come from.

'There,' Jim gasped, pointing.

Up ahead, Amy saw a slim, dark figure, with a smaller shadowed figure next to it. Jack and Claire. It had to be!

'Come back!' Jack was shouting. 'That's my money!'

Claire was tugging on his sleeve. 'Let's just go home. Jack, I want to go home.'

'But he took my money!'

'Jack!' Jim yelled, as they approached.

Both kids turned to look at them, their eyes wide and fearful. Yeah, Amy thought, they both knew they were for it now.

'*What* did you think you were doing?' Jim stopped just a pace in front of them, looming over Jack like he was six again and had been drawing on the walls.

Claire rushed to Amy's side, throwing her arms around her waist. Amy held her tightly to her, reassuring herself that everything was fine, and her heart could stop racing any time now.

'He said he had Henry,' Jack said.

Amy could see the pleading in his eyes – how badly he wanted his dad to understand. But Jim wasn't watching. And Amy wasn't sure she blamed him, this time.

'You brought Claire – your twelve-year-old sister – to a strange place, in the middle of the night, to meet a man

166

neither of you knew, who had already asked you for money.'
Amy's voice came out clipped, the anger barely contained.
'Never mind that it was a stupid and dangerous thing for *you*
to do – you're nearly eighteen, and I get that you want to
make your own mistakes. Although if you could refrain from
making the really stupid ones that could get you *killed* that
would be great—'

'The point is,' Jim interrupted. 'It wasn't just your life or
well-being you were putting at risk. It was Claire's too.'

Jack looked shamefaced. No, more than that – he looked
horrified. Like it hadn't occurred to him before now that
there was any risk at all.

Well, wasn't that what growing up was about? Learning
to think about the consequences?

'I told you not to make contact with that man until you'd
spoken to your father,' Amy reminded him. 'But you thought
you knew better. Is that it?'

'I thought . . . I thought he had Henry,' Jack stammered.
'And I thought that if we waited too long, we might lose
our only chance of getting him back.'

'He wanted money, right?' Jim guessed. 'A reward for
finding the dog?'

'Yeah.'

'So where did you get it?'

Jack's eyes shifted to the side, avoiding his father's gaze.
'I . . . I took it out of my savings account yesterday. One
hundred pounds.'

There hadn't been much more than that in there to start
with, Amy remembered. He'd been saving for a new guitar.
Before everything had happened with Jim, she'd hoped they

might be able to top up his savings so he could buy it for Christmas.

No chance of that now.

'He took it all?' she asked.

Jack nodded.

'And he didn't even *have* Henry.' Claire's words were muffled by the way she was pressed against Amy's side, but Amy could still hear the tears in her voice.

She looked up at Jim, who stared back with an expression of frustration, waning anger and disappointment. Never a good mix.

'Come on,' Amy said. 'Let's all get home.'

'I'll drop you off.' Jim's words were a stark reminder that they weren't a whole family any more. They were broken – a broken home.

And Amy just wasn't sure they'd ever feel complete again. Not without Henry there.

HENRY

'Where are you going?' Willow asked, as I jumped down from my basket that evening. A nice little post-dinner snooze had set me up for the night, I reckoned. And I had plans.

'Out,' I told her, unhelpfully.

Willow looked lazily over at me as I padded to the door. 'Out of the room, out of the Palace, or out of our lives?' She made it sound like it didn't much matter to her which one it was.

'I'll be back later,' I replied. 'Sorry to disappoint.'

Remembering the route to the Palace cinema took some work. I knew we'd gone there from the Post Office, so I headed there first so I could retrace my steps.

As I got closer, though, I realised I could have just followed the buzz of noise. There was already a host of Palace staff queuing up to find their seats, all chatting and eating popcorn. Apparently cinema night was a big hit, even when they were showing an old film.

Weaving through the legs of the crowd, I followed my nose to try and find Oliver and Sarah, although the competing scents of popcorn and other people were confusing.

169

Finally I found them towards the front of the queue, just making their way inside. I brushed up against Sarah's legs, and she looked down at me in surprise, then giggled.

'Looks like we have a chaperone,' she said. Then her eyes widened. 'Not that we need one! I mean, not that I'm expecting—'

Oliver reached down and picked me up in his arms. 'None of the other Palace dogs would let me do this, you realise? They won't be touched by anyone except the Queen, unless it's strictly necessary.'

'Henry's a special case,' Sarah said. 'I think he's adopted us.'

'I think he has, too.'

They stared at each other over my head, until I stretched up to lick Oliver's cheek to remind them I was still there.

'Looks like we're going in,' Oliver said. 'Henry, you planning on watching too?'

I barked, and Oliver placed me back on the ground so I could trot in ahead of them.

Inside, the cinema was dark, with rows of deep red seats. I'd never been allowed in a *real* cinema – dogs aren't, generally – but from what I'd seen on the TV programmes Claire watched sometimes, it looked about right.

Oliver led Sarah towards a row somewhere in the middle, and I hopped up onto the seat between them. I twisted around a few times to get comfortable, then settled down with my head on my paws. I was looking forward to a good Christmas movie, but I figured I could enjoy the film and still keep an eye on my friends.

But before I was even properly comfortable, the whispers

started. My ears pricked up as I listened to the chatter from the rows behind us. And in front of us, actually.

'Who's that Oliver's with?'

'Why would he bring her!?'

'Have you heard her talk? Her accent is hilarious.'

'I don't think she'll last six months here.'

And then, somewhere in the middle of it all:

'Hang on, have they brought one of Her Majesty's Corgis with them?!'

Sarah shifted uncomfortably in her chair, and Oliver reached across my back to take her hand.

'Ignore them,' he murmured.

'That's getting harder.' Sarah gave him a small half-smile. Even in the darkness of the cinema, I could tell she was sad.

'Are they holding hands?' I heard from behind me.

Oliver turned round in his seat, his expression hard. 'I'm sitting right here, you realise. And I have ears. So, if you have any questions . . . go ahead and ask.'

Nobody said a word after that.

Sarah smiled gratefully, and I settled back down again, happily watching as the credits rolled. But then Sarah was stroking my fur, and the warm room and that familiar popcorn smell made it feel almost like I was back home again. Home, and warm, and safe, and loved. With my family.

I smiled, and let my eyes close as I enjoyed the sensation . . .

'Henry. Henry . . .' Sarah's gentle voice woke me, and I realised the lights had come up again. The film must be over. I'd missed it. That was a shame. But it looked like

Sarah and Oliver had enjoyed it; they were both smiling down at me.

I shook my head a little as I stood up. Apparently cinemas were really good places for naps, even unintentional ones.

'We should get this guy back up to the Corgi Room,' Oliver said. 'They'll be missing him.'

I didn't think that was very likely, but I followed them out, anyway, listening to them chatter about the film.

'I'd forgotten how much I loved it,' Sarah said. 'I mean, I remembered that it was great – one of my favourites when I was little, even. But there were all sorts of details I'd missed or forgotten.'

'It's a classic,' Oliver agreed. 'I think sometimes, when we see something after a long time, it's like we see it in a whole new light. Appreciate it anew, maybe.'

'I think you're right.'

'And sometimes it works the opposite way with people.' Oliver's voice was a little darker as he said it, and Sarah turned to look at him with concern.

'Is that what happened with your ex?' she asked.

Oliver shrugged. 'Sort of.'

'Tell me?'

For a moment, I thought Oliver was going to say no. Then he sighed. 'We'd been dating for almost three years when I proposed. She said yes immediately, and we started the wedding planning right away. But . . . she had this trip planned, with a few of her friends. They were heading off to Australia for a month, while I was hoping to be doing my pilot admissions training. Obviously, you know how that turned out. But when she got back from Australia . . .'

172

'You didn't see her the same way any more?'

'The other way round, I'm afraid.' Oliver gave her a small smile. 'She didn't see me the same. She'd seen the world, and it was a much more exciting place than anything I'd shown her. She decided she didn't want to be tied down, even if it meant not being with me any more. She gave back the ring a few days before she headed off to Thailand.'

'I'm sorry,' Sarah said. 'You didn't want to go with her?'

Oliver shook his head. 'That wasn't the life I wanted. I didn't know what *was* at that point, but I knew I wouldn't be happy just following her around the world. I wanted to make something of myself. Do something I enjoyed and that I found meaningful.'

'And you are.' Sarah smiled up at him.

He smiled back. 'I am. So really, I think everything worked out for the best. Don't you?'

'Definitely.'

I agreed. If Oliver had run off to Thailand, he wouldn't have been here to meet Sarah. And that would have been no good at all.

'So, now you know all my deepest darkest secrets, what about you?' Oliver bumped his elbow against Sarah's arm as he asked.

'How do you mean?'

'Well, I don't believe you only came to the Palace because you realised you were never going to win the pub quiz . . .'

Sarah gave a quick smile as she looked down at the carpet we were walking along. 'No, I didn't suppose you would.'

'So? Do you feel ready to tell me the real reason you left home?' Oliver's voice was kind and gentle, and I could tell he wasn't just asking from idle curiosity. He wanted to know so he could help Sarah. Just like me.

Sarah obviously heard that in his question, too, because she started to talk – the same way she'd talked to me, when she'd been cleaning around the Palace.

'I mentioned my ex, David, when we met at the Post Office?'

'You said things didn't end well,' Oliver said.

'Yeah. Well, they weren't all that great in the middle, either, as it happens. The beginning . . . that was good. In the beginning he was romantic, kind, generous. I really thought he loved me. I could see our whole future laid out before us.'

It sounded like me and the Walkers, I realised. Before Jim left. Before I got lost.

'What changed?' Oliver asked.

'I don't know,' Sarah admitted. 'I don't know if I changed, or he did, or if we were both always that way and just didn't want to admit it. It happened so slowly it felt normal. But one day . . . it was like I woke up. Like I woke up from a terrible dream and realised that all the things he was saying about me weren't true. That I didn't have to stay and listen to it any longer. So I left.'

'What sort of things was he saying?' Oliver's voice was tight, clipped, and he held his hands tight at his side as we walked. Like he was struggling to control himself.

I had a feeling he wanted to bite David the ex as much as I did.

Sarah shrugged. 'Oh, you know. He'd complain about my weight, tell me I needed to lose a few pounds. Or stone. He'd tell me I was going nowhere, that I wasn't ever going to make anything of myself. That I was holding him back. That I was . . .' Her voice caught. 'That I was nothing without him.'

'But you are.' Oliver grabbed her hands and held them tight. I jumped to one side to avoid being caught between them. Clearly, none of us were walking any more. 'Look how far you've come.'

'Dusting a lot of candlesticks?'

'Finding a job that mattered to you, called to you, and doing everything you had to do to get it,' Oliver corrected her. 'And don't forget what they say – once you've worked at the Palace, you'll be in demand everywhere. You could work anywhere in the hospitality industry that you want, after this. Five-star hotels, millionaires' mansions. The sky is the limit.'

'And if I don't want to leave?' Sarah stared up into his eyes. She looked vulnerable in the dim lighting of the corridor. Even scared.

I wanted to jump up and protect her, but I knew I couldn't. I had to trust Oliver to look after her as well as I could, otherwise I knew I'd never be able to leave her.

'Then you could go far here, I'm sure,' Oliver said. 'You can do anything you can dream of. I just know it.'

'No one has ever told me that before,' Sarah whispered.

'Then I'll have to make sure I tell you often.'

Sarah smiled. 'How can you have such faith in me? You barely know me.'

'I have good instincts about people,' Oliver said. 'Well usually. And I can just tell, you're someone special.'

'I think you're pretty special, too,' Sarah said, smiling again.

Never mind the movie I'd missed; this was straight out of one of Amy's DVDs.

Yeah, I was *definitely* the dog with the best plans *ever*.

Day 7

Friday 20th December

HENRY

I'd imagined that, after my late night at the cinema, I'd take it easy the next morning. Oliver and Sarah were grown-up humans. They could probably take it from here themselves. I deserved a morning off.

But apparently the Palace had other ideas for me.

'Come on, you lot,' a footman said, as he opened the door. 'Quick breakfast this morning, and then we've got to get you all on the road.'

'Where are we going?' I asked Willow, while Vulcan was eating his breakfast.

Willow gave a lazy shrug. 'Hard to say. We're always in high demand, you know. Could be we're needed for an event somewhere in the Palace, or outside. Road suggests outside, I suppose.'

'Outside?' That was where I needed to be. But only a very specific part of outside – the part where the Walkers lived.

I had a feeling that wasn't where they'd be taking us.

'Maybe She is back,' Candy mused. 'Or maybe we're being taken to wherever She is! Normally She *always* takes us with Her.'

'Except that Vulcan had that upset stomach,' Willow said. 'And She had to go and collect the New Dog.'

They all looked at me – the wrong new dog – then.

'So maybe we're all being taken to join them now?' I asked. That sounded bad. That sounded like I might be about to be outed – and if they kicked me out on the street wherever the Queen was, I might never find my way home, and the Walkers would have no idea where to look for me.

Suddenly, I'd lost my appetite for breakfast.

I spent the morning panicking. We were loaded into a car in the most comfortable transport crates I'd ever experienced, before the car started pulling away from the Palace.

I put my paws up against the wall of the crate, and peered out of the car window through the bars. From the front, the Palace looked even more impressive – and familiar. I could almost imagine Amy and Jack and Claire standing out there by the railings, waving at our car as we passed.

But, of course, they weren't there.

As the Palace began to disappear into the distance, I settled back down in the crate. If I was going to be out on the streets of some strange town by this afternoon, I might as well try to get some rest before then.

I might need all my energy just to survive.

'So, Henry, where do *you* think we're going?' Candy pressed up against the side of her crate to talk to me through the mesh wire. She was practically panting with excitement at the idea of a day trip.

'I wish I knew,' I replied.

Outside the window, the streets of London passed us by.

Shop windows, stations, a whole world I was no longer free to explore.

Then, suddenly, the car came to a stop.

'We're here,' Candy whispered.

'But where's here?' Vulcan pulled himself up to look out of the window, but the view didn't seem to give him any answers.

I wished Sarah had been allowed to come with us. Or Oliver. Neither of them would let me be left in the middle of nowhere, all alone.

A nameless Palace staff member, dressed in an ordinary black suit and red tie, pulled open the back of the car, and we were all clipped onto leads and helped out. I glanced around, curiously. As far as I could tell, we were on just another London street. And there was no sign at all of Her Majesty.

For now, I was pretty sure that was a good thing.

'Come on, then,' the man said, and tugged across the pavement, towards a door that was painted a deep blue.

Above the door was a sign. I couldn't read the words, but the picture of a dog in a bath tub were pretty clear.

Oh no. This was worse than even I'd dreaded.

We'd been brought to the Puppy Parlour.

Amy had tried taking me to our local Puppy Parlour a few times when I was smaller. When she didn't know me so well. The one near us wasn't half as nice as the parlour the Palace dogs used, though.

The moment we were inside, the person running the parlour flipped a sign on the door over – presumably to show that the place was now closed to any other customers. I couldn't imagine that the Queen would want her dogs being primped and clipped alongside everyday dogs – or that Willow, Vulcan and Candy would stand for it.

'Hi, Quentin,' the owner said, smiling widely. 'And hi, you four!'

'Thanks for squeezing us in today, Jasmine,' Quentin – the Palace staff member – said. He looked like a Quentin, I decided. I'd known a dog in the local park called Tiddles once, and he'd looked anything but – being a giant, hulking, slobbering Doberman. But Quentin was definitely a Quentin. 'I know we'd normally arrange for you to come to us, but this was a bit last minute, for the photo shoot.'

'It's no problem at all,' Jasmine said. 'Always a pleasure to pamper Her Majesty's prize pooches.'

'Great. Well, I'll just leave you to it?' Quentin asked.

Jasmine nodded. 'Give us a couple of hours, and these four will be sweet-smelling, coiffured and ready for their close-ups.'

Hmm. I wasn't sure I liked the sound of this.

'Don't worry,' Candy whispered, as she was led past me by another groomer. 'You'll love this. It's great!'

For Candy, maybe. My experiences of groomers was of soap in my eyes, a rushed clip job, and someone complaining about the state of my nails – or claws, as I preferred to call them.

I should have known, though, that the Palace dogs would get a rather different experience.

Jasmine walked me to my own private room, where a fresh bath was being run. 'Now, let me see,' she said, as she perused a shelf full of bottles. 'What sort of a dog are you? Citrus? Floral? No . . . woody, I think.' She plucked one bottle from the middle of hundreds of others, and tipped some of the

contents into the bath. A cascade of bubbles shot up immediately, covering the surface of the bath. 'Don't worry,' Jasmine
said. 'We have matching shampoo and conditioner for your
coat, too.'

I had to admit, I was rather more eager to hop into this
bath than I had been previous ones.

'Come on then,' Jasmine said. 'In you get.'

The water was just the right temperature, and the bubbles
were soft and soothing on my skin. I even liked the scent
– not too overpowering, unlike the one at the parlour Amy
took me to. (After the first few times she gave up and just
bathed me at home. Let's just say I had made my displeasure
known.) That one had made me stink of flowers for days,
which Sookie had found hilarious.

After the bath, I was dried, groomed and clipped, which
was more relaxing than I expected. Then my claws were
trimmed, without any comments on the state of them.

Overall, it was a surprisingly pleasant experience.

Which is why I felt a sudden jolt of panic when Quentin,
looking over the four of us, nodded and said, 'Time for our
next stop, then.'

'They said something about a photo shoot,' Candy said,
as we were lifted back into the car. 'We often get tidied up
a little before one of those.'

'A photo shoot?' I'd heard the words, of course, but that
didn't mean I had any idea what they entailed. 'What's one
of them?'

'Usually, we get taken somewhere with Her, and made to
sit around in stupid poses while someone takes our picture,'
Willow explained. 'Goodness knows where today's will be.'

Wherever it was, it took us a long time to get there. And I was growing more and more nervous by the second.

If we were going to meet the Queen, that was it for me. I didn't think my fancy doggy manicure was going to last long out on the streets.

Eventually, the car pulled off the main road we'd been travelling on and started approaching another building. This one looked just as giant as Buckingham Palace, but it was made of grey stone, and had funny bits of building sticking up at the top of the walls.

'Windsor Castle,' Vulcan said, happily. 'I think this is my very favourite of all our homes.'

'How many do you have?' I asked, incredulous. I'd assumed that the Palace was more than enough home for three dogs.

Willow frowned. 'Do you know, I'm not actually sure. Obviously there's Windsor, and Buckingham Palace.'

'And Sandringham, and Balmoral,' Candy put in.

'Do we still count the one in Ireland?' Vulcan asked.

'Hillsborough Castle? Yes, I imagine so,' Willow said. 'So that's how many?'

'I think we've forgotten a couple,' Candy said.

'Never mind.' My head ached just imagining how many Palaces these dogs had the run of. 'Let's just say it's a lot of palaces.'

'But this one is my favourite,' Vulcan repeated.

I could see why, I thought, as we pulled up the driveway of Windsor Castle. Vulcan liked to think he was intimidating, the big dog of the Palace. Windsor Castle looked like *exactly* his sort of place – all threatening grey stone walls and battlements. It looked like a proper castle from one of Jack's old books on medieval wars and stuff. (He'd gone through a phase of wanting to be a knight when he was eleven. I was his trusty steed.) Of course Vulcan would love it.

Especially if Her Majesty was there, and it meant he got to see the back of me.

The car pulled inside the castle proper, and swung to a stop before a large door. Outside it stood a collection of new people – one carrying a heavy and expensive-looking camera, along with what I assumed were bags of other photography equipment.

Quentin climbed out of the car and shook hands with the new people, before coming round to let us jump down.

'So, where do you want them, Tessa?' Quentin asked, as he clipped our leads on.

'Well, the magazine really wants a full, glossy feature on how Windsor Castle does Christmas. So lots of shots of the decorations inside the castle, and a few of it looking festive and frosty from the outside.' Tessa, who seemed to be in charge of everything, checked her clipboard. 'We were thinking some photos of the dogs on the Long Walk would be perfect, as well as some shots of them inside, by the Christmas trees, reflected in the odd bauble, that sort of thing. Maybe even under the mistletoe. In fact, we have a few props we hoped to use . . .'

One of the men with Tessa came scurrying forward with a large bag, which he held open for her. Tessa reached in, and pulled out a shiny golden crown. Bending her knees, she reached down to place it on my head. 'What do you think?'

'Perfect.' Quentin's smile was a little weak, I thought. But nothing compared to the glare Vulcan was giving me as Tessa placed a red Santa hat with a fluffy white pom-pom on his head.

'Great!' Tessa beamed. 'Then let's get started!'

'It's just as well Her Majesty isn't here to see this,' Quentin muttered under his breath, as he led us into the castle.

Candy and I exchanged a quick look, as I felt my spirits start to soar.

'She's not here,' I said.

'Looks like.' Candy beamed at me. 'Seems your secret is safe for a little longer, Henry.'

Suddenly, this photo shoot seemed like a *brilliant* idea.

It turns out that posing for photos is kind of boring. The photographer – Juan – spent a lot of time saying, 'No, no, no!' when one of us moved out of position (okay, it was usually me. And usually when a particularly sparkly decoration caught my eye). But it was fun to see the inside of Windsor Castle, with its many, many Christmas trees, festive greenery twined everywhere, and the lights.

But the best part was when Tessa, possibly sensing that Juan was close to a breakdown, suggested that we take the shoot outside.

Tessa reached down to straighten my crown (it had a tendency to slip over one ear) as we left the castle walls through a large arch and stepped out into grounds. Ahead, a long, long straight path disappeared into the distance in front of us.

'I thought maybe the dogs could stretch their legs on the Long Walk for a little while,' Tessa said to Juan. 'I'm sure you'll be able to get some fantastic shots of them frolicking in the gardens.'

Juan didn't look fully convinced, but he nodded, all the same. Quentin let us off our leads, waved his hands at the Long Walk, and we ran.

Winter was really here now, and even with the sun sparkling overhead in a crisp, clear blue sky, there were shadowed parts of the ground that were still covered in frost. It crunched under my paws in a way that made me smile, even as I shivered.

The Long Walk really was very long. I chased along it, crown slipping, enjoying the freedom of being outside the Palace, even if it was only for the afternoon. Candy ran alongside me, sometimes, looking happier than I'd ever seen her. Her ears flapped in the wind, and she grinned at me as we dashed ahead of Willow and Vulcan who were walking along properly.

All too soon, though, it was time to head back.

Tessa plucked the crown from my head as I climbed back into my crate in the car. I was tired, worn out from racing around the Long Walk, and cold from the frost.

As I circled round to settle down, head on my paws, I heard Vulcan mutter, 'Well even if She wasn't here today, She has to come home soon. Then we'll see.'

I knew he was right. And I knew there was nothing I could do about it.

So instead, I snoozed all the way back to the Palace, dreaming of a world in which I was the king of all I surveyed. Including the kitchens.

AMY

The school hall was packed.

'You know, if there aren't enough seats, I can totally head home again,' Jack said, unhelpfully.

Amy grabbed his sleeve and dragged him with her, through the crowd, heading towards two empty seats she'd spotted on the other side of the central aisle.

'This is Claire's Christmas Concert, and she wants us both here.' Amy quickened her pace in time to toss her handbag onto the first seat, before the large man in the green jacket could reach it. Actually, was that Claire's history teacher? Too late to worry about that now, anyway.

Jack threw himself into the second seat, his coat still on and the collar coming up to his ears. 'Fine.'

Sighing, Amy slipped her own coat from her shoulders and sat down, placing her bag in her lap. Was it so much to ask for just one nice night out, the three of them all in the same place, her and Jack cheering Claire on? Just one, normal, family Christmas event, with carols and song sheets and mulled wine in the interval?

Picking up the programme she'd been handed at the door, she scanned through the list of carols the choir was singing, pieces the school orchestra were playing, and songs that the audience would be expected to join in with, but hardly ever did. It was comfortingly familiar – practically exactly the same as last year, even if everything else in her world was different.

She sat back in her chair, and let the discordant sounds of the orchestra tuning up and the clamour and chatter of all the other parents fade away. This concert was something she looked forward to, every single Christmas. And having missed out on most of her work's Christmas night out, she was *not* letting this night be ruined.

'You didn't tell me *he* was coming,' Jack muttered, his voice dark.

Amy looked up, knowing without Jack having to say exactly who *he* was.

'I didn't *know* he was coming.' Even last night, in all the chaos of finding the kids and bringing them home, they hadn't discussed their separate lives at all. Hadn't talked about whose turn it was to do all the things they used to do together.

It took her a few moments to find Jim, sat a few rows back on the other side of the hall. But it took only seconds to realise who the petite brunette next to him was.

Bonnie. The famous – infamous – Bonnie.

They hadn't met before – why would they? Jim had gone out of his way to keep them separate. But that didn't mean she hadn't wondered. What she looked like, how she dressed, or walked, or talked. What it was about her that made Jim up and leave a marriage that was about to celebrate two decades of togetherness.

Maybe that was it, she thought, as she watched him take

Bonnie's coat and fold it neatly under his chair. Maybe he'd just grown tired of the same old, same old. Maybe he'd needed a change of pace, some excitement in his life, something new.

While she got stuck with keeping the old life he was bored of running on her own.

She looked away, before she got caught up on Bonnie's hairstyle, or the dress that was just slightly shorter than Amy would ever dare wear. Or before Jim noticed she was staring, at least.

She had to focus: she wasn't interested in Jim's future, any longer, except for how it affected her children. Amy had her own future to concentrate on.

'He's got no right to be here,' Jack said, his arms folded tightly across his chest as he stared mulishly ahead at the empty stage.

'Claire is his daughter too,' Amy reminded him evenly, to stop herself from yelling, *You're right! Let's get a mob together to run him out of here!*

'You don't think he gave up the right to call himself our father when he walked out and left us?' Jack looked her in the eye as he asked the question, and Amy knew he was looking for the slightest tell that she was lying as she answered.

'I think that he's the only dad you get, whatever he's done. So you have to think very carefully about the relationship you want to have with him.' Jack was almost an adult now, and he deserved her total honesty, however difficult the question. He deserved the right to make his own decisions about his own future, the same way that she was.

Amy knew that she couldn't force Jack to keep his dad in his life. But she could strongly encourage it. Because whether

Jack knew it or not, he needed Jim. Last night had proven that to her. Amy could be mother and father every day of the week, but there was going to come the point when Jack needed to talk to someone else. And she would far rather that someone else be Jim than some other seventeen-year-old mate who knew as little about the world as Jack did.

Thankfully, the lights went dark and the curtain went up before Jack was able to come up with an argument against her comments. With a deep breath, Amy settled back into her chair, determined to enjoy what had always been one of her favourite Christmas traditions.

The interval came almost too quickly, after a moving performance of 'O Holy Night' from the orchestra and choir. Amy, still wiping her eyes, got to her feet quickly. She knew from experience you had to be quick out the door if you wanted to make it to the front of the refreshments queue before they called everyone back into the main hall again.

Unfortunately, she wasn't the only one who knew that.

'Amy!' Jim sounded surprised to see her, which was kind of crazy since it was her daughter up there in the choir too. At least he seemed to be alone; Bonnie must have run to the bathrooms, or stayed to look after the seats. 'And Jack. Nice to see you've come to support your sister tonight.'

There was an edge in his voice, a hint of the censure he just couldn't avoid giving – a reminder that the night before he hadn't been such a good brother. Of course Jim couldn't just leave it, just for one night, while they were all at Claire's concert. Because he wasn't around the rest of the time, he was going to ruin tonight instead.

Great.

'Jack, why don't you head back and keep an eye on our seats,' Amy said, keeping her gaze on Jim. 'I'll get us drinks and meet you back there.'

Jack, obviously eager to get away from his father, disappeared back into the hall without a murmur.

'You're trying to keep him away from me?' Jim asked, his cheekbones turning hot and pink with colour.

'I'm trying to make sure neither one of you makes a scene at Claire's school concert,' Amy corrected him. 'You have to understand his point of view, Jim.'

'I don't see him trying to understand mine!'

'Perhaps you should try setting him that example, then.' Amy tried not to sound exasperated, but it was hard.

Jim seemed to expect that life should go on exactly the way he wanted it – all the bits he liked about his old life copied and pasted over to the new one, while he dumped the stuff that didn't work for him any more. Like her. And the kind of responsibilities – financial and otherwise – that meant he couldn't just drop everything and go skiing for Christmas.

Well, as the person left to deal with all the stuff he chose to leave behind, Amy felt she still had the right to call him out on his behaviour – even if she no longer had that right as his wife.

Which, judging by his current behaviour, she was growing more and more glad about by the day.

'Jack is still only seventeen, Jim,' Amy said, keeping her voice soft. 'Yes, he's almost an adult in lots of ways, but in others – like understanding the behaviour of people with almost three times the amount of life experience he has – he's still a child. You can't expect him to understand what you've chosen to do when he has no life experience of his own to match it up with. He's barely even had a girlfriend that lasted more than a month.'

'I suppose.' Jim frowned in the way he always used to when he was puzzling out a new idea. 'I guess I just expected him to want me to be happy.'

'I think he'd rather that *he* got to be happy first,' Amy said, drily. Then she sighed. 'I'm sure he will understand, eventually. But you're going to have to give him time. And you're going to have to try to understand him, first.'

'Understand a seventeen-year-old boy? That should be easy,' Jim joked. 'After all, I used to be one.'

'Very true.' Amy thought about the boy Jim had been at seventeen, and the girl she'd been back then, too. 'But I don't suggest you start reliving your misspent youth. Especially since I believe your new girlfriend is on her way over here right now.'

She nodded towards the door from the bathrooms, and Jim turned quickly in time to watch Bonnie walking towards them.

'So, do you want to introduce us, or would you rather let me cut in front of you in the refreshments line?' Amy asked, eyebrows raised. She was quite proud of the way she kept her cool, actually.

Even if she hadn't been concentrating on how brilliant her own future was going to be, she might have battered both of them with little Tommy Finn's double bass for ruining the future she'd always planned on.

'Uh, you go ahead,' Jim said, looking unsettled at the idea of both of them in the same place at the same time. 'I'll just . . .' he trailed off.

'Good plan,' Amy said, as if he'd said something sensible, for once.

Breezing past him, she reached the front of the queue and selected mulled wines for herself and Jack. And a couple of mince pies. Just because.

HENRY

I slept most of the way back to the Palace. Racing around Windsor Castle all day had been tiring enough, but the added tension of fearing being found out to be a fake Royal Dog had really worn me out.

Of course, that meant that once we'd got home (and when had I started thinking of the Palace as home?) and been fed our dinner, I wasn't in the slightest bit sleepy.

Sarah took us all back to the Corgi Room after dinner, and the others curled up in their baskets quickly enough. Sarah petted me for a while when I made it obvious I wasn't going to head for my basket, just yet.

'Sounds from Quentin like you four have had quite the adventurous day,' she said, stroking my smooth fur. 'And a lot of pampering too. Your coat is beautifully shiny.'

I preened a little at that.

'And you didn't miss much here,' she went on. 'Just the usual dusting, cleaning and so on. I didn't even get a chance to meet Oliver for his morning break today.'

That was a shame. I'd hoped that even without me here they'd have carried on their fledgling relationship. But it seemed like they still needed me to push them along.

Or maybe not. Even as I had the thought, the door to the Corgi Room opened, and Oliver's head appeared around the edge of the door, followed swiftly by the rest of him once he saw Sarah.

'I thought I might find you here,' he said, smiling. 'Catching up on all Henry's adventures?'

'Something like that,' Sarah replied. 'What about you? Come to hear all the latest gossip from Windsor from our furry pal?'

'Actually, I came to invite you to a party.'

Sarah's eyes widened. 'A party?'

'Absolutely!' Oliver shut the door behind him, and came in to perch on the edge of the table that held our food bowls and so forth. 'Every month or so, the staff throw a corridor party – so called because it literally takes place in the staff corridor, outside our rooms.'

'So this party is basically at my house, and you're inviting me to it?' Sarah asked, grinning.

'Well, it is in the men's corridor not the women's, this time . . .'

Sarah laughed. 'I'm kidding. And I'm pretty sure no one else here would have thought to tell me about it, so thank you.'

She was right, I realised. If it wasn't for Oliver, Sarah would have been left out, again. And then she'd have headed back to her room from here and walked straight past it, knowing she wasn't wanted there.

Thank goodness for Oliver.

'Anyway,' he went on. 'Everyone brings a bottle of something alcoholic to drink, and someone tends to bring speakers to play some music, and we all just chat and get to know each other a bit better.'

'Sounds nice.' Sarah sounded dubious, though. Probably because she was sure that none of *them* wanted to get to know her better.

But they should, I realised. If they knew Sarah like I knew her, like Oliver knew her, they'd *have* to like her. How could they not?

Which meant we had to get her to this corridor party.

'It'll be a great chance to get to know the other staff here,' Oliver said. I caught his eye, and I could see he knew Sarah was wavering too.

'I'm just not so sure it's a good idea,' Sarah said.

Not good enough. I had to do something.

I jumped up to my four paws with a sharp bark, and bounded to the door, ducking behind Oliver, and pawing at the wood.

Maybe Sarah would go to the party if I went with her.

'Looks like Henry wants to join the party,' Oliver said. 'But I'm sure he'll only go if you do. You wouldn't want to let a dog down, would you . . .?'

Sarah rolled her eyes. 'Henry's had plenty of adventures already today.'

I barked again, and she laughed.

'Come on,' Oliver said, obviously sensing she was weakening. 'Never mind Henry – *I'd* really like it if you would go to the party with me. Please.'

She looked up, and I saw their gazes lock. For a long moment, they just stared at each other.

Then, Sarah whispered, 'Well, when you put it like that . . .' and I knew we were in business.

★★★

I hadn't had cause to visit the staff corridors of Buckingham Palace before; Sarah didn't seem to spend all that much time there anyway, so I just caught up with her out and about around the Palace and its grounds. Still, I was interested to see where she and Oliver lived – and if it was nicer than the Corgi Room (I suspected not).

There wasn't much chance to see inside the rooms, though. When we arrived, the party was already in full swing, and the corridor rang with music and conversation, people shouting over each other to be heard. There were plenty of bottles and glasses laid out too – apparently a lot of fun was being had.

'While the cat's away,' Oliver murmured, close to Sarah's ear, just loud enough for her – and my excellent ears – to hear.

'Looks like everyone is enjoying themselves.' Sarah sounded more nervous than I'd heard her since I arrived at the Palace.

'And we will too. Come on.' Oliver grabbed her hand and dragged her into the crush. I followed behind, keeping as close to their heels as I could.

'Who brought a corgi to the party?' someone cried upon seeing me.

'What, are you worried he's going to report back to Her Majesty?' someone else asked, and everyone laughed.

Clearly they didn't know the sort of corgi they were dealing with. I knew how to party: Amy and Jim used to hold New Year's Eve parties every year, and I would dance and jump and celebrate with the best of them.

Oliver had brought drinks for them both, although as far

as I could see neither he nor Sarah did much more than sip at them. They stood off to one side, chatting between themselves more than actually joining in the party.

Every now and then, though, someone would stop by to talk to Oliver, and he would introduce them to Sarah. Oliver was clearly a well known and liked member of the household staff, I realised. Hopefully just being his friend would be enough to convince the others that Sarah was worth getting to know. She certainly seemed to be relaxing, the more and more people she said hello to. And they all seemed to be smiling and friendly to her.

Obviously this had been a brilliant idea. Good of Oliver and me to come up with it, really.

'I just need to go talk to Russell, over there,' Oliver said, after a while. 'Will you be okay here with Henry?'

Sarah gave him a half-smile. 'I think I can hold my own without a guard dog.'

'Of course you can.' Oliver smiled and started moving away. 'It's Henry I'm worried about,' he called back over his shoulder, making Sarah laugh.

The moment he was out of sight, though, lost in a sea of people, Sarah tensed up again. I knew she didn't feel comfortable with the other Palace staff yet – the same way I didn't feel truly comfortable around Willow, Vulcan and Candy. It's hard to be somewhere you know you're not wanted.

But *Oliver* wanted Sarah here. And so did I.

Hopefully that would be enough, in the end.

But then, Harriet from the Post Office came over to say hello, on her way to fetch another drink. And then another housemaid stopped for a quick chat before being whisked off to dance by one of the footmen. I sat happily at Sarah's feet, watching her gaining in confidence by the moment.

She could do this – even without Oliver. And she was finally starting to realise that. Brilliant.

'You're Sarah, right?' A red-haired woman who looked just a little older than Sarah approached us. She had a smile on her face, but it was the sort of smile I didn't trust, not entirely. Not like the smiles of the others who'd stopped by to chat. I shuffled a little closer to Sarah, just in case she needed me. 'You're here with Oliver.'

'That's right.' Sarah turned towards the voice, returning the bad smile with one of her brilliant ones. 'On both counts, I suppose.'

'I'm Jessica.' Her smile twisted, just a touch. Just enough to tell me that I was right to trust my instincts.

This one was up to no good.

'Oh. Yes, I think we met on my first day,' Sarah replied, her smile fading and her voice a little tight. Was this one of the people who'd been making fun of her? I wondered.

'You seem to have settled in just fine,' Jessica said, glancing over Sarah's shoulder to where Oliver was talking to his friend. 'Getting Oliver on your side is a big coup.'

'He's not . . . it's not about sides.' Sarah's brow creased up with confusion. 'He's just my friend.'

'Of *course* he is. And you've even befriended the Queen's dogs.' She glanced down at me with visible disgust.

Not a dog person, then. Good. We wouldn't want one like her, anyway.

'Henry's a very friendly dog,' Sarah said, neutrally.

'Well, I suppose that will stand you in good stead with

Her Majesty,' Jessica said, suddenly all smiles and friendliness again. 'She *loves* it when other people dote on her dogs. Especially when the dogs love them back. You should definitely make a show of your closeness with Henry when the Queen gets back.'

'Hello, Jessica,' Oliver said, appearing suddenly beside us. I was glad. I didn't know exactly what Jessica was up to, but I was sure it wasn't nearly as friendly as she wanted us to believe.

'Oliver.' Sarah smiled up at him, relief glowing from her face.

'I was just saying hello to our new girl,' Jessica said, already edging away.

'Yes, she was telling me how much the Queen loves it when her staff get on well with her dogs,' Sarah elaborated. 'She suggested that I make a fuss of Henry in front of her, when she gets back.'

Oliver's eyes narrowed as he stared at Jessica. 'Did she now.'

'It was a joke!' Jessica burst out, stepping back again. 'A prank – you know, like we always play on the newbies. Just the usual hazing for new staff members. Or have you forgotten, now you're a high and mighty senior footman? You used to like making an apple pie bed, or putting food colouring in someone's toothpaste, just as much as the rest of us.'

'A prank?' Sarah asked, obviously confused.

'The Queen is very particular about her pets,' Oliver said. 'Remember, I told you how normally no one else is allowed to pet them, except her? Henry is obviously the exception, but you still wouldn't be very popular if you made a fuss of him in front of Her Majesty.'

'So you were trying to get me into trouble,' Sarah said, looking at Jessica with disappointment.

'It was a joke,' Jessica muttered again.

'Not a very funny one.' Oliver glared at her again, until Jessica decided to take the very sensible course of getting away from him. He turned back to Sarah. 'I'm sorry about her.'

Sarah shrugged. 'I told you they didn't like me.'

'It might be my fault too,' Oliver said. 'Ever since I got promoted to senior footman . . . I think a few people feel I've forgotten where I started. I haven't, of course, but . . . sometimes that's how it is around here.'

'Well, I'm right on the bottom rung, and they can *still* find a reason to dislike me!'

'They're not all like Jessica,' Oliver insisted. 'Most people who work here are lovely. Like family, even, once you get to know them. But it does take a while to settle in.'

Sarah straightened her shoulders. 'Well, I'm in it for the long haul. So they'd just better get used to me.'

Oliver beamed. 'Good for you.'

'But for now . . . maybe I should just head back to my room. I think I've had enough partying for one night.'

Oh no. That would absolutely not do. I had to find a way to keep Sarah at the party. If she left now, then that Jessica would have won. And that was unacceptable.

'We haven't even had a dance, yet,' Oliver said, but Sarah shook her head.

'I'm not great at dancing.'

Well, I was. And I was going to get Sarah dancing one way or another.

The music blaring from the speakers changed to something I recognised from one of Amy's movies – and apparently everyone else there knew it too, because a lot of them got up to dance. I barked my approval and then, with a quick glance up at Sarah, dove into the crowd of dancers, ready to shake my furry stuff.

'Is Henry . . . is he dancing?' I heard Oliver ask, over the buzz of the music. I was too busy making my paws move in time and shaking my stumpy tale to look over, though.

The dancers around me spread out a little, giving me room to move, clapping along in time as I danced. Then, as the song reached my favourite bit, I darted over to Sarah and barked up at her, encouragingly.

'I think he wants us to join him on the dance floor,' Oliver said.

Sarah was shaking her head again, but this time I had the crowd onside.

'Come on, Oliver! Come on, Sarah!' people were shouting.

Laughing, Oliver pulled Sarah onto the designated dancing area to join me, and she buried her head against his shoulder as his arms came up around her.

Then, just as if I'd orchestrated it, the music changed again – this time, to a slower, softer song. I backed away and sat on the sidelines, watching as Sarah and Oliver swayed in time to the music.

Perfect. Like a happy ever after in a movie.

Just like I'd planned.

Day 8

Saturday 21st December

AMY

'Now, are you sure you two will be okay without me today?' Amy looked nervously back at her children as she wrapped a fluffy scarf around her neck. 'Remember, I'm only at the surgery if you need me, and your dad is only a phone call away too. There's stuff to make sandwiches in the fridge, and if you could remember to feed the cat . . .' she trailed off as her two children stared at her impassively. Even Sookie was sitting alert next to the radiator, watching her. Judging her, in that way cats always seemed to.

Henry never judged her.

Amy sighed. 'Look, I know that staying home while I go out to work isn't the most exciting way to spend the first day of the holidays, but—'

'Actually, Mum . . . we did have a sort of plan for today.' Jack was looking faintly guilty before she even asked what the plan was, which didn't bode well at all.

She unwound her scarf. This might take a while.

'What plan?' she asked.

'Jack thought we could go into London again, on the train,' Claire said, excitedly.

Amy's chest tightened. Last time they'd gone to London,

they'd come home a family member short. She really wasn't sure she could bear risking that again.

'We could put up some actual Hunt for Henry posters, for local people who maybe wouldn't see it online,' Jack explained. 'And maybe we could even check out the Dogs and Cats home at Battersea. See if he's ended up there by mistake.'

'He's microchipped, Jack,' Amy pointed out. 'I'm sure they'd have checked that.' But what if they hadn't? Had she even called Battersea? She couldn't remember if it was on her list of places to check in with. If it wasn't . . . it had to be worth a try, right?

'What if something went wrong with the microchip?' Claire asked. 'I've been reading up, and sometimes they do. They might have him and have no idea that he's ours.'

They both looked so excited, so eager, Amy wanted to say yes. Even if it all came to nothing, at least they'd be doing something. And doing it together, which made her feel kind of warm inside. With the age difference, it wasn't often that Jack and Claire found a common interest. But for Henry, they were working together. That felt good.

The only problem was, could she bring herself to trust them both again after the stunt they'd pulled the other night?

'Look, this is different from the guy who said he had Henry,' Jack said, reading her mind in the way he only ever seemed able to do when he could use it to get what he wanted. 'We're not going to meet anyone else, or do anything dodgy. We've told you exactly where we're going, and we'll text and tell you our train times if you want. It's not like I've never been into London without you before.'

That was true. Jack was seventeen, perfectly old enough to take the train into town on his own. He went often with his friends, on the weekend, and had even volunteered at a city centre animal shelter the summer before, in preparation for his vet's training. She didn't have to worry about Jack finding his way around the big city.

But taking his baby sister with him? That was a different proposition altogether.

'And I'm twelve now, Mum,' Claire added. 'It's not like I'm a baby any more, or anything.'

'You'll always be my baby,' Amy said, absently, and Claire pulled a face.

'Mum!'

'I know, I know.' They were both growing up. And she couldn't keep them home and safe and with her twenty-four hours a day – however tempting that might sometimes be. It was just . . . she'd lost so much she'd taken for granted recently, it was hard to risk anything more.

'Maybe I could get someone to cover for me at the surgery. Then I could come with you.' She'd only taken the extra shift at the Saturday clinic because they were desperate for staff, and because the extra cash would come in *very* handy this month. The chances of finding someone else willing to work the weekend were limited, she knew. But maybe . . .

'Mum.' Jack gave her a serious look, and suddenly he was more man than boy. More parent than child, even. 'We'll be fine. You know we will.'

And that was the problem. She did know that. They were capable, sensible children – usually, at least. She didn't have an argument against the plan except that she didn't want to spend the whole day worrying totally unnecessarily.

She sighed. 'Okay. Fine.' Claire squealed and threw her arms around her mum's waist. Even Jack managed a proper smile. 'But I want you to text me every hour to check in. Okay?'

'Sure. We will,' Jack promised.

Claire grabbed a pink floral folder from the kitchen table and stuffed it into Amy's hands. 'Look! These are what we're going to put up, and show around.'

Amy opened the folder. Inside were page after page of copies of the photo of Henry in his Christmas cracker hat, along with the link to the 'Hunt for Henry' Facebook page, and the word 'Missing!' in a large font. Underneath, was a full description of Henry, starting with the words: 'Much loved family pet.'

Would it help? Probably not. But at least they'd feel like they were doing something. Amy could understand the need for that.

'Maybe don't attach anything to the Palace railings though, yeah?' she suggested. 'I have a feeling the Queen wouldn't like it . . .'

Jack grinned. 'We won't, Mum.'

'In that case . . . good luck!' She gave them both a hug and reached for her scarf. 'And I really, really hope you find him.'

'Um, Mum?' Jack said, giving her the guilty look again. 'I don't suppose you could lend us any money for today could you? Only . . .'

Only he'd given all his to a scam artist to try and get Henry back. Of course.

Amy sighed and reached for her purse, doing some quick mental calculations about the cost of train tickets, and how much today's extra shift would bring in. Apparently her children weren't as entirely grown-up and self-sufficient as all that *just* yet.

HENRY

I awoke to the sensation of being stared at. Cautiously, I opened one eye, and found Willow, Candy and Vulcan standing around my basket, all looking at me.

I opened the other eye. 'What?'

'Where, exactly, did you disappear to last night?' Willow asked.

'Sarah carried you back and put you to bed,' Candy added. 'It was really, really late.'

'And you let her *hold* you.' Vulcan shuddered. 'You didn't even have the excuse of being sedated, or anything.'

'Unless you were?' Candy asked. 'I mean, had you been to the vet's or something? What happened?!'

'I was at a party,' I said, closing my eyes again. 'Up in the servants corridor.'

There was a shocked silence. Then all three of them started talking at once.

'Did anyone see you?'

'What were you doing *there*?'

'That really is taking this being friendly thing too far!'

Apparently more sleep was off the table.

With a sigh, I got up to my paws, and hopped down from my basket.

'Look, Oliver wanted Sarah to go with him, so I went as her guard dog. Some of the other staff haven't been very nice to her.' Understatement of the year, but I knew that the other dogs wouldn't necessarily understand how that felt.

'Probably because she doesn't know her place yet,' Vulcan said, obviously trying to sound wise.

'Her place is here, at the Palace,' I said firmly. 'And with Oliver.'

'Perhaps,' Willow said. 'But it does take a very special sort of person to work for Her.'

'Sarah is special,' I snapped back. 'Much more special than the rest of them.'

Candy stood staring balefully at me, but she didn't speak out to defend Sarah, either.

'We'll see,' was all Willow would say. I could tell she didn't believe it though.

I didn't have to stay and listen to this. Turning my back on the three of them, I stalked out of the Corgi Room and down the corridor, muttering about snobbish dogs who wouldn't know a good person if they bit one. Which they probably would.

Over the last week I'd explored most of the Palace, a room at a time. I'm sure it had many more secrets – maybe even more secret passageways, like the mirrored door Sarah had shown me in the White Drawing Room – but this morning I wasn't in a hurry to hunt them out. Instead, I just wandered the corridors, thinking.

There was so much about the world inside Buckingham Palace that didn't make sense to me. But the most confusing thing of all was the attitude of the other dogs. In my experiences, people who cared about you, who took care of you, who were kind to you – those were the people you devoted yourself to. And for me, here, that person was Sarah.

At home, of course, it was the Walkers – and I couldn't help but miss them, every day, however kind Sarah and Oliver were.

But who was it for Willow, Candy and Vulcan?

I stopped, halfway into a new room, as a thought struck me.

The Queen. That was who they loved – who cared for them, loved them and was kind to them. She fed them, walked them, brushed them . . . and She wasn't here. Willow had said that She nearly *always* took them with Her, whenever She travelled, but this time She hadn't. And, in fact, She'd taken a new dog instead.

Of course they were grumpy and difficult. They were missing their Person, the same way I was missing the Walkers.

In a way, we were all in the same boat. Except the Queen would be back soon, and I would be out on my ear – still without my family.

I heard a door shut somewhere behind me, and trotted all the way into the room to keep thinking about this. The room I was in had a strange light in the centre, a bit like an upside down umbrella. There was all the usual gold on the walls, and regal decorations – things I'd almost become used to over the last week.

But the most interesting thing was the fact there was also an open door. That led to outside!

Glancing back over my flanks, to check no one was watching me, I padded over to the door. It was a glass one, like a giant window, and obviously it had been left ajar by accident. I pushed it with my nose to open it fully, and looked out.

In my excitement to find an open door, I'd forgotten one very important thing: I was still on the first floor.

The door didn't lead, as I'd hoped, to a new area of outside I'd not explored yet. Instead, it led to a long, stone balcony, looking out over the forecourt to the Palace.

I pressed my nose between two of the stone columns that made up the balcony wall, and looked out through the gap.

The first thing that struck me was how *far* I could see – in the distance, I could see tall buildings and oddly shaped structures, then a long, straight road lined with trees and parks, all the way up to a roundabout with a large, stone statue topped with a golden figure. All those places I'd never been – all those parks I'd never run in.

A pigeon flew past, and I almost jumped out to chase it – before I remembered the huge drop down to the ground. I stepped back, more securely on the balcony, and watched the pigeon as it fluttered down to the ground.

And then I saw something far more familiar.

There were the railings I'd stood at with Amy, Jack and Claire. There was the road we'd walked down. There were the bushes I'd disappeared through.

This was where I'd lost my family, and now I was imprisoned here at the Palace, until someone learned the truth about me.

I was about to turn back and head inside, out of the

freezing December wind, when something caught my eye. A dark head and a lighter one, pressed up against the railings down below. A bright red, puffy coat I recognised from an epic shopping trip with Amy and Claire. A battered bag covered in patches that Jack would never throw out.

And they were holding up a white piece of paper, trying to show it to whoever was on the other side of the railings – one of the police guards, by the look of things.

Jack and Claire.

They'd come looking for me after all! They hadn't forgotten me!

Frantically, I barked my loudest, jumping up to try and get my front paws on the top of the balcony, in the hope of being seen over the top.

But Jack and Claire never even looked up. I was too far away for them to see or hear me.

'What are you doing out here?' A cross voice behind me made me jump back down to the floor of the balcony. I turned to find Jessica standing behind me in the open door, her hands on her hips. 'If you fall off there, there'll be hell to pay. And you just know it'll be my fault, somehow. Come on, in with you.'

She tried to get me inside by waving her arms towards the door, but I turned back for one last look at my lost family.

Down below, Jack and Claire were turning away too. Walking away from the railings. Away from the Palace.

Away from me.

I watched, until they were almost out of sight. And then I followed Jessica back inside, whimpering slightly as she locked the balcony door behind us.

I wondered if that might be the last time I ever saw Jack and Claire, ever again.

The corridors and rooms of the Palace felt vast and empty, as I made my way back towards the Corgi Room. I no longer saw the splendour of the Palace, or noticed the golden threads in the carpet under my paws. I missed the scruffy stripy carpet of the hallway at the Walkers' house, and the pile of shoes that never quite made it onto the shoe rack (and so were ripe for the occasional chewing).

I missed home. And I missed my people.

'What's up with you?' Candy followed me across the room as I slunk back to my basket.

'Nothing,' I lied.

'Homesick?' Candy guessed, as she jumped up into my basket with me.

'Maybe.' Definitely.

'You know, Christmas with the Royals isn't so bad. You might even have fun.' Candy pressed her nose against my side. 'It might even make you want to stay with us.'

'If that's even an option.' I was still waiting to be discovered and tossed out on my ear.

'I think it could be,' Candy replied. 'She is a bit of a soft touch when it comes to corgis. I don't think She'd throw you out with nowhere to go.'

I tilted my head to one side. I hadn't considered that possibility before, but now that Candy said it – rather than Vulcan spreading his poison – it almost made sense. After all, a Queen who hand fed and brushed Her dogs, took them almost everywhere with Her, walked them Herself and didn't like others touching them . . . that was a Queen who loved dogs. And a Queen who took in an old friend's pet after they died, just to make sure the dog had a good home in its old age . . . that wasn't a Queen who would throw a dog out into the snow at Christmas. Was it?

And it wasn't like there wasn't enough space at the Palace for one more small, well-behaved corgi.

It just wasn't the same as being at *my* home for Christmas.

I settled down a bit more comfortably in my basket, as Candy curled herself around my side.

'So, tell me a little more about Christmas at the Palace,' I said.

Candy shrugged. 'Well, first of all, we don't spend it at the Palace. Well, not this one, anyway.'

'Wait.' I sat up straighter again. 'You have this incredible Palace, all decked out for Christmas, and you don't even spend Christmas Day here?'

'No. We go to Sandringham.' Candy tilted her head. 'We have a family Christmas lunch here before we go, though. So I suppose that's why they put up a few baubles and things.'

'A few baubles . . . have you even walked around to look at all the decorations in this place?'

'Well, I've seen a few of them. On my way to dinner or a walk, and such.'

All this magnificence, and the dogs who lived here didn't even appreciate it.

'That's it.' I hopped back down from my basket. 'You're coming with me.'

'Where are we going?' Candy asked, but she followed me all the same as I trotted towards the door.

'I'm going to show you this Palace through *my* eyes, for a change,' I said. 'Come on.'

I started with the Grand Staircase, making Candy stop and stare at all the brightly coloured baubles hung from the garlands that twined down the bannisters.

'They are very pretty, I suppose.' Candy stared at her reflection in one of them. 'So this is what you wanted me to see?'

'This is just the start,' I assured her. 'Let's keep going.'

I knew my way around the Palace well enough now to lead Candy to all my favourite spots. I took her through the Bow Room, with its enormous tree, laden with red and gold decorations. I took her through banqueting rooms with sprigs of holly and bright red berries in vases on every table. And with every part of the Palace I showed her, I talked about how Christmas was at home, with the Walkers.

I saved the best for last, though. Just when Candy was starting to complain that her paws were sore, I led her to the Grand Entrance, with its three huge trees all lit up and sparkling.

'Do you see, now?' I asked. 'How this place must look to people who weren't born here.'

'I think so,' Candy said. 'But *your* Christmases, with the Walkers . . . they sound just magical.'

'*This* place is magical,' I admitted. 'This Palace . . . it's like something out of a movie. But Christmas at the Walkers' . . . that's my home. That's what feels right to me.'

'I think I can understand that,' Candy said, leaning against my side, as we stared up at the trees, twinkling in the night. 'We always spend Christmas at Sandringham, so that's where my best Christmas memories are. This Palace . . . it's so huge, and the Queen is always so busy when we're here. But when we're away and it's just us and the family . . . that's the best time. We all get red stockings on Christmas morning, filled with treats and toys. And there's always a long walk on Christmas morning – even in the snow some years. Then we all snuggle by the fire . . . That's Christmas to me, you see. Not all the decorations and fuss.'

'That makes sense,' I admitted. 'For me, Christmas is curling up with Jack and Claire as they open their presents. It's a walk in the park while Amy's cooking the dinner, and watching a Christmas movie together once it gets dark.'

'I hope you get that again for Christmas,' Candy said. 'Because I know it's what will make you happy. But . . .'

'But?' I prompted.

She gave me a small smile, and rested her head against mine. 'But I wish you could stay with us, too, at the same time. Does that make any sense?'

I swallowed a lump in my throat. 'Yes. Yes it does.'

Because as much as I still wanted to go home, to my family, I wasn't quite ready to leave the Palace behind yet, either. Or the people – and dogs – who lived there.

AMY

Amy made it home from the clinic before Jack and Claire returned from London. She sat at the kitchen table, a mug of tea at hand, and read back through each of the text messages she'd received – on the hour, every hour – through the day.

They started out so full of hope, so optimistic that any moment now they were going to catch a break or find a lead. But as the day had worn on, they'd grown less certain, less hopeful. Now it was fully dark outside, and the last one read:

Still nothing. Heading to station now. Home soon.

Still nothing. That was how this whole season had felt, for Amy. Like she was still getting nowhere, no matter how hard she tried. Like trudging through a snowdrift, and getting blown backwards by the wind. Like when she finally got a night out, and the chance to feel like *Amy* again, singing karaoke with Luke Fitzgerald, only to be dragged back to the real world by Jim's phone call.

The future felt an awfully lonely place, right now.

She shook her head. She couldn't let the kids see her moping around like this, and they'd be home any second.

Instead, she got to her feet and turned the radio on, tuning it in to whoever was playing Christmas music right now. Then she pulled a couple of packs of chocolate Christmas decorations out from the cupboard. The kids had always loved hanging them on the tree – and insisting they had to eat whichever ones didn't have threads attached to hang them with. It was always amazing how many defective ones they found – and how many extra threads she found hidden around the place afterwards.

Amy had just hunted down the scissors to open the packet, when the front door crashed into the telephone table, indicating that the kids were home at last.

'Hey, how did it go?' She met them in the hallway with a smile on her face, but neither Jack nor Claire returned it.

'Waste of time.' Jack brushed past her to throw his coat over the end of the bannister, and add his shoes to the pile that never quite seemed to make it onto the shoe rack. Amy smiled sadly at the shoes – all unchewed, without Henry there. Just another sign of their loss – like the small pile of food scraps she kept finding under the kitchen table after dinner, which she knew were there because Claire had forgotten, again, that there was no Henry around to eat up the bits she didn't like.

'We looked everywhere,' Claire said, quietly. 'No one had seen Henry. Not even at the Dogs and Cats home.'

Amy wrapped an arm around her shoulders and held her close. 'At least you tried.'

'Don't know why we bothered,' Jack muttered. 'Henry's never coming home. Just like Dad.'

Ouch. Amy's heart contracted at the pain in her son's voice.

She had a feeling that chocolate tree decorations weren't going to come close to fixing this, but they were all she had to offer right now.

'Come on,' she said. 'I've got chocolates to put on the tree. We can put a Christmas movie on and I'll make hot chocolate too, if you like. What do you say?'

It took some cajoling, but no one could turn down her hot chocolate. Amy hummed 'Baby, It's Cold Outside' under her breath as she added the whipped cream and chocolate sprinkles, and carried the mugs through to the lounge. She smiled as she noticed that a few chocolates were already missing, and that *The Muppet Christmas Carol* was playing on the TV.

'I love that you both still love the Muppets,' she said, handing out the mugs.

Claire rolled her eyes. 'Mum, we put it on because it's *your* favourite. Not ours.'

Amy's throat felt tight. 'Then, thank you, sweetheart.'

'This chocolate has no string,' Jack declared, tearing the thread from the wrapper without even trying to be stealthy about it. Then he handed it to Amy. 'You better eat it.'

She did.

For a moment, while the Muppets sang, the Christmas tree lights twinkled, and the world tasted of chocolate, Amy started to think that maybe, just maybe, things were getting better.

And then the phone rang. Again.

She was starting to hate phones.

'Hi, Jim.' Amy tried not to sigh at the sound of his voice, but it was hard. She signalled to the kids that she was taking the phone through to the kitchen, and saw them exchange a look. Had they been talking about Jim and her on their day trip to London? Probably. She'd give up hot chocolate for a year to know what they'd each said.

'Amy. Hi.' Jim sounded stiff, constrained. Amy wondered if Bonnie was right there, listening in, making sure he said whatever they'd agreed on. Like she'd used to have to do when he called his mother to tell her when they'd be visiting.

'What's up?' Amy sank onto one of the kitchen chairs and stared at the clock on the wall. It had stopped six months ago, so it wasn't much help in actually telling the time, but it did emphasise how long the pause before Jim spoke felt.

'Bonnie and I were thinking it would be nice to have the kids round on New Year's Day. Once we're back from France.'

'Oh.' Amy didn't miss the way it was *Bonnie's* idea too – or that it meant that they were living together, and he planned to introduce the kids to her. A new year, a new start – and a new family for her children. Just what they wanted, she was sure. Not.

But moving on – that was what *she* wanted. Wasn't it?

'We thought it would help you out, too,' Jim went on, suddenly eager. 'You know, give you a break from the kids.'

Amy blinked. 'Wait. Are you honestly trying to tell me that you introducing our kids to your new girlfriend is doing me a favour?'

Jim sighed. 'I don't want this to be difficult. I just wanted to spend some time with Jack and Claire over the holidays.'

Which is why you're going skiing for most of the two weeks they're off school. Right.

She didn't say it, because this *was* what she wanted, really.

She wanted the kids to have a good relationship with their dad. She wanted Jim to make an effort to be an important part of their lives. And more than anything, she wanted to move on, to get to the next stage of whatever this was.

Jim wasn't coming back, she knew that. And maybe Henry wasn't too.

Which mean the only thing left was to suck it up and find her own future. Make a new life in a new situation. Maybe even go on a date, or two. Find things that *she* wanted to do, just for herself – not because anybody else needed her to.

Find out who Amy was, now.

The New Year was as good a time as any for that.

'Fine,' she said. 'Let me know what time you want them, and where, and I'll drop them off for you.' She just hoped the kids would be alright with the new arrangement, too.

'Great.' She could hear the relief in Jim's voice. Some small, mean part of her felt angry about giving him what he wanted, but she forced herself to focus on the bigger picture.

He had a new life. It was time for her to find one for herself, too.

Hanging up the phone, she headed back through to the lounge, where the Muppets had been swapped for something on YouTube, as far as she could tell.

'What did *he* want?' Jack didn't look at her as he asked the question.

'Your dad was calling to invite you both over to his new home on New Year's Day.' Amy braced herself for the response.

'What? I'm not going.' Jack shook his head so hard Amy was half afraid it might come loose.

'I already told him that you would *both* be there,' Amy

replied. 'He's your father, Jack, and this is important to him. *You're* important to him?'

'Really? Then why did he leave?' Jack didn't wait for her answer. 'And you had no right to tell him I'd be there. I'm not a kid any more, Mum. I get to make my own decisions, you know. And I'm never going to decide that I want to spend the day with him. Never again.'

'For someone who claims to be an adult, you sound an awful lot like a whiny child,' Amy snapped, and regretted it almost instantly. 'I'm sorry. I just—'

But it was too late. Jack threw the TV remote down onto the floor and stalked out, muttering under his breath. She heard his bedroom door slam, and knew that she wouldn't be seeing him again before morning. Perfect.

Claire looked at her, her gaze full of judgement.

'I know, I know,' Amy said, rubbing her forehead. She sighed. 'Shall we watch more Muppets?'

'No, thanks.' Even Claire's tone was clipped. 'I'm going to go call Lucy.'

And just like that, Amy was all alone again.

Another perfect festive night in.

Well, at least she got control of the remote.

Amy flipped the Muppets back on, and went to fetch her bags of Christmas presents and wrapping paper. Unlike her children, she didn't have time to sulk. There was far too much that still needed fixing around here, if she wanted to find that fabled future, where everything didn't feel so difficult all the time.

Day 9

Sunday 22nd December

HENRY

I felt much cheerier as I trotted out into the gardens with Sarah the next morning. The Palace, after all, had a lot going for it – and I might as well enjoy it. Waking up with Candy in *my* basket this time, curled around me for warmth, might possibly have had something to do with my good mood, too.

After we'd finished looking at the decorations the night before, Candy and I had retreated back to the Corgi Room, where we found Willow and Vulcan already asleep. Not ready for the night to end, we'd jumped up into my basket, where Candy had whispered stories of royal celebrations and palaces for me, until I'd fallen asleep.

I'd almost forgotten about spotting Jack and Claire altogether, for a time.

After Sarah had fed us that morning, I'd smiled a good-bye at Candy, and followed the housemaid out to keep her company while she worked. But I had high hopes that Candy would fancy another storytelling session again tonight!

As Sarah and I walked out into the gardens we found Oliver waiting for us, a little way along our usual path.

'Good morning, you two,' he said, smiling widely as he spotted us. 'Thought I might meet you guys here.'

Sarah's answering smile was every bit as bright. 'Isn't it a beautiful day?' She tipped her head up to stare at the bright blue skies, and let the weak winter sun shine on her face.

'They're saying it might snow later.' Oliver fell into step beside us as we continued our walk. 'I can't believe it though – look how blue that sky is.'

Sarah shook her head. 'No. They're right. I can almost smell it. I just wish it would hurry up.'

Oliver laughed. 'You sound like a child waiting to build a snowman.'

'And what's wrong with that?' She raised her eyebrows as she waited for an answer.

'Nothing at all,' Oliver replied, very sensibly, in my opinion.

We carried on down the path, the three of us walking in step. In so many ways, it felt like the perfect, normal morning – I hoped they would carry on doing this for years to come. Everything seemed perfectly in place.

Which, really, should have been my first sign that it was all about to come crashing down around our ears.

'Sarah?' A footman I didn't recognise approached us. 'Sarah Morgan?'

She frowned as he grew closer. 'Is there a problem?' I could hear the nerves in her voice. Oliver obviously did, too, because he reached out to squeeze her hand.

'There's someone at the side entrance demanding to see you,' the footman said, apologetically. 'I tried to get him to call you, but he won't leave. I'm sorry, but I think you're going to have to deal with him.'

'Of course.' Sarah's frown deepened as we all made our way towards the side entrance.

'Any idea who it could be?' Oliver asked.

'None at all.'

'I wouldn't worry about it.' Oliver gave her a reassuring smile, then let go of Sarah's hand, but he still stayed close by her side. I was glad. For all Oliver's reassuring words, I had a very bad feeling about this.

And I was right. As usual.

As we reached the door, Sarah stopped, suddenly, in her tracks, as the man who'd come calling for her came into view. He was wearing jeans and a jumper under a thick jacket, and shifting from foot to foot as if he was cold. Or nervous.

'David.' Sarah's eyes were huge with surprise.

'Your ex,' Oliver said, his voice tight.

'I don't . . . I don't know what he's doing here.' Sarah sounded lost and confused. I pressed up against her leg to reassure her that I was still there.

'I thought that might be the case. But since he says he's not leaving until you talk to him, I suggest you find out,' the footman said, opening the gate to let David in. 'I'll be on hand if you need any help with him.'

'Sarah!' David rushed forward and swept Sarah up into a hug. Oliver stepped back, his smile long gone and his eyes serious.

'What are you doing here?' Sarah asked, her face muffled against David's shoulder. I couldn't quite tell if she was pleased to see him or not. I'd assumed she wouldn't be, but she hadn't pushed him away.

From the look on Oliver's face, he wasn't sure either.

'I'll . . . I'll catch up with you later, Sarah,' Oliver said.

Sarah spun round, pulling away from David's arms. 'Oh, yes. Of course. Thanks, Oliver.' Then she turned back to David.

I watched Oliver walk away, his shoulders slumped, and hoped that all my hard work hadn't been for nothing.

Sarah led David into the gardens, so they could walk while they talked. I trotted along at Sarah's side, of course, my lead still in her hand. I'd been half afraid she might send me back to the Corgi Room. I really didn't want to leave her alone with her ex-boyfriend, though.

He didn't look much like Oliver, I thought, studying him. He had dark hair, but that was about where the similarities ended. He was shorter, softer, and his blue eyes were weak and watery. When Oliver looked at you, there was no weakness at all. Oliver knew what he wanted, and he worked hard to get it. David, from what little I knew of him from Sarah, didn't know a good thing when he had it. Even if I hadn't known anything about him, my stomach told me he wasn't someone to be trusted.

I had to find a way to get Sarah away from him.

'Why are you here, David?' Sarah asked again, when we were a little way away from the Palace, and any prying eyes. She'd stopped walking in the middle of the path, right by one of my favourite bushes to explore.

I tugged on my lead a little, but Sarah stood firm, staring at David. Oh, I didn't like this at all.

Twisting my head round, I tried to see if there was any way I could wiggle free from the lead attached to my collar.

Then I could run for the bush, and Sarah would have to follow me, and she'd forget all about this David fellow.

'I saw the card you sent to Mum,' he said, his voice over-eager. 'And of course, I knew what it meant.'

Sarah's eyes narrowed. 'Which was?'

I glanced around me again, still looking for an escape, a way to get Sarah away. Maybe if I pulled really hard, really suddenly . . . I was just studying the best places to run for, when something else caught my eye. Was that someone standing behind the bush, listening in?

'It meant that you were still thinking about me, even though you moved all the way to London. That we were still linked. Still meant to be together.' David leaned in closer, and I dashed round to stand between them, so he couldn't get *too* close to my Sarah. Or, Oliver's Sarah, more accurately. 'I knew it meant that you loved me too.'

'Wait, what?' Sarah took a step back, and David almost tripped over me trying to stay close to her. That was surprisingly gratifying.

But then something else grabbed my attention. Had that bush just moved? Yes! It had. There was definitely someone hiding there. But who? And why?

I stared at the mass of green leaves, until I caught a glimpse of red hair, and then the side of a woman's face.

Jessica. What was she doing here? From the little I knew about her, I couldn't help but think she was probably looking for another way to cause trouble for Sarah, after Oliver foiled her plot at the corridor party.

But I couldn't worry about that right now. I had to get

Sarah away from David, before he ruined everything for her and Oliver.

'I made a mistake, letting you go,' David said, his tone sincere. I still didn't believe him, though. Nobody who could make Sarah feel as small as he had deserved any second chances at all, as far as I was concerned. 'I know that now. I realised, when you were gone, how much I still love you. And when I saw that card, I knew it was a sign – a sign that you felt the same. And so, of course I had to come.'

His foot connected with my side as he tried to push me out of the way to get closer to Sarah. I yelped, indignantly, but by the time I'd turned round to consider giving him a good nip on the ankle, it was too late.

David was kissing Sarah.

His hands pressed against her back, holding her tight against him, and I couldn't see Sarah's expression at all because his stupid big head was in the way. I barked, as loud as I could, trying to get Sarah to snap out of whatever thrall he had her in, but it was no good.

This was terrible! I hadn't put all this effort in to showing Sarah how great life at the Palace could be, and how much she deserved that, only to have her go back to the man who told her the exact opposite.

And then, just to make things worse, Jessica stepped out from behind the bush, a vicious smile on her face. I tried to dart away from Sarah to chase Jessica, to stop her before she did anything to get Sarah into trouble. But Sarah still held my lead tight, and I wasn't going anywhere.

With one last look at the kissing couple, Jessica raced towards the Palace before Sarah even knew she was there.

And I was very afraid that I knew exactly where she was going – or rather, who she was going to tell about all she'd seen.

Oliver.

This was a disaster.

AMY

Sunday mornings, Amy had always believed, should be time for lie-ins, coffee, and quiet contemplation. Or, in weeks of great stress, at least a time for pancakes.

After the disaster of Jim's phone call the night before, Amy had decided this was definitely a pancake morning. So, while the coffee percolated on the kitchen counter, she mixed the ingredients for her famous breakfast pancakes, and hoped there was enough maple syrup left in the bottle to serve all three of them.

Sookie, normally disinterested in cooking unless there was fish involved, twined around her legs as she moved about the kitchen. Amy was starting to get the feeling that the cat had appointed herself family guardian in Henry's absence – or maybe she was just taking advantage of the lack of dog to spend more time indoors.

Either way, Amy was glad of the company, even if it wasn't quite the same as having Henry home. Sookie didn't like walks, for one thing, and Amy was missing the daily fresh air and thinking time. She supposed she could take a walk *without* a dog, but somehow it never seemed to happen. Luke had even let her borrow Daisy the day before on her lunch break, but the Dalmatian wasn't nearly as interested in squirrels and smells as Henry was. Plus, Amy had been so terrified of losing someone else's dog, she hadn't been able to relax the whole walk.

Luke had laughed when she'd told him that. 'I'll have to come with you too, next time, then,' he'd said, and Amy had smiled.

'It's a date,' she'd replied. Only to then spend the next three hours wondering how much he'd read into that easy slip of the tongue.

She shook her head. She had to concentrate on cooking – not mooning over a divorced doctor who was just being kind to her because he knew what she was going through.

'Ooh, pancakes!' Claire's enthusiasm as she hopped up onto one of the stools by the breakfast bar was enough to brighten Amy's morning – and distract her from fretting about what she'd said to Luke.

Even Jack looked slightly less grumpy than he had when he thumped down the stairs. He looked at her for a long moment, and Amy held her breath, waiting to hear what he'd have to say. Would it be another rant about his father? Or – heaven forbid – an apology?

Neither, as it turned out.

'I'll go fetch the Sunday papers, shall I?' he said, already grabbing his trainers.

'That would be lovely,' Amy said, neutrally. 'I'll start flipping pancakes when you get back.'

The Sunday papers were another family tradition. Jim had always liked to have the real thing on a Sunday, rather than just reading the news on their phones or tablets like they did the rest of the week. Jack liked the cartoons and the film and music reviews, Claire liked looking at all the fancy, expensive photos in the colour supplements. And Amy liked that everyone tended to be quiet and happy for half an hour on a Sunday morning, while they all sat around the table together.

'We haven't done Sunday papers in months,' Claire commented, as Jack slammed the front door behind him. 'Not since . . . well, not since Dad left.'

'No,' Amy said. 'We haven't. But it was nice for Jack to offer to fetch the papers, don't you think? Especially since he'd normally take—' she cut herself off before she said the name 'Henry'.

Because Jim wasn't the only thing still missing from the perfect family portrait, was he?

Amy sighed, and turned back to her pancake mix. One thing at a time.

Jack returned with the papers – and an extra music magazine, Amy noticed – and he and Claire sat at the table divvying them up while Amy heated the pan and added the first dollop of batter.

'Oooh, look!' Claire held up the front of the colour supplement for Amy to see. 'Christmas at Windsor Palace! I bet they have fantastic decorations. Even better than the trees we saw outside Buckingham Palace.'

They had to be better than the tiny fake tree and half a holly garland that she'd put up, Amy thought. She hadn't even managed to dig out that wicker reindeer of Claire's. It was just as well the kids had eaten the chocolates she'd bought for the tree, too. When she'd looked at the tree after they'd all been munched, she'd realised it didn't even have enough branches to hold them all. And the fake holly garland that she usually wound around the bannister had lost half its leaves – something she suspected might have been Henry's fault, actually. So now, whenever she looked at it – half bare and still shedding – she thought of Henry and missed him all over again. Which was ridiculous. No one should get that teary over fake greenery.

Claire was still oohing and ahhing over the pictures of Windsor Castle, and Amy leant over her shoulder to take a look as she placed the first plate of pancakes on the table.

'Oh, look at the corgis!' They looked so much like Henry it made Amy's heart hurt. 'And the Dorgis are pretty cute, too.'

'Look at this one wearing a crown!' Claire pointed to the page, then frowned. 'Wait . . .'

She leafed quickly through a few pages to find a close-up of the corgi in the crown, this time seated on a throne-like chair, panting up at the camera.

'Look! Jack, look! It's Henry!'

Amy's heart lurched at Claire's words, at the certainty behind them. Could it be?

But no. That was crazy. Henry had run away, sure – but he hadn't somehow made his way to Windsor Castle, right?

'It's a corgi, Claire,' Jack said, dismissively. 'Of course it looks like Henry.'

'It doesn't just look like Henry. It *is* Henry.' Claire's mulish certainty didn't waver for a moment. 'He's even wearing the collar I bought him for Christmas last year!'

The collar, Amy had to admit, was distinctive. A red, mock croc leather one with a gold buckle, and a gold tag that just read 'Henry'. Claire had saved up to buy it for him herself, so he had something special to open on Christmas morning, too. Of course, Henry had been far more taken with the chocolate doggy drops that Jack had bought him, but still. It was the thought that counted.

And in this case, the similarity.

Amy leant closer, peering at the photo, noticing that the dog's name tag had been twisted so she couldn't read the name. 'It does look a lot like him . . .' Like, exactly like him. But then, she'd never really been great at telling one dog from another, unless they were lined up next to each other. She'd once almost taken the wrong corgi home from puppy training class, when Henry was little. She probably shouldn't be trusted on this one.

Amy shook her head. 'It can't be him, Claire. It's just not possible.'

'Why not?' Claire asked. 'These are the Queen's Corgis – and we lost him at Buckingham Palace. Of course it could be him!'

'Don't you think the Queen might have noticed if she suddenly had an extra dog?' Jack asked.

'Maybe not! It's a big Palace . . .' Claire was clutching at straws, and everyone knew it.

Well, everyone except Claire.

'I'm going to write to her. Ask for my dog back.'

'Write to who?' Amy asked. 'Wait, you're going to write to the Queen?'

'Yes!' Claire jumped down and ran to the junk drawer

where they kept the envelopes and stamps (along with used batteries, torches that didn't work and half-used birthday candles). 'No, that's stupid.'

'Very stupid,' Jack agreed, as he tucked into a plate piled high with pancakes drenched in maple syrup.

Claire shot him a sharp glare. 'I meant because it'll take too long to get a letter there and read. Christmas post and all. I've got a much better idea.'

'Which is?' Amy asked, suddenly nervous.

'I'm going to do what everyone does when they need to get the attention of a big company or important person,' Claire said, happily. 'I'm going to tweet her!'

HENRY

I was just about to bite David on the ankle when Sarah pushed him away.

'No.' She wiped at her mouth as she stumbled back. Her hair was rumpled out of its usual neat ponytail, and her cheeks were flushed pink – but more with anger than with passion, I realised.

I should have had more faith in Sarah. *Of course* she wasn't going to take this idiot back. Why would she? Especially now Oliver and I had shown her that she was worth so much more.

'No? What do you mean?' David looked completely dumbfounded by the word. His cheeks were bright red too, but I was pretty sure that was with embarrassment. Served him right.

I sat right at Sarah's feet, stopping David from getting close enough to try again, and smirked at him.

Sarah wasn't his any more. She was ours.

'I mean no,' Sarah said, her voice clear and strong. 'I'm not going to kiss you. I don't love you any more – in fact I'm not even sure I ever did. How could I love someone who told me I wasn't good enough, that I was fat and useless and a waste of space?'

'I didn't—' David protested.

'Yes,' Sarah snapped, 'you did. I know because they're carved in my brain and my heart. I remember every awful thing you ever said to me – and I remember them a hundred times more often than anything kind you ever said. Not that there were so many of those to remember in the first place.'

'I was trying to help you!'

'Help me?' Sarah's eyebrows shot up so high they almost disappeared into her hair. 'How on earth was that supposed to work?'

'Well, you know . . . I was giving you motivation. Trying to stir up some ambition in you. I didn't mean to make you feel bad,' David tried, but even I could see that this was a lost cause. Sarah wasn't going to buy his justifications any more.

In fact, she laughed right at him. 'Don't you see? That only makes it worse! You thought so little of me that you could say those terrible things to me without even worrying for a moment how they would make me feel.' She shook her head. 'You don't love me, David. You just hate the fact that I've escaped from you, that I'm here living my own life, making my own future – doing all the things you told me I never would. You hate the fact that I'm proving you wrong, every moment of every day. Just by living my life the way *I* choose to.'

Sarah's face was pink with the cold – or with righteous anger, I wasn't sure. Either way, she looked magnificent. Her pale hair shone around her face like a halo, and her eyes blazed with surety.

While David's watery blue eyes looked more uncertain with every passing second.

'But the card you sent . . .'

Sarah cut him off. 'I sent a Christmas card to your mother because she, unlike you, has always been kind to me. I didn't want her thinking that I'd forgotten that, just because I'd moved away. I'm not that kind of person.'

'And you didn't send me one because . . .?' If ever there was a stupid question . . .

'Because to be honest, David, I've hardly given you a second thought since the moment I arrived at Buckingham Palace.'

He was getting it now, that much was clear. But he couldn't help but give it one last try. 'Sarah, I—'

She didn't let him get any further. 'No. Whatever you have to say, I don't have to listen any more. You treated me badly, and I know now that I deserve much, much better than you. And I'm going to get it. Which means that it is time for you to leave.'

If I could have cheered, I would have. As it was, I gave a happy bark and jumped to my paws.

But then I remembered Jessica's gleeful face as she'd run back to the palace, and I realised that the job wasn't done yet. I had something else to fix.

I persuaded Sarah to let me off my lead and back into the Palace by means of dragging her off course towards the nearest door. Shaking her head at me, she unclipped my lead and I raced inside, leaving her to show David the exit. Fast, I hoped.

I didn't want to spend a moment longer in his company, any more than Sarah did.

Racing up the stairs, I made my way to the staff quarters. I had to find Jessica and keep her away from Oliver. I dreaded to think what she would tell Oliver. Hopefully, he was busy working and she hadn't been able to talk to him yet.

But I was too late. I knew that the moment I entered the staff corridor and I heard her voice.

'You should have seen them, Oliver,' Jessica said, sounding disgusted. 'They were kissing, right there in the Palace gardens. Making a complete show of themselves. If they'd been seen by one of the Royals . . .' She shuddered.

'I don't need to know this, Jessica.' Oliver's voice was clipped.

'Are you sure?' Jessica asked. 'Only, you did seem to be getting very close to our Sarah. This must be very hard for you to hear, I'm sure. But I thought it was important that you know.'

'Why? Why on earth—?' He leaned back against the wall, rubbing a hand over his neatly styled hair.

'Because she was playing you, Oliver!' Jessica sidled up to him and pressed herself to his side. 'She let you think she was one of us, that she was going to stay and be here with you. But it was a lie. She was only ever here to make her boyfriend jealous. And now that plan has worked, she'll be leaving to go back with him.'

'She said that?' Oliver asked. 'You actually heard her say that?'

Jessica shook her head sadly. 'Oh, Oliver, I didn't have to. It's blindingly obvious to everyone except you. Sarah never fitted in here – and maybe she didn't want to. Maybe she never bothered because she knew she wouldn't be staying. It was all just part of her plan.'

'But she worked hard to get this job,' Oliver said. 'She wanted it, I know she did.'

'Perhaps. But perhaps she never wanted it as much as a happy ever after with her boyfriend.'

Suddenly, I remembered a conversation between Sarah and Oliver. One where she'd told him all the things she'd wanted, before she came to the Palace. A home, a family, a husband, all back in her home village. I had a feeling he was remembering the same one.

He honestly believed that she'd gone back to all those old dreams, the ones she'd left behind when she applied to be a housemaid for the Queen.

And I didn't know how to tell him that he was wrong.

'Oliver, you know what it's like, working here,' Jessica said, still standing far too close to him for my liking. 'It takes a special sort of person.'

'I thought Sarah *was* that sort of person,' Oliver said, sounding forlorn. 'She's . . . I thought she was special.'

Jessica pulled a face. Oliver didn't see. 'Maybe she wasn't as fantastic as you seemed to think.'

'Maybe.' But Oliver still sounded doubtful. Good.

'You need to stick with the sort of people you know you can trust. People you know belong here.'

'People like you?' Oliver guessed.

Jessica smiled. 'Exactly.'

But as she leant in towards him, Oliver pushed away from the wall. 'To be honest, Jessica, I think what we both need to do is get to work. Don't you?'

He raised an eyebrow at her until she blushed. 'Right. Yeah. I'll see you later, though?'

'I imagine so.' He watched Jessica walk away, then looked down at where I was sitting, watching.

I barked at him, willing him to understand everything I couldn't say.

Don't give up on Sarah, I thought, as hard as I could.

But Oliver didn't get the message.

He sighed. 'Not now, Henry, okay? I've got a Christmas card I need to write. Now, before I lose my nerve.'

Day 10

Monday 23rd December

HENRY

I didn't see Sarah or Oliver again before the end of the day. And by the next morning, the Palace was far, far too busy for me to even think about getting them together for a quiet talk to sort things out.

'What on earth is going on here today?' I asked Willow, as we watched staff members hurrying about the Palace, carrying furniture and silverware and who even knew what else. I'd come down from the Corgi Room for my usual morning explore, and found the State Rooms in absolute chaos. Men and women in Palace uniforms were all bustling about cleaning and arranging tables and chairs. One was even measuring the distance of the table mats from the edge of one of the tables. Another was polishing glassware, before setting out several of them at each place.

This was definitely not just another day at the Palace.

'Today is a day for staying out of the way,' Willow said, shifting back a little to sit against the wall behind us.

'I thought you told me that the rule at the Palace was that the staff had to always get out of *our* way,' I reminded her.

'Usually, yes,' Willow agreed. 'But tomorrow is the day of

the Buckingham Palace Christmas Lunch. So today, everyone will be more than a little bit crazy getting ready for it. It's usually safest to just keep out from underfoot for once.'

As if to prove her point, a housemaid came bustling through with a giant silver serving platter – not dissimilar to one of the ones I'd sent flying on my first day in the Palace – and almost stood on me. I gave a sharp bark, and hurried out of the way.

Willow and I retreated to a quiet spot under the curve of the grand staircase, where we could still watch all the comings and goings without risking life and paw. From there, I saw a couple of footmen ferrying in a parade of suitcases. They were followed by a smartly dressed older couple who were carrying nothing.

'So, what's the deal with this Christmas lunch?' I asked. 'I thought Candy said that the Queen usually went to the Sandy Palace for Christmas?'

'Sandringham,' Willow corrected me. 'And yes, She does, along with us and certain other members of the family. This is a sort of pre-Christmas celebration, for the whole extended Royal Family, before She leaves for Sandringham.'

Of course. Hadn't Candy said something about a Christmas lunch here at the Palace? This must have been what she was talking about.

'It's normally held earlier than this, I feel,' Willow went on. 'Presumably it had to be held up until She returns from her current trip.'

The Queen. 'So She'll be back for it, then?' I felt a tight knot forming in my stomach at the thought.

'Oh, most certainly.' Willow gave me a knowing look.

'She's never once missed it. And once She's back . . .'

'I know.' The moment the Queen returned, it would be time for me to learn my fate. Would I continue forever as a Palace dog? Or would I be sent away – and if so, where to? The streets? A dogs' home?

I could hardly bear to think about it.

So I decided not to. At least, not until I had to.

'Are there good scraps for us to eat at this lunch?' I asked, instead.

Willow rolled her eyes. 'You know the rules. No scraps from table.'

I sighed. I did know. But it was Christmas! Amy always let me have a few special bits at Christmas. Some turkey, maybe some stuffing. Gravy, of course – not as good as the Queen's, but still very tasty. I knew things were different at the Palace, but surely there were allowances?

Besides, despite Willow's insistence on the no scraps rule, Candy had let slip that the Queen sometimes let them eat scones at afternoon tea. I couldn't help but hope that maybe I'd get to experience *that* before I left the Palace . . .

'So, who will be here tomorrow then?' I asked, allowing Willow to let loose on her favourite subject – listing all the Very Important People in the Royal Family that I had never met, and would never be as important as. I zoned out after the first few. It wasn't like the names meant anything much to me, anyway.

But her distraction let me focus on all the activity without interruption. I watched as housemaids and footmen raced around getting everything ready for what must be a very grand lunch, and an awful lot of guests. Back at the Walkers, it was usually only the four of them, Grandma, Sookie and I for Christmas. Here, they looked like they were preparing for a guest list of a hundred!

'Of course *they* won't be invited again this year,' Willow said, censoriously. 'Not after last time.'

I had no idea what she was talking about. But I also had something far more important to worry about: across the way, I spotted Sarah, hurrying about her business. Her eyes were red, all the way around, and her nose looked pink too. Like Claire, when she'd been crying about something some mean girl had said at school. (Amy never let me bite them, as much as I wanted to, though that didn't stop me barking and growling at them.)

'Excuse me,' I said to Willow, cutting her off mid flow. 'I have to do something.'

I chased Sarah through several rooms – and what seemed like hundreds of pairs of legs – before I finally caught up with her.

'Oh! Henry!' She looked down in surprise as I brushed against her calves. 'I'm sorry there hasn't been time for a walk this morning. Everything's rather busy and—'

'Sarah!' Someone yelled her name and she stopped, spinning round to attention. 'Are you honestly wasting time talking to a dog? Today, of all days?'

'Absolutely not,' Sarah lied. 'I'll see you later, Henry,' she whispered, as she bustled off again.

I sighed, and slunk back against the wall, out of the way again.

Clearly, corgis weren't a priority today. For anyone.

★★★

It was teatime before Sarah made it up to the Corgi Room. She still looked quiet and sad, and I just knew it had more to do with Oliver than a very busy day at the Palace.

Sarah sank to sit down on the floor and I walked over to sit beside her, my head pressed against her leg reassuringly. 'Oh, Henry. How did this get so messed up?'

I rested my head in her lap and looked up at her, eyes wide. It was my best 'tell me everything' look. It always worked with my family. Even with Jack. Sarah was a pushover compared to that.

'He sent me a card, you know? Oliver, I mean. Saying he was happy that David and I patched things up, and that he'd enjoyed being my friend at the Palace. My friend!' She shook her head in astonishment. 'And the worst thing is, David and I *didn't* patch things up. No, wait, that's the good part. The best part. I made the right decision and it didn't change a single thing – except for the worse. I'm still here, all alone – and Oliver's avoiding me.'

She sighed, and scratched between my ears, but I couldn't even enjoy it, I was too worried about Sarah and Oliver.

'I really thought we were getting somewhere, Henry. I really did. But I should have known. I shouldn't have got my hopes up. The likes of Oliver Kinchen-Williams was always going to be too good for me. Friends is more than I should have even expected.'

She was wrong, of course. I knew she was wrong. But how did I make her see that?

'Maybe I never should have come to the Palace.' Sarah let out a sob, and suddenly I wasn't alone on her lap. Candy darted down from her basket, pressing up against Sarah on the other side. And then to my surprise Willow jumped down, making her way across more leisurely, before placing her head directly under Sarah's hand for petting.

I glanced up at the only still occupied dog basket. Vulcan rolled his eyes at me, then hopped down to pad across to join us and I felt my heart swell towards these dogs, my friends.

'Oh, you lot,' Sarah said, her voice full of tears. 'You four are my best friends at the Palace.'

'She really is desperate, in that case,' Willow muttered.

'But this will help,' Candy replied. 'We always make people feel better.'

'We hardly ever make people feel better,' Vulcan said, rather more honestly.

'Well, Henry does, anyway.' Candy nudged me with her nose. '*Henry* always makes people feel better. It's a talent he has.'

'I don't know how to make Sarah feel better,' I admitted. I wished I did. I wished there was a way I could talk to her, make her understand that everything would be fine. Make Oliver understand too.

Willow made a small, amused noise. 'Seems to me the answer to that is obvious.'

'Really?' I asked. 'How.'

'Fix whatever went wrong.' Willow shrugged. 'Simple as that.'

If only it was . . .

Wait.

Maybe it was.

Just maybe . . .

I sat up a little straighter, and drew the other dogs' attention. 'I've got a plan.'

AMY

'Claire, can you give me a hand with these bags?' Amy struggled through the front door, shopping bags making her too wide to fit easily through the gap. Where had Claire even gone? She'd been sitting in the car with her just moments ago, but by the time Amy had opened the boot to retrieve the Christmas food shop, Claire had disappeared into the house already. When, exactly, did children learn that skill of being a million miles away at the precise moment they could actually be helpful?

'Hang on!' Claire called, from somewhere inside the house.

'Kind of hard to,' Amy yelled back. 'These bags are really heavy!'

Where was Jack when she needed him? Teenage boys weren't generally the most useful of creatures, but they were really good at carrying shopping bags – if you could find them. He, too, usually managed to turn up just as she finished unpacking the shopping, stopping just long enough to snaffle some sort of snack that would ruin his dinner.

Amy dumped the bags she had onto the kitchen table, then turned round to go back for the rest – only to be stopped by Claire's squeal.

'They've replied!' she cried, across the hallway.

Amy hurried through to the lounge, where her daughter was sitting on the sofa with her laptop open on her knee.

'Who's replied?' And to what? With Claire, it could be anything from a new friend at school, to a boy one of her friends liked, to a teacher answering a question about homework. Or, in this case . . .

'The Royal Family! Or, well, whoever manages their social media accounts, I suppose.' Claire turned the screen to show the notification. 'It's probably not actually the Queen, is it?'

'Probably not,' Amy agreed. 'She's probably a bit busy for Twitter. So, what does it say? "@TheRoyalFamily replied to your tweet." That's not very informative.'

'Wait a minute,' Claire said. 'That's just the notification. The actual message should be around about . . . here.'

Amy couldn't help the tight, anxious feeling in her stomach as she waited for Claire to open the right tab in her browser and read the tweet. As much as she wanted to believe that this would lead to Henry coming home at last, it seemed like too much of a long shot. Even *Christmas* miracles were few and far between these days. It was hard to believe that the Walker family would get one, when so many others didn't.

Just as Amy had been afraid would happen, Claire scanned the message, and her face fell. 'They say I must be mistaken, but that they hope we're reunited with our pet soon.' There was no emotion in her voice, no feeling at all, but Amy knew the disappointment she must be feeling. Mostly because she was feeling it too.

Oh, Henry. Where are you?

Amy hugged her daughter tight, the shopping in the car

forgotten for the moment. 'At least you tried. It was always a long shot, sweetheart. But you gave it your best. That's all you can do.'

'But, Mum! They're wrong!' There was a desperation in Claire's voice Amy didn't like. She was pinning all her hopes on this ridiculous idea of Henry being at Windsor Castle, and as fantastic as that would be, Amy knew it wasn't going to happen. And now she had to convince Claire of that, too – if only so it didn't hurt even more later, when it became clearer that Henry was never coming home.

Amy sighed and wished, just for a moment, that she had someone to share this burden with.

'Claire, think about it logically, sweetheart,' she said, as gently as she could. 'Buckingham Palace is one of the most tightly guarded places in the world. But even if Henry had somehow found a way in, someone would have noticed that he didn't belong there. The Queen must know her own dogs. The Palace staff certainly would. The chances of a strange dog just being allowed to stay at the Palace . . . they must be astronomical.'

'I know it's Henry,' Claire said stubbornly. 'And I'm going to prove it.'

So much for talking her out of it, then.

Pushing Amy away, Claire turned back to her laptop.

Amy watched for a moment, then she got to her feet and went back to carrying in the shopping. Alone, since it seemed everyone else had other priorities tonight. She'd done what she could, for now. Claire was a sensible girl. Eventually she'd realise how ridiculous this idea was. And Amy would deal with the crying and the upset when she did.

Amy was just putting the last of the shopping away when

she heard Jack come in. When she'd finished, she headed back through to the lounge to check on Claire – and stopped in the doorway.

There on the sofa were her kids, Claire curled up beside Jack, who seemed to have taken over control of the laptop. They were both talking quietly, pointing to things on the screen, debating something or another.

Amy smiled softly. It wasn't the way she'd have wanted it to happen, but if nothing else, at least all the turmoil of the last few months had brought Jack and Claire closer together.

She just hoped they'd let her in, too.

'What are you two up to?' Amy made her way in, and settled onto the edge of the sofa beside them.

'Getting proof,' Claire said, sounding determined. That usually boded trouble.

'Proof of what?'

'That the Queen stole our dog,' Jack said.

Amy winced. 'I'm not sure that—'

'Look!' Claire spun the screen round so Amy could see what they'd been working on.

It was two side by side photos of corgis – one, the dog with the crown from the Sunday papers, the other the shot of Henry from last Christmas, wearing a paper cracker crown and the collar Claire had bought him. The same collar that the Queen's dog seemed to be wearing.

'How can they deny it?' Claire asked. 'It's clearly the same dog!'

'And other people are starting to see that too,' Jack said. 'I posted the side by side photos online, and people are already sharing and commenting on the Hunt for Henry page.'

Oh, that didn't sound good. Amy was all for anything that would bring Henry home safely – as long as it didn't also bring the police to her door on Christmas Eve because she'd accused the Queen of dognapping. Did this count as treason? She wasn't sure – but it wasn't really the sort of risk she wanted to take.

'Maybe we don't want to make too big a deal about this,' Amy started, but Jack interrupted her with an uncharacteristic whoop of joy.

'And it just got picked up by an online news site I sent it to!' he crowed. 'Henry is totally going viral.'

'Oh good,' Amy said, weakly, and wished she'd bought more mulled wine.

There was just no way this was going to end well.

HENRY

I had to wait a little while to put my plan into action, but I decided that was for the best. It gave me longer to talk the others into it.

Willow, in particular, wasn't happy with the plan. 'It doesn't sound very dignified,' she said.

'And I don't understand why we have to do it at all,' Vulcan added. 'Can't the humans solve their own problems?'

'Sarah's been kind to us all,' Candy put in. 'We should be kind to her too.'

'But she's *staff*,' Vulcan whined. Apparently he was never going to get over that distinction.

'She's my friend,' I said firmly. 'And we are going to help her. And this is how.'

We decided to wait until dinner time to put the plan into action, working on the theory that everything is easier on a full stomach. Plus, feeding us was usually Sarah's last duty of the day, and I was pretty sure Oliver would have finished work by then, too. It was all coming together perfectly.

But then something else cropped up to disrupt our plans.

'Good news! You all get a nice brush and a wash after dinner, ready for Her Majesty coming home tomorrow.' Sarah was trying to sound cheery, I could tell, but she wasn't doing a very good job. The final, official confirmation that the Queen would definitely be back at the Palace the next day wasn't doing wonders for my mood, either.

Candy and I exchanged a glance. I gave a small shake of my head to say, not now. It would have to wait until after the other three at least were all clean and tidy. Then I'd have the perfect chance to put my plan into action. (The fact it might also get me out of yet another grooming session was just an added bonus.)

Sarah took each of us out, one by one, to be bathed, clipped, brushed and dried. Given that we'd all been fully pampered at the parlour just a few days before, I hoped that it wouldn't take too long. But still, I spent every moment, every second, tense, waiting to put my plan into action. To fix things for Sarah, at last.

Finally, it was my turn. Sarah approached me, my lead in her hand, ready to walk me to where the groomer had set up. As she got closer, I gave the other dogs the nod. 'You all know what to do.'

Sarah leaned down to clip the lead to my collar and I waited, waited, waited . . . Now!

The moment she was just about to clip it on, when she was already engaged in bending down so she couldn't get back up again too quickly, I dodged out of her way and ran for it.

'Henry! Henry!' I could just make out her calling my name over the sound of Willow, Candy and Vulcan all barking at the same time. They'd keep Sarah occupied, I knew – just long enough to give me a head start. I didn't want to get too far ahead, or how would Sarah know where to chase me? But I also knew my legs weren't long enough to outrun her without a *little* bit of help.

The barking died down, and I knew that Sarah must be on my tail. Now, the other dogs just had to keep the rest of the staff distracted. The last thing I needed was another member of staff deciding to help out by scooping me up before I got to my planned destination.

Keeping my head down, I raced through the state rooms, not even glancing up at any of the staff dodging out of my way. I didn't have time to worry about them right now.

'Henry!' I heard one of them call, indignantly.

'That blasted corgi,' another one muttered. 'Why did she have to take in another one, anyway?'

In the Blue Drawing Room, I crashed straight into two footmen carrying a giant display of festive greenery, sending white candles and red holly berries flying everywhere. I barked an apology and kept running, even as I heard them yell my name after me.

It was nice to know that everyone in the Palace had got to know me, at least. After ten days in the Palace, apparently I'd made quite an impression. Although I couldn't see any of them speaking up for me with the Queen, right now . . .

Then I was in the State Dining Room, ducking under tables and chairs and weaving between legs, desperately trying not to get stood on. I had no more time to worry about what the Queen would think; Sarah was what mattered most now.

Glancing back over my flanks, I saw Sarah dashing after me, and gaining fast. I needed to move.

I ducked through a doorway, and then another and another and soon I was in the private parts of the Palace. I was sure the staircase I was looking for was around here somewhere . . .

There!

I'd only been up to the staff corridor twice, but that was enough. Finding Oliver's room, though, that was a little harder. Still, I've found that if you bark long and loud enough, eventually everyone will come out to find out what all the noise is about. One by one, the doors to the staff bedrooms opened, as footmen and kitchen staff stared at me – or shouted, depending on their natures.

'Henry?' Oliver stood in the open door to his bedroom, looking at me with confusion. 'What are you—'

I darted between his legs and grabbed a lone shoe from where it sat by his wardrobe. Then I ran again, knowing he'd have to follow me. Oliver was very particular about his clothes, I'd noticed, and his shoes were always perfectly shiny. He wouldn't risk me destroying one of them – any more than Amy would let me run off with one of her best high heels!

Back down the staircase I flew, fast enough that I could race past Sarah and be ahead again before she even realised what was happening.

'Henry!' she called after me. 'Come back here! It's only a bath, for heaven's sake!'

Then I heard another crash, and a thud.

Screeching to a halt, I spun to check that she was okay.

Oliver had obviously caught up faster than I'd anticipated. He and Sarah were sitting practically on top of each other, tangled up at the bottom of the stairs, after what must have been a pretty spectacular crash.

I stayed long enough to hear Oliver ask, 'Are you okay?' and Sarah respond, 'We need to catch Henry.'

They were fine. And so, I ran again.

Back through the hallways, back to the State Rooms, back through the tables and chairs and legs, treading on a few stray holly berries on my way.

As I reached the Grand Staircase, I dodged to one side to avoid hitting a footman, and accidentally caught my collar on the edge of a green garland, twined through the bannister.

'Henry!' I heard Sarah call behind me. There wasn't time to unravel myself, so I kept running – straight into a tall, balding man in a grey suit.

'What in heaven!' The man turned to try and see what had hit him, but unfortunately that just helped the garland to wrap around him further.

'Your Royal Highness!' Oliver cried, pausing to help unwrap what I realised, a little late, must be one of the Royal Family, here for the lunch. Oops.

Shaking the garland free, I kept running, just a little slower to make sure I didn't lose Sarah and Oliver. Sure enough, in a few moments they were right behind me again.

My plan was nearly complete. I had Oliver and Sarah together again, working for a common cause – catching me. All I had to do now was get them exactly where I needed them.

I screeched to a halt as I reached the Grand Hall, right by the main entrance. I was panting hard from my exertions, but I knew it had all been worth it. Outside the Palace, snow was just starting to fall, flakes of fluffy white sparkling in the Christmas lights, against the blackness of the night. It was a perfect winter evening – and perfect for romance.

Glancing up, I saw exactly what I was looking for – what I'd seen when I'd explored this area on one of my first days at the Palace. Mistletoe. Even a dog knew what that meant.

Sarah and Oliver ran in behind me, both a little out of breath, and stopped at my side.

'Henry! What were you thinking?' Sarah scolded, even as she kneeled at my side to make sure I was okay.

I sat still, and stared up at the ceiling.

'What's he looking at?' Oliver asked, frowning.

They both followed my gaze, and I knew the moment they spotted it, because Sarah's cheeks turned pink, and Oliver started to smile.

'I think he's trying to hint at something,' Sarah said, still looking at the huge bunch of mistletoe hanging overhead.

Oliver took a step back. 'I don't think that would be appropriate. I mean, under the circumstances. Given that you're, well, back with your ex—'

'But I'm not!' Sarah protested. 'I don't know what you heard, or saw, or whatever, but David and me – that's over. Completely. And that's what I told him when he came to see me. My life is here now.'

'Really?' Oliver moved closer. 'You're sure?'

'Surer than I've ever been about anything.' Sarah smiled up at him, and Oliver returned it.

I waited, patiently. I knew what came next. It happened in all the movies I watched with Amy and Claire. Mistletoe plus snow plus confessions from the heart equalled . . .

Slowly, tentatively, Oliver dipped his head to Sarah's level. Placing a hand under her chin, he tilted her mouth towards his, and kissed her.

I smiled.

This was why I'd come to Buckingham Palace, even if I'd not known it at the time.

My work here was done. I could leave without worrying about Sarah.

Leaving the two of them kissing under the mistletoe, with the lights from the three Christmas trees twinkling all around them, I headed back up to the Corgi Room. I wanted to spend one more night in my basket, with the dogs who had become my friends – or at least, in Vulcan's case, no longer my enemies – all around me.

Tomorrow, the Queen would be here.

And who knew what would happen then?

Day 11

Tuesday 24th December
Christmas Eve

HENRY

I slept strangely well (helped by Candy in my basket, again) but woke with butterflies already fluttering around in my stomach. Today I would find out my fate. As soon as break-fast was over, Sarah showed up to take us all for a morning walk, before the Queen came home.

Sarah, I couldn't help but notice, looked decidedly bright and smiley for someone who'd spent the better part of yesterday evening chasing me all over the Palace.

'Oh, you,' she said, grinning at me as she clipped on my lead. 'Not running off anywhere this morning, are you? I suppose you must have got what you wanted last night. Or what *I* wanted.' She placed a kiss between my ears, and led us all off to the garden.

I had to admit to a certain amount of pride in how yesterday evening had turned out. Obviously Oliver and Sarah had worked out all their differences, and I had a feeling that from here on, they wouldn't let anything so silly come between them again. Those two were made for each other. I was just glad to have helped them realise that.

The only downside was now I had nothing to distract me from what happened next.

'Are you ready?' Candy asked me, as we trotted around the gardens in the new fallen snow. 'To meet Her Majesty, I mean.'

I considered the question carefully, as I took in my surroundings. Here I was, in the grounds of the most opulent building I'd probably ever be allowed in. Me, Henry Walker, living in a Palace. I'd eaten freshly caught and cooked rabbit from shiny silver bowls. I'd been pampered and groomed to within an inch of my life. I'd slept in a special basket kept above ground to avoid draughts. I'd even worn a crown!

And now I was going to meet the Queen of England. And the Queen would decide my fate.

'I don't know,' I answered, honestly. How could anyone ever really be ready for that?

'Probably depends what she says when she realises there's an imposter in her house,' Vulcan said, smirking just a little.

'Henry's not an imposter,' Candy protested.

'More a . . . surprise guest,' Willow said. Which was far nicer than she'd managed on my first few nights here.

'*Uninvited* guest,' Vulcan muttered. Which was about the same. Vulcan didn't change, I thought. Not for anyone. But knowing a bit more about him – who he'd lost, and how he must miss them, as well as his kindness to Sarah last night – made it easier for me to ignore him.

'Either way, I'm not supposed to be here.' I kicked at a small pile of snow that had built up along the path.

If the Queen threw me out, I wasn't going to miss all the fancy food and the Corgi Room or any of that. (Okay, maybe the gravy. Yes, I'd definitely miss the gravy. Maybe she'd let me take the recipe with me?) I was going to miss the friends

I'd made here. Oliver and Sarah. Candy and Willow. Even Vulcan. (Okay, maybe not Vulcan.)

Maybe I *was* ready to meet the Queen. I just wasn't sure I was ready to say goodbye.

After our walk, Sarah began to lead us back up to the Corgi Room – only to be stopped by a harassed-looking Oliver who came running up to meet us.

'What's the matter?' Sarah moved immediately to his side, resting one hand on his arm.

Oliver smiled and shook his head. 'Nothing to worry about. Just the usual Christmas Lunch chaos. But the most important thing right now is: we just got word that the Queen will be returning to the Palace earlier than planned.' He checked his watch. 'In fact, they're about five minutes out. You're to take the dogs straight to the Grand Entrance to meet her.'

Sarah's eyes widened. 'Me? Are you sure? I've never even—'

'They like you,' Oliver interrupted, his tone soothing and kind. 'More than any other member of staff here, in fact. Henry especially. They'll sit and wait with you – and no one else wants to try and make them do that after last night's antics!'

'Okay, then,' Sarah said. She still looked a little panicked though, to my eyes.

'Best behaviour, everyone,' I muttered to the other dogs catching Vulcan roll his eyes. I knew that any messing around now could only get Sarah – or me! – into even more trouble.

Sarah kept us on our leads as she led us to the Grand Entrance. There, a whole host of activity was taking place, ready for the Queen's arrival, not to mention the arrival of all the other lunch guests. Sarah stood carefully to one side, while we all sat patiently at her feet. I saw her glance up at the mistletoe and smile, though.

My heart was pounding against my ribcage, and I knew my ears were almost flat against my head. This was it. The moment I'd been both dreading and hoping for ever since I was brought into the Palace. Any moment now, I would know my fate.

A rustle of noise went up around the gathered staff, as a long, black car pulled in through the recently opened gates. Without me even asking, Candy, Willow and Vulcan all shuffled round to sit in front of me – although whether they were planning to guard me or hide me, I wasn't entirely sure. I appreciated their efforts, all the same. Even if I didn't expect them to work.

The car slowed to a halt, just before the entrance, and Oliver dashed forward to open the back door. As I watched, a petite, silvery-haired woman wearing a lavender coat and hat stepped out, and everyone waiting to greet her bowed or curtsied.

Her Majesty Elizabeth the Second, by the Grace of God of the United Kingdom of Great Britain and Northern Ireland and of Her other Realms and Territories Queen, Head of the Commonwealth, Defender of the Faith. (Yes, Willow had made me memorise her regnal title. Although heaven only knew when she expected me to actually use it. It wasn't like I could impress the Queen herself by barking out the list now, was it?)

She was imposing enough in her own right – not because she was tall or threatening, but rather because she wasn't. All that dignity, composure and authority enclosed in a rather petite form only made her more impressive.

Rather like corgis, I suppose.

But then, the Queen did something that confused everyone – except us dogs. She reached back into the car, and lifted out a small, furry form. Monty the corgi, I presumed. The dog whose place at the Palace I had stolen, without anyone even noticing.

Nobody said anything, of course, but I could see Sarah's gaze flicking frantically from the four of us to the dog in Her Majesty's arms. Oliver was still holding the car door, his mouth hanging open a little.

Yes, this was most definitely *it*.

Her Majesty came straight over to us, placing Monty-the-other-Corgi down on the ground. She greeted Willow, Vulcan and Candy in turn.

And then she stared at me.

Not knowing what else to do, I stared back.

Please, I thought at her, as hard as I could. *Please, don't throw me out. Help me find my family, or let me stay. Just don't send me out there alone, away from all my friends and family. Please.*

The Queen straightened up to stand tall again, and turned to the assembled staff.

'One seems to have acquired a new corgi, in one's absence.'

And that was when real chaos truly broke loose.

It took a while for the humans to figure out exactly what had happened. The Queen kept all five of us with her in her private study while the matter was being investigated. It seemed that word was spreading around the Palace pretty quickly, though.

While we waited, Willow, Candy and I explained the events of the last week and a half to Monty, who seemed utterly bemused by the whole thing.

'So you ran away? From your family?' he asked. 'Why?'

'I wasn't running from them, exactly,' I said. 'There was just a lot of noise, and I saw a nice fat pigeon to chase . . . and then there were the gardens to explore . . .'

'Basically, he's too nosy for his own good,' Vulcan sniffed, disapprovingly. He didn't seem much more impressed with Monty than he had been with me, despite the other dog's apparently superior pedigree – or rather, his late owner's.

Finally, a rather shamefaced woman in a navy suit was shown into the Queen's study.

'Susan Yeats, Ma'am,' the footman at the door said, introducing the woman. 'Marketing Manager here at Buckingham Palace.'

Susan gave a quick curtsy and waited, her gaze darting round the room, for the Queen to speak first.

Her Majesty put down her pen, and gave her full attention to Susan. 'Have we discovered where this rather lovely corgi originated?'

I shot a smirk to Vulcan. A compliment from the Queen was worth all of his rude comments.

'We think so, Your Majesty.' Susan stepped forward, holding out a sheet of paper in a shaking hand. 'It appears that a young girl contacted us a few days ago, upon seeing photos of the dogs at Windsor in the Sunday papers. Apparently they were walking their dog near the Palace a little over a week ago, when he ran off, and they've been hunting for him ever since. She recognised her pet, Henry, in the photos and tweeted the Royal Family Twitter account to ask if it could be her dog.'

Claire! Claire had seen my photo and realised it was me! I wiggled with happiness at the news.

'And I assume they said that was impossible?' the Queen said, drily.

Susan winced. 'Yes, Ma'am.'

'I still don't fully understand how the staff failed to notice that we had acquired an extra dog, here at the Palace.'

'Um, well, it seems that there was some confusion over your new corgi,' Susan said, her cheeks pink.

'Over Monty?' The Queen raised her eyebrows. 'Are you suggesting that this was *Monty's* fault?'

'No! Absolutely not, Ma'am. Only that the staff were not familiar with Monty, so when they found another corgi in the gardens, they assumed that it must be him, and that you'd decided not to take him with you on your trip after all.'

Steepling her fingers on her desk, the Queen stared at Susan over them. 'And no one noticed that he was wearing a tag that said Henry?'

Susan's blush deepened. 'As I said, Ma'am, there was some confusion. Over the new dog's name as well as his location, it seems.'

Since Monty had informed us, upon his arrival, that his full name was Montague Hercules Henry Pentrose-Smythe, I wasn't surprised that no one at the Palace had been able to remember it. And Henry was *one* of his names, at least.

'I see.' The Queen gave a small shake of the head. 'This does not seem to have been the finest hour for my staff, does it? But I am sure they will all redeem themselves at this afternoon's Christmas lunch.'

'I'm sure they will, Ma'am,' Susan said, nodding a little overenthusiastically.

'But first, the question of Henry must be resolved, don't you think?' Getting up from her chair, the Queen crossed to where I sat, huddled behind the other dogs. Candy tried to cover me, but the Queen gently nudged her aside.

I stood up, ready to face my fate.

'He is a very handsome dog,' the Queen said, petting me. 'And he seems to have made plenty of friends here at the Palace, from what I've heard.'

'Yes, Ma'am,' Susan said, not mentioning last night's rampage through the Palace, which was nice of her.

The Queen sighed. 'But it would be rather bad form to keep a dog from his family. Especially at this time of year.' She stood, and turned to face Susan again. 'I think you'd better find a way to get Henry home in time for Christmas. Don't you?'

I barked my agreement. I was going home!

'And see if you can't make it up to his family for dognapping their pet?' the Queen added. 'One really doesn't want to get a reputation for such behaviour.'

AMY

Amy tossed her handbag onto the kitchen table and unwound the scarf from around her neck. Christmas Eve at last. She'd finished her Christmas shopping – finally – and the surgery was closed now until the 27th. She was officially on holiday for at least the next sixty hours, and she planned to relax for every single one of them.

Well, once she'd finished wrapping the presents.

Christmas dinner was all ready in the fridge – a smaller spread than most years, admittedly, but the kids liked roast chicken more than turkey, anyway. Probably. And nobody really needed Christmas cake *and* Christmas pudding, right? Luke had even given her a bottle of her favourite wine to enjoy with it, which was a lovely treat.

The Christmas stockings might be a little more boring than previous years, but everyone needed shower gel and vitamins, so it wasn't like they wouldn't be useful. Jack and Claire had each chosen one gift that they really wanted so, even if that was all she could give them this year, at least Amy knew they'd be appreciated. Even Sookie had a tin of extra special cat food for a Christmas treat, and a new squeaky mouse.

It would be a quiet, relaxed, small, family Christmas. Even

Granny was off on a cruise with Aunty Mary. But that was fine; Amy liked the idea of it just being them, this year. It had been such a hard few months, and things were so different from the year before. It felt right to spend that time together, close and together, building up reserves to burst into the new year and make it great, for all of them.

Yes, a small family Christmas was perfect.

The only thing that was still missing, really, was Henry.

Amy pushed the thought aside as the phone started to ring. It had been nearly two weeks. If Henry hadn't found his way home by now, it was highly unlikely they'd see him before Christmas. Or ever. Not that she planned on saying that out loud in front of the children any time soon. Christmas was a time for hope. She would let them keep theirs a little longer.

'Hello?' she said, picking up the phone, her mind still half on timings for cooking the Christmas dinner.

'Ah, hello. Would it be possible to speak to Miss Claire Walker, please.' The well-bred voice on the other end of the line sounded almost embarrassed to even be asking.

Amy frowned, all thoughts about preheating and so on dismissed. Who would be calling for Claire on Christmas Eve? 'Could I ask who is calling?'

'This is Susan Yeats from Buckingham Palace.'

Oh God. What had those kids done now? She'd known this internet campaign was going to get them into trouble! Amy's mouth felt dry, as she tried to find the right words to fix whatever had gone wrong.

'Right. Of course. Listen, if this is about the tweets . . .'

Jack stuck his head around the lounge door, and Amy

made expressive hand motions towards the stairs while mouthing the words 'Get Claire! Now!' Jack looked confused, but ran upstairs all the same, hopefully to fetch his sister.

'You have to understand, Ms Yeats, my daughter Claire is only twelve years old, and she's devastated by the loss of her dog,' Amy went on, hoping to play into the sympathy vote.

'I understand, Mrs Walker. In fact, that's why I'm calling—'

'Oh, I know, I know, and I'm so sorry!' Amy interrupted. 'I don't know why she's so convinced that the dog in the photo is Henry, but she is. I've tried to talk to her about it . . . but it's Christmas, and she's just clinging onto hope, I think.'

Jack and Claire came thundering down the stairs, stopping at the bottom to listen into the call.

'Who is it?' Claire asked, softly.

Amy put her hand over the mouthpiece. 'It's Buckingham Palace!'

Claire's eyes widened.

'Oh hell,' Jack muttered. 'Now we're for it.'

'I totally understand, Mrs Walker,' Susan said, on the phone. 'And I promise, no one is in any trouble about the tweets. At least, not at your end. If you could just let me speak to Claire? I'd really like to give her this news myself.'

Mystified, Amy handed the phone over to Claire.

'Hello?' Claire said, her voice small. Then she listened for a little while, nodding along to whatever Susan was saying, her eyes getting wider all the time.

'What is it?' Amy whispered sharply. But Claire didn't answer.

Jack was standing right behind his sister, obviously trying

to listen in, but by the way he shook his head he wasn't getting anywhere either.

What on earth was going on? It couldn't possibly be . . . Amy felt a small bubble of hope starting to build in her chest, but she swallowed it down. It didn't do to expect too much, or let herself hope for anything that mattered. She only ended up disappointed.

No, most likely the Queen had heard about the missing dog and wanted to send a Christmas card, or something. That was all. And that would be a lovely Christmas surprise for them all, really, wouldn't it?

But then Claire's mouth dropped open, her face lit up, and she started to bounce on the balls of her feet. 'Thank you! Thank you, thank you, thank you!'

She dropped the phone, and threw herself into Amy's arms.

'What's happened?' Jack asked, obviously frustrated.

'They've found Henry!' Claire cried. 'He's coming home. Tonight!'

HENRY

'I don't think I'm ready to say goodbye to him.' Sarah knelt on the floor before me in the Corgi Room, stroking my fur over and over, like if she was still touching me, I couldn't leave.

Oliver placed a hand on her shoulder. 'No one is ever really ready for goodbye.'

'He's right,' Candy said. She was sitting nearby – not in her basket, not right next to me, but close. 'Goodbyes are the hardest.'

'When we had to say goodbye to Holly, last year . . .' Willow shook her head. 'She was the Queen's other last Corgi, until Monty – and, well, you. When she died, we knew we probably wouldn't be getting another brother or sister. That the three of us were all that was left.' I could hear the pain in her voice – and I knew Vulcan must be feeling it too. Candy had said he was closer to Holly than any of the others.

'And then you came along,' Candy added. 'And everything was different.'

'It'll be different with Monty, too,' I said, feeling a little embarrassed by all the emotion. Monty hadn't been shown to the Corgi Room yet, he was being brushed by the palace staff first.

'He's not you,' Candy said, simply.

Vulcan rolled his eyes. 'What they're both trying to say is, the Palace won't be the same without you. Now, as to whether that's a good thing or a bad thing . . . that probably depends on who you ask.'

I barked a laugh. Trust Vulcan to cut across all the mushy stuff.

'I'll miss you too,' I said. 'All of you.'

'Even Vulcan?' Candy asked.

'Even Vulcan.'

I rested my head against Sarah's knee, and whined a little to show her that I'd miss her, most of all. We'd looked after each other, when we were both new at the Palace, and a little scared and unsure. The thought of never seeing her again made my heart hurt.

'Do you know, if it wasn't for Henry, I don't think I'd have ever had the courage to really talk to you,' she told Oliver.

'If it wasn't for Henry, I know we wouldn't have such a romantic story about our first kiss,' he replied, and Sarah laughed.

'I'm serious,' she said. 'He gave me a confidence I couldn't find on my own. Made me believe I belonged here.'

'And here I was thinking I did that.' Oliver pretended to look hard done by, until Sarah reached over and squeezed his hand.

'You, too,' she said. 'You made this place home for me. Made me believe I could stay – made me want to stay! But Henry . . . he made me believe in myself.'

'Then we all owe him a lot,' Oliver said. 'Because I can't

imagine not having you in my life. But I know that it wasn't all me, or even all Henry, that helped you find your place here.'

'No?' Sarah asked, confused.

Oliver shook his head. 'You did that. Yourself. You worked hard, you were your lovely, loyal self, and you won people over. Me and Henry included.'

He leant in to kiss her, lightly, on the lips, and Vulcan rolled over onto his back in disgust.

'This is unbearable,' he said. 'When are you leaving? And are you taking these humans with you?'

'Unfortunately not,' I replied, just as the door opened to reveal a footman, already dressed in a warm, winter coat. 'But I think the answer to your first question is: now.'

Sarah and Oliver got to their feet, Sarah holding me in her arms as she stood.

'Goodbye, Henry,' she said, against my fur. 'I'll miss you.'

'Maybe we can see if we might be able to visit him, back at his home,' Oliver suggested. 'After the holidays.'

My ears perked up at that, and I barked my approval.

Sarah laughed. 'I think Henry loves that idea. And so do I.'

She dressed me in a warm jacket, and clipped on my lead, before placing me on the floor and handing the lead over to the footman.

'Bye, Henry.' Oliver scratched between my ears, then stepped back to hold Sarah's hand as I was led out of the room.

To my surprise, all four other dogs followed.

'You can't all go to Surrey,' the footman told them. 'Her Majesty would miss you too much.'

Still, they all traipsed down to the side entrance with me, where they sat and waited.

As the footman tried to encourage me out of the door, I took a moment to look back at my friends. Willow, who had taught me everything I knew about the Palace and the Royal Family. Candy, who had cheered me up when I was sad, who I'd grown closer to than either of the others. Vulcan, who had . . . well, been generally nasty the whole time, but who looked genuinely sad to see me leave, now it came to it. Even Monty, without whose absence I'd never have been allowed into the Palace in the first place.

'Goodbye, everyone,' I said. My eyes felt itchy. Like I'd been rolling in cut grass in summer. Maybe it was the snow.

'Goodbye, Henry,' Willow said.

One by one, they each stepped forward (in order of seniority, of course) and touched my paw.

'Good luck,' Vulcan said, his voice a little scratchy.

'I'll miss you,' Candy whispered.

Monty didn't say anything, just gave me that same bemused look he always seemed to have.

I glanced up and saw Sarah trying to hide her tears, with Oliver's arm around her shoulder. Even though I would miss Sarah a lot, I was glad she had Oliver, they were going to be fine now they had each other.

And then, it was time to go.

My heart was a little heavy as I took my last look at the Palace, from the car, as we drove away. It was lit up in the darkness of the winter night, glowing like Christmas lights on the tree of London. There was, I knew, no other place quite like it in the whole wide world. And even though I'd never set paw in there again, I had a lifetime's worth of stories to tell about the Christmas I became the Queen's corgi.

In no time at all, though, Buckingham Palace, and all my friends, were out of sight – and I was speeding towards the only other place in the country I wanted to spend Christmas.

Home. With my family.

At last.

I was almost asleep by the time we reached Redhill. Outside, the night was black and cold, with the glistening snow lying over everything. But as we started to approach my neighbourhood, I sprang up to try and see out of the window. There was Claire's primary school, that I used to walk her to in the mornings, when she was smaller. There was the doctor's surgery where Amy worked. There was the local park where I had such excellent walks. There was the corner shop where Jack took me on a Sunday morning to buy the papers. And there . . .

There was my front door, a shiny, silver number seven on the front.

I was home.

As the big, black car came to a stop, the front door opened and my heart lifted. There they were – Amy, Jack and Claire, all dressed in their Christmas pyjamas from last year, waiting for me.

I hopped down the moment the driver let me out of the car, and dashed towards them. Jack swept me up into his arms, holding me close against his chest while Amy and Claire petted me and told me how much they'd missed me.

I wished I could tell them the same, but I think they knew.

'Excuse me, ma'am?' The footman who'd brought me spoke to Amy.

'Thank you so much for bringing our Henry home!' Amy reached out to hug the surprised footman. 'I can't tell you what it means to us.'

'It was, uh, our pleasure,' the footman said. 'He's certainly livened up things at the Palace, by all accounts.'

'I bet he has,' Amy murmured, but she was smiling at me as she said it.

'We actually have a few things here for you,' the footman went on. 'From the Palace. Sort of a thank you for letting us borrow your dog.'

'Borrow?' Jack said, but Amy shushed him.

'Oh, well, that's very kind. But you didn't have to . . .' Amy trailed off as the driver appeared, almost completely hidden from the waist up behind a giant wicker hamper. The footman rushed to help him with it.

'Wow.' Claire stared at it, eyes wide. 'Henry must really have made an impression on the Palace.'

'Looks like,' Jack agreed. 'But are they rewarding us for letting him stay there, or for taking him away again?'

Amy laughed. 'I don't care. I'm just glad to have him home.'

Not as glad as I was to be there.

The footman and the driver placed the giant hamper on the kitchen table, gave Amy strict instructions that it wasn't to be opened until the next day, then left again, driving back through the night to the Palace.

And then, it was just us Walkers – all except Sookie, who I hadn't seen at all since my return.

'So, what do we do now?' Jack asked, sitting on the stairs to pet me some more.

'It's Christmas Eve,' Claire pointed out. 'And Henry is home. We should do something as a family.'

Amy grinned. 'Hot chocolate and a Christmas movie? And doggy chocolate drops for Henry.'

'Perfect!' Claire raced for the lounge. 'I'm getting the best seat though. Come on, Henry! You can sit with me.'

I barked my approval, and trotted after her.

Yes, it was good to be home.

Day 12

Wednesday 25th December
Christmas Day

HENRY

'So. You're back then.'

I awoke on Christmas morning to a grumpy, fluffy cat, staring malevolently at me from just outside my basket. It was just like I'd never left at all. I closed my eyes again.

'Looks like it. Where were you last night, Sookie? You missed the whole, grand homecoming.'

'You know me,' Sookie said, with a feline shrug. 'I hate those big, emotional scenes. Besides, I heard them say earlier that you'd be back. Figured they wouldn't need me so much any more.'

'Need you?' I'd hoped that Sookie might be trying to look after our family in my absence, but I hadn't truly expected her to do a very good job of it.

Sookie sighed. 'I never realised quite how *needy* humans were until you went away. I suppose it's just as well you're back, really. Means I can get back to doing important things, rather than babysitting the family.'

Sookie's really important things, as far as I'd ever noticed, were napping, yawning, eating and prowling around the neighbourhood like she owned the place.

'Well, I'd hate to keep you from *really* important things,' I said. 'So I'm happy to take back the responsibility for the family again.'

'Glad to hear it,' Sookie said, stalking off to curl up in her usual spot – on the radiator in the hallway.

I watched her go, wondering if she might actually have missed me – and not just because of the family.

Amy came down the stairs first, stopping to make a fuss of me on her way to turning the oven on. 'Oh, it's so good to have you home. You're our Christmas miracle, Henry.'

I pressed my face against her hand to show her how glad I was to be home, too.

'Can we open the presents yet?' Claire asked, as she bounded down the stairs next. She, too, stopped to pet me. 'I'm brushing your coat out later, Henry. Don't try and stop me.'

Amy gave her a smile. 'And Happy Christmas to you too.'

Claire rolled her eyes. 'Happy Christmas, Mum,' she said, giving Amy a hug. 'But seriously. The presents.'

'You know there's just the one present for each of you from me this year, right?' Amy sounded anxious. Normally, there'd be piles and piles of presents waiting for the kids on Christmas morning. This year, things seemed to be different.

'I know, Mum. Besides, having Henry home is the only present I *really* wanted.' Claire got down on the floor beside me again, wrapping an arm over my back.

'Well, that makes the whole thing a lot cheaper!' Amy joked.

'But that doesn't mean I don't want to open the present from the Palace,' Claire replied.

'Oh, that . . .' They both turned to look at the giant hamper, wrapped in red and green paper, with a tartan ribbon tied round it. Amy bit her lip. 'You'd better go get your brother, then. He'll never forgive us if we open it without him.'

While Claire ran upstairs to wake Jack, and Amy turned back to getting food out of the fridge for breakfast, I took the opportunity to have a sniff around the hamper, see if I could figure out what was inside.

The wrapping smelled, weirdly, of the Palace. The same pine scent of the Christmas trees, along with the smell of the polish that Sarah always used, and another, deeper scent that just reminded me of the place. But under that I could smell other things too – spices and fruit and sugar and deliciousness. I had a feeling that Jack and Claire would be *very* happy when they opened this present!

'He's coming.' Claire jumped the last few stairs and flew into the kitchen. '*Now* can we open it?'

'Wait for me.' Jack stumbled into the kitchen a way behind her, and dropped into one of the wooden chairs around the table. I jumped up into his lap. Somehow, I just didn't want to be too far away from my people today.

Jack gave me a tight hug, and I knew he felt the same. I'd missed them all, of course, but I'd worried about Jack most of all. A boy needed his dog, especially when he was nearly a man. I was the only one he could talk to, and I wanted to be there for him.

'It's so good to have you home, Henry,' Jack whispered in my ear.

Claire looked to her mother for permission, then began tearing away the layers of paper, while Jack reached over me to untie the bow. Amy abandoned the fridge and pulled up a chair, so I escaped from Jack's lap to hers when he got a little too frustrated with the tightly tied ribbon.

But then the last of the paper fell away, and we all sat and stared at the gifts before us.

It wasn't just a hamper. Oh, sure, there was Christmas cake and mince pies and pâtés and sweets and all sorts of other delicious-looking things, but that wasn't all. There was breakfast – pastries that smelled freshly baked by the Palace kitchens, and fruits and jams to go with them. There were Christmas decorations, like the ones on the trees at the Palace – red crowns with golden stitching. There were Christmas crackers, biscuits, and a set of handbells of different notes for playing Christmas carols on. There was also a stack of wrapped boxes in the middle of them too. Amy, Claire and Jack all exchanged a look, then dove for the presents, ripping one open each, all laughing and joking as they revealed the contents.

'What did you get?' Claire asked, leaning across to Jack.

'Some kind of board game. You?'

'Same – Cluedo.'

'Me too.' Amy held up another box, this one with brightly coloured triangles on it. 'Looks like the entertainment for the day is sorted. And we can have our very own royal Christmas!'

'There's something else in here,' Claire said, digging deeper into the hamper, until she pulled out a large, red stocking. It had a yellow label on it. 'It's for Henry!'

She held it out to me, and I batted it with my paw.

'I think you might have to help him with that,' Amy said, laughing.

Grinning, Claire opened the stocking for me and pulled out bags of chocolatey dog treats in the shape of Christmas puddings and a soft toy in the shape of a turkey. I wolfed down a couple of the treats, then settled down in my basket with the toy.

'Wait, there's something else for Henry, here.' Jack held up another square parcel, this one thinner, and wrapped in green paper. 'It says, "From Sarah and Oliver". Who on earth are they?'

'No idea,' Amy said, frowning. 'Why don't you open it for him?'

Jack peeled off the paper, and revealed a silver-edged square. 'It's a photo frame.'

'And a photo,' Claire pointed out. 'I think that might be the actual gift!'

'Those must be the other dogs at the Palace,' Amy said, peering at it. 'And I guess those two must be Sarah and Oliver.'

I barked sharply, standing up in my basket. That was *my* present – and I wanted to see it!

Amy laughed. 'Here you go, Henry.' She stood the frame on the floor, just by my basket. 'But we might need to move it somewhere safer, later.'

I settled down again and stared at the photo. There was Sarah and Oliver, surrounded by Willow, Vulcan, Candy and Monty. Goodness only knew when they'd managed to have it taken, but I was very glad they had. Now I had a reminder of my magical Christmas at the Palace – even though I knew I'd never forget it. But right now, with all the hugs and the petting and the promises of brushing, I felt every bit as royal and important here with the Walkers as I'd ever done at the Palace.

Smiling to myself, I cuddled my turkey toy, and looked at

my photo. Around me, my family talked and laughed and joked, and for a moment it was almost as if I'd never been away.

One thing was for certain, though. I knew I never wanted to leave again.

AMY

Amy smiled as she watched Jack and Claire fighting over who got to be the Scotty dog in Monopoly. They'd all already played a round of Cluedo while eating the pastries sent from the Palace (Claire won), and had a quick quiz from the Trivial Pursuit set while she'd finished prepping dinner for the oven. While it cooked, they'd all taken time to shower and dress – while Henry snoozed in his basket with his toy turkey.

And Amy . . . well, she might have taken a few minutes to have a little cry from sheer relief and happiness that everything seemed to be falling back into place. Henry was home, and the spectacular hamper from the Palace had more than made up for any lack of presents under the tree. And best of all, the kids seemed to be genuinely, truly happy for the first time in months.

Maybe, just maybe, this Christmas wouldn't be the disaster she'd been dreading, after all.

Her phone beeped, and she picked it up to see a message from Luke. She'd texted him that morning to wish him a Merry Christmas – and to tell him the fantastic news about Henry.

Wow! What a brilliant Christmas present. I look forward to hearing all about Henry's adventures with royalty . . . I'm away for the holi-days, but maybe we could take Henry and Daisy for a New Year's Day walk together? If you don't have other plans?

Amy considered. The kids would be with Jim and Bonnie that day. And she had said that she wanted to start the new year fresh, looking to her future . . .

She typed a response, then looked at it a little longer before pressing send. Could she do it? She took a breath and pressed the button.

It's a date.

Luke's response was almost immediate.

That's what I was hoping x

Amy grinned at the screen. Yes, this Christmas didn't seem like a disaster at all, any more.

Lunch was the usual mixture of bad cracker jokes (even crackers from Buckingham Palace had terrible jokes in them) and paper hat wearing, and Amy slipped Henry extra chicken scraps under the table, even though she knew Jack and Claire were doing the same thing. He deserved them.

Claire sat a paper hat on Henry's head, and took a new photo of him, home with his family, to share with the Hunt for Henry page – so that everyone who'd kept an eye out for Henry, or tried to help over the last couple of weeks, knew the story had a happy ending at last. Claire even tweeted it to the Palace as a thank you for bringing their Henry home.

'Do you want us to clear up, Mum?' Jack asked, as they polished off the last of the Christmas pudding.

Amy stared at him in amazement. 'Um, that would be great. Thank you. But why don't we all do it together later? I thought we might take Henry out for a Christmas Day walk first. And then I think this year, of all years, we should really sit down together to watch the Queen's speech. Don't you?'

Jack grinned. 'Definitely.'

'Have I got time to Skype Lucy first?' Claire asked. 'I want to show her the decorations from the Palace.'

Amy checked her watch. 'Ten minutes,' she called, as Claire dashed up the stairs.

Pouring herself a glass of red wine, Amy carried it through to the lounge, knowing Claire would be more like twenty. She'd made sure the Queen's speech was set to record, just in case they were late back from their walk. Henry definitely deserved the chance to get out and jump around in the snow. Although whether their local park would live up to the gardens at the Palace was another matter . . .

It was hard to imagine that Henry – *their* Henry – had been living at Buckingham Palace for nearly two weeks, and no one had even noticed. To think of him wandering around the state rooms, barking at royalty . . . it was downright bizarre. But he seemed happy to be home – and Amy was even happier to have him there.

Amy flicked the television on, and was just sitting down when the phone rang. With a sigh, she pulled herself up again – only to find that Jack had beaten her to it.

'Hello?'

Amy loitered in the doorway, waiting to hear who it was on the other end. Probably her mother, she decided, calling from the ship phone on the Christmas cruise she was taking with Aunty Mary.

Then she caught Jack's eye, and saw a hundred emotions go through them all at once. Not Granny, then.

'Hey, Dad,' Jack said, and Amy understood.

Her breath felt tight in her chest as she waited to see what would happen next. Would Jack blow up at Jim again? Hang up like he had every other time Jim had called since he left? Or would her Christmas miracles keep coming?

'Yeah. Merry Christmas,' Jack said. 'Hey, did you hear the news about Henry?'

And just like that, Amy knew they were going to be all right.

Resting her head against the door frame, Amy took a sip of her wine and listened as Jack regaled his father with the story of Henry's adventure.

'No, I swear! The Palace sent this whole giant hamper of presents when they brought him back last night, along with a note saying sorry for "borrowing" our dog!'

There was another pause, but even that was a good sign – it meant that Jack was actually listening to Jim. Another first.

'New Year?' Jack said, looking up at Amy.

'Your choice,' she whispered. Because Jack was right; he was almost an adult now, he got to decide for himself the people he let into his life.

She just hoped he chose the right ones. She hoped she would, too.

There were a lot more changes and challenges coming in their future, Amy knew, but at last she honestly felt she could meet them. She could handle Jim, and Bonnie, and Jack becoming an adult, and Claire growing up every day, and work, and Henry and Sookie, and the house, and everything else that came her way. And she'd do it by keeping her family together, happy and loving, and remembering how lucky she was to have them all.

The future was wide open, and the only thing Amy felt when she thought about it now was excitement.

'Yeah. I think I can make it.' He smiled. 'Great. I guess I'll see you then. Bye, Dad. You want to talk to Claire? Okay.'

He dashed up the stairs, phone in hand, calling for his sister, and Amy took the chance to finally settle onto the sofa and check the TV guide for the rest of the afternoon. Maybe there'd be another good film on again later that they could all watch together.

As she sat down, Henry hopped up beside her, snuggling in against her hip. Amy petted him behind the ears, enjoying the feeling of having him home where he belonged. He was part of her family too, after all.

'We missed you, Henry,' she whispered. 'It wouldn't have been a family Christmas without you.'

HENRY

Claire and Jack came back downstairs together, both smiling, which seemed to make Amy relax even more, too. I sat up, my ears perked, ready to hear the word I was waiting for.

'Walkies, Henry?' Claire said, and I jumped down, barking my agreement.

Outside, the snow had settled over everything, making the world look magical and white. Wrapped up in their coats and scarves, Jack and Claire laughed and joked as they made their way to the park, taking it in turns to try and shove snow down each other's back.

Me, I trotted along contentedly at Amy's side, taking in all the familiar sights, sounds and smells of my home town. Amy didn't let me off my lead when we reached the park, which I suppose was understandable, but she seemed happy to follow me around as I reacquainted myself with various corners and hidden places between the trees and the benches.

Everything seemed more or less as I'd left it – apart from the snow. I wondered if Candy and the others had snow at Sandringham.

Wondered if they were thinking about me at all, this Christmas Day.

But then Jack came to take my lead, and we raced across the park together, Claire following, while Amy brushed the snow off a bench and sat to watch us. There were plenty of other dogs and their owners in the park, and I barked a Merry Christmas to each and every one of them.

By the time Amy declared that it was time to head home for the Queen's Christmas message, my paws were cold and sore, I was panting from my exertions, and I had quite simply, never been happier.

Back home again, Claire and Jack hurried into the lounge after hanging up their coats, and piled onto the sofa next to me and Amy, just as the BBC credits rolled. The TV screen cleared to show a familiar figure sitting behind a familiar desk, a twinkling Christmas tree in the background.

'There she is,' Claire said. 'Isn't it weird to think that Henry has actually *met* her.'

'Shh,' Amy said. 'I want to hear what she has to say.'

So did I. This was the woman my friends loved more than anyone, and that was more important to me than what she was Queen of. This was the person who had sent me home to my family. The woman who had made our Christmas complete.

The least we could do was listen to her message.

I tucked my paws up under me to warm up, and paid attention.

'Christmas, for many of us, is a time for family, and for togetherness. But we must never forget those who do not have a family around them, especially in their hour of need.' Her Majesty looked so serene, so authoritative. I wished she had the other dogs with her, so I could see them again.

'Family is not always a matter of birth. Our communities, our schools, our churches, our businesses, our whole country – they are all a family of sorts. Each of us belongs to more families than we can count, communities we can rely on to support us, and which we must try to support in return.

'This year has been a trying one for the country, in many ways. But I have been heartened to see, in amongst the darkest times, great hope. Hope for the future, and for our country, in the actions of individuals, and communities – in the actions of the many different families that make up this land. Kindness and compassion have brought us together, when some would try to drive us apart.'

At her words, Amy reached out and wrapped an arm around Claire's shoulder, pulling her closer. Jack did the same on the other side, until we were all huddled together. Family.

Just then, Sookie hopped up onto the sofa and, with a brief glance my way, settled down to sit at the far end of the sofa, beside Jack. Even she felt it, I realised – the need for us all to be together today.

'This Christmas, perhaps more than any that has come before, we need that togetherness,' the Queen went on. 'And I know that as a family, as a country, we will both give and receive help, hope and heart. We will stick together, even when times are hard. And in doing so we will continue to create each day anew, a country – and a family – we will be proud to leave for our children and our grandchildren.'

Amy pressed a kiss to Claire's head, and I nuzzled her thigh.

We were together, all of us, once more. And I knew in my heart that, now I was home, we could manage anything.

Together.